Everyone's reading

JULIAN F. THOMPSON

Author of

THE GROUNDING OF GROUP 6
"An extraordinary novel, by turns harrowing and hilarious."

> Robert Cormier, Author of
> *After the First Death*

FACING IT
"Julian Thompson is fresh, inventive, funny and mischievous."

> Norma Fox Mazer, Author of
> *Taking Terri Mueller*

AND NOW...
A QUESTION OF SURVIVAL
"Julian Thompson is a real find."

> Norma Klein, Author of
> *Breaking Up*

"An author with a remarkable literary style and inventiveness...Everyone will be looking for more feats by this talented author."

> *Publishers Weekly*

A QUESTION OF SURVIVAL

JULIAN F. THOMPSON

AN AVON FLARE BOOK

A QUESTION OF SURVIVAL is an original publication
of Avon Books. This work has never before appeared in
book form. This work is a novel. Any similarity to actual
persons or events is purely coincidental.

AVON BOOKS
A division of
The Hearst Corporation
1790 Broadway
New York, New York 10019

Copyright © 1984 by Julian F. Thompson
Published by arrangement with the author
Library of Congress Catalog Card Number: 84-91075
ISBN: 0-380-87775-9

First Flare Printing, July, 1984

FLARE TRADEMARK REG. U. S. PAT. OFF. AND IN OTHER
COUNTRIES, MARCA REGISTRADA, HECHO EN
U. S. A.

Printed in the U. S. A.

WFH   10   9   8   7   6   5   4   3   2   1

For love of peace, and Polly

1. The Breeding of Zack and Toby

Zachary Izak Plummer had had his license for just exactly two months on the day he drove the Rabbit home from school to find The Egg being buried in his parents' back lawn, beside his mother's cutting garden.

The Rabbit in question is not a long-eared, four-legged heavy breeder, but a car. I wouldn't want you to get a picture of a kid with a whip and a hat and a rope legally pursuing young Cottontail, P., from Stockton Country Day to Catamount Hill. Not every Egg has to do with reproduction or breakfast or a nest, either.

"You were lucky to be born in March," Zack's friend Cristabel Ayer had told him once. "You know why?" Toby Ayer didn't have a middle name. Her father had wanted to christen her Belle Ayer, because he'd always wanted a new one of them, but her mother had vetoed that.

"When you're born in March, that means you were bred in June, when your parents felt good," Toby'd gone on. Toby was a girl; she was his friend. But not *his* girl, though maybe more than just a friend, if he understood what she was saying. Who knew? Man cannot live by bread alone. And if you stop breeding, it doesn't mean you're dead.

"It's an established fact that most people feel better in

1

June than any other month," she said. "Healthier, happier, more optimistic, even—stuff like that. And the way the parents feel when they're doing it—you following this?—is the way their kid is going to *be*. It's all part of something called prenatal patterning." She'd licked her middle finger and smoothed a sleek brown eyebrow.

"No kidding," Zack'd said. He tried to throw a movie on the inside of his skull: his parents, seventeen years younger, laughing and bouncing hopefully around a big, wide bed, naked, both with just the first faint markings of a tan. It didn't really work. He couldn't get his mother into it at all, and his father looked disgusting.

"How come you know all that?" he asked.

"Because I'm almost four months older than you are," Toby'd said. "And a voracious reader, considering my background. I heard Miss Signorelli, the librarian, tell that to Mrs. Bates, my homeroom teacher in the fifth grade. Which is one reason why it's so unfair for me to be fertilized by some pale, pathetic, gloomy, February sperm, probably just getting over a cold." The first time Zack ever laid a hand on Toby, she threw him over her hip and onto the mat at the Kyong Kim Academy of Adapted Traditional Karate, and knocked his wind out. Since that day, he'd managed to touch her in a number of different places, and the only really soft spot he'd discovered was her heart. Not only did she never get sick, she never even said she was tired.

She never even said she was *bored*, if you want to hear Unbelievable.

2. Lifely Serious

So this is a storybook about Zack Plummer and Toby Ayer, and their parents and some other Americans in 1982. Don't kid yourself, it is lifely serious.

If you don't treat life seriously, you're missing most of the fun it has to offer. And all of the best laughs. Death is much less serious than life, in case you were wondering. But only if you've treated life seriously.

Death can be a howl.

3. The Egg

The Egg was eighteen feet long and made of fiberglass. In Zack's opinion, it was shaped a bit more like a meat loaf, or a really full leech. It was an underground shelter that could be stuffed with three months' worth of food and drink and entertainment. There was space for materials and devices that might prove handy in the postdisaster world: radiation detectors, lead-lined jockstraps, and guns. You could have the darn thing—stocked, hooked up, and planted in the ground—for fifty thousand dollars. Some pessimists, or maybe you'd call them optimists, ordered a space-age metal marker to put over the whole business, but that was an extra, of course.

4. Rodman Plummer

Rodman Plummer, Zachary's father, had thought the matter over and decided he'd be double-bleeped if he was going to take the limp-wrist route, a murmured *"Que sera, sera"* to chances of a Big One touching down on Wall Street, say. He'd always been short, and so he had the small man's attributes of quickness, cuteness, do-I-smell-a-rat?

When something was right and needed getting done, he did it. His wealth was not a handicap, in this regard.

Once upon a time, he'd read in a magazine in a dentist's waiting room that some of the Jewish people, back during the time of the Holocaust, had sung as they walked to the gas chambers. At first, that struck him as an incredibly brave and cool and faithful thing to do. He'd glanced at the door to the hall that led to the rooms with the dentist's chairs. But then, on second thought, he felt it was just a touch too passive to be altogether admirable. Even *fatalistic*, you might say. He was pretty sure that as an Episcopalian, he wasn't meant to be fatalistic.

In any case, being Jewish in Germany in 1942 was obviously a completely different ball game than being Episcopalian in Connecticut in 1982. Hell, in 1942, he was only nine years old, so even now he was a lot too young to die

The more so when you figured that he'd never really smoked and always kept in shape with tennis, squash and paddle, plus a daily set of stretches and a jog. He wasn't about to let that kind of sweat and character go down the tubes. He owed it to his family. "When a man takes care of himself, he's taking care of his family"—that was one of his father's maxims. Nowadays, his father was taking care of himself, year round, on Captiva Island, thank the Lord.

"As far as the Desmonds and the Montagues are concerned—should there ever be a question, which I doubt—we've just installed a brand-new, thousand-gallon septic system." Mr. Plummer smiled as he spoke to wife and son that evening over dinner.

Rodman Plummer's smile was still downright boyish, the sort of smile that prep school teachers love to have in class: a bright and blue-eyed, done-the-homework, good-sport sort of smile.

"The thing is built for four—the three of us and Pal, in this case," he went on.

Pal was Mr. Plummer's sometime hunting dog, with whom he sometimes got together weekends for a bird or two. He was an amiable fellow, smooth-haired, liver and white, with different-colored blue-gray eyes; much like his master, in other words, except for the difference in the eyes. He'd been born and raised in Morristown, New Jersey. "He's part German short-haired pointer," Mrs. Plummer had told a friend one day when Pal had made a sudden appearance on the croquet lawn, "and part New Jersey ass-hound." When her friend said, "Apropos of nothing, where was Rodman from, originally?" Mrs. Plummer made as if she hadn't heard.

"You know how some people get," Rodman Plummer continued. "There isn't any sense in shaking up the neighborhood."

5. Belinda Plummer

Belinda Plummer nodded pleasantly and cut herself a tiny bite of broiled chicken. She was dieting that week—a matter of a pound or two—which meant that dinner menus would include a lot of things you had to cut—or *could* cut, anyway—and eat in tiny bites: whole carrots instead of creamed spinach, for example, Granny Smiths as well as chocolate ice cream. Belinda Plummer would never have been dieting if she'd thought for a minute that she'd have to use The Egg, someday. Her diet, she felt, was a small, affirmative feminine gesture, on a stage given over to large, male melodramas.

She was ten years younger than her husband, and a deep-dyed product of her special times. She dealt with the wider world the way she did with her family and friends: she still believed that peace could be insisted on.

"I think that Daddy's trying to tell us to button our lips, Zack-o," she said softly, affectionately.

She winked at her chicken, but spoke to her son. Loving both of them at the same time was no problem for her. All *three* of them, that is. Or four, counting Pal. She was as tall as her husband, and almost as broad-shouldered. She could drive a golf ball "three dollars in a cab," as one of

7

her caddies once put it, and her flat first serve, to the backhand corner, was usually seen as a blur. But she'd never laid a fingertip on Zack, when he was small, and she thought that things like tournaments were silly.

Zachary winked back, but looking at his bread and butter, knowing that she'd see.

"The thing I'd like to know," he said to his father, "is how you're going to explain to Mr. Montague why an '82 septic tank has a hatchway wide enough for the Callipygian Venus, not to mention *Mrs.* Montague, to walk right down and *into* it. I mean, why *would* anyone want to go down a ladder and into a tankful of . . . septums?" Belinda Plummer giggled. "Or whatever you want to call them."

"Tomorrow," said Mr. Plummer, "the hatch gets covered by a birdbath. The Egg people bring it over. Then all the guys who had anything to do with the installation eat the records of the transaction and kill themselves. Look, I don't kid around. They guaranteed me absolute security. There's a premium, of course, but I was happy to pay it."

Zack nodded appreciatively. Every time he'd decide his father was a complete and utter asshole, the guy'd come up with one of these little takeoffs on himself, and some of them were pretty good, he had to admit.

"And what kind of Venus did you say?" asked Rodman Plummer.

"Callipygian," said Zachary. "Means 'having beautiful buttocks,' if you must know." His mother giggled again.

"Hey, that's pretty good." Rodman Plummer nodded. It made him feel rather cool and liberal to have a word like "buttocks" used at the dinner table, without embarrassment on anybody's part. Their young man was growing up; he wondered why they hadn't had a lot more children.

"Callipygian," Rodman Plummer repeated. This bit of esoteric knowledge gave him a happy sense of having received a tiny dividend from a rather hefty investment. Stockton Country Day was up to four and a half big ones a year, not counting extras, which seemed to be everything but the teachers' ultraliberal opinions.

8

6. Coincidence

It could have been that very same evening, on the other side of town, that Toby Ayer was told by her father, Harold, that he had signed her up for the month of July at the Francis Marion Institute.

Oh, what the heck, let's say it *was*. Most of us get some kind of a little thrill out of a coincidence. Seems as if it makes us part of a Larger Picture: "What? I can't believe it! I mean, at the very same moment I was going . . . cha-cha-cha, *you* were doing/saying/being . . . blah-blah-blah?" It can be a pretty thin paste that holds relationships together, *amigo*.

Now here comes the complete coincidence. The setting is the Ayers' big kitchen, L-shaped, nice work area, counter with stools, and beyond that a round maple table with four maple chairs. A cut above your average dinette suite, and a lot like the setup in the Shake 'n Bake commercial. Imitation cast-iron electric chandelier.

Toby, sixteen, wearing green turtleneck (no bra), tan straight-leg corduroys, gray sweater-vest, having heard the word about serving thirty days at FMI, just smiled and shook her head and said:

"You can stick that up your ass, you . . . *Callipygian*."

9

Toby had a real wide smile, and smooth dark skin. Her brown hair was parted in the middle and done in two braids that hit her on the clavicles. She couldn't make her eyes bigger or her nose shorter, but she'd worked for that body, as hard (if nowhere *near* as busty) as a Barbie doll's.

7. Mothering

"Now, Toby, don't be fresh," her mother said. "That's no way to speak to your father." But everyone knew she didn't mean it. How do daughters learn to fold the wash, or make a really tasty apple crisp? Or talk to people, great and small, including living relatives?

Mrs. Ayer was a nurse by choice, and a mother by tradition, you might say. Or evolution, expectation—whatever. It wasn't anything she'd ever thought about, except to realize it was happening. As a process, it could be compared to having her second set of teeth come in. That's what you had to expect, at a certain age.

8. Harold Ayer

Harold Ayer had gotten very busy with the tuna-stuffing-noodle casserole. Between mouthfuls, he looked up, out of the tops of his eyes, keeping his head down in the manner of Lady Diana, the Princess of Wales. Otherwise, the two of them were quite dissimilar in looks: he with a much shorter haircut than her ladyship, going bald, and a ski-jump nose, and jowls. When he was feeling frisky—off-watch at the Institute, for instance—he looked like a basset hound with plans to pinch the waitress. Now he just looked wary, ill-at-ease.

It wasn't being told to stick it up his ass that bothered him. His wife, unwittingly, had used the buzz word "fresh," his nickname many years before. "Fresh" Ayer, the other kids had called him at St. Rose's—that's the grammar school. It wasn't fair; he wasn't such a wise guy as all that. And what would happen was that one big bruiser in his grade'd say to someone just as tough, "Say, Michael, how about getting a little fresh air, after school?" And then they'd get him. The nuns were completely unconscious, of course. Harold Ayer didn't like to think about those days; he'd hate it if his wife and children knew what a wimp he'd been then. He'd been doing all right for quite a while.

Meanwhile, Toby was making her stock response to her mother's standard statement. "Oh, Mom. Gimme a break. I didn't ask to be born."

To which her brother, Devon, eleven, had irritatingly learned to add, "So what? Neither did anybody else, stupid."

9. Laying Down the Law

The Law, according to Harold Ayer, seemed to consist of all those things that God, the United States, the state of Connecticut, the town of Stockton, and "your mother and myself" said. And as long as a person—a "child"—was under eighteen years of age, she/he had to obey it. At eighteen years and one day, you stopped being a child and it became "your funeral."

For over a year, Toby had been arguing that her father's use of age eighteen was arbitrary, inflexible, and possibly sacrilegious. She pointed out that if God had wanted a girl to spend the first eighteen years of her life without a mind of her own, He could have arranged it easily, at the time of the Creation. And if Mayor Peter Kohlman, of the town of Stockton, ran *his* house by such a rule, would we see his daughter Lisa, born just two weeks *after* her, going with a nerd like Matthew Minterman? Could her father think that Mayor Kohlman liked the idea of Lisa's going with a boy who had seen *Blue Lagoon* fifty-four times?

Or what about this one? Suppose she lived into her early seventies—died at seventy-two, let's say. Would Thomas Jefferson agree that all the major decisions for a full twenty-five percent of her life should be made, unchecked and

14

unbalanced, by a man who wears thin black socks with brown shoes?

She'd tried the Thomas Jefferson argument, for the first time, that very night, and all her father'd said was, "Sorry, Tobe. That's just the Way It Is. This July, you're up at Francis Marion; That's It."

Which is when she told him to stick it up his ass, and her mother said to not be fresh but didn't mean it, and she and Devon got in their lines about being born.

10. Florence Ayer

The argument between Toby and her father continued for the entire casserole and on into dessert, which was scratch brownies with raisins in them, made by one of them, guess who.

The brownies didn't do much good.

"Sheesh," she finally said. "Moth-er! Aren't you going to say something? This is perverted. Four weeks with a bunch of creeps, running through the forest? Is that what you want for your daughter? The social life of a Green Beret?"

Florence Ayer shook her head: a sympathetic shake, as well as "no." She had gained twelve pounds in the past two years, feeling that it didn't really matter. She looked like a nurse who'd been around, capable and steady, but who'd still be fun at a party, or in a bar and grill.

"She's got a point there, Hal," she said to her husband, not looking at Toby. "Devon, take your elbows off the table." She slid her engagement ring up and down her finger—three, four times. A few years before, he'd wanted to get her one with a bigger diamond, on their fifteenth, but she'd vetoed the idea. She loved that little snowflake of a ring. He hadn't asked her again, and it still fit perfectly.

16

"The place is not exactly what you'd call a resort," she said, and smiled to keep it light. She was going to go there for a week with him, herself, and set up a dispensary.

That was going to cost him seven days and six nights in Puerto Rico.

11. Pouring Out of Hartford

"No-o-o," said Harold Ayer, trying to match her tone, "it's not." He had that long, houndlike upper lip, but a fat, wet lower, like a baby's. "But then, of course, it's not meant to be," he added. "A resort," he finished.

As a matter of fact, that was one of the main things he liked about the Institute: it was nothing like Puerto Rico, or arguing with a teenage girl. It was more of a man's world. No fag comics drinking a banana daiquiri up their nose. Forget psychology, discussion groups, and all that jazz.

"But when the day comes, God forbid," he said, "when they start pouring out of Hartford"—he nodded, looking grim—"you may be pretty goddamn glad it's there." He held up a finger. "I'll tell you one thing: the only people who're going to make it are the people who can take care of themselves. I can guarantee you that much." He nodded. Guaranteed.

Toby rolled her eyes. The pouring out of Hartford bit, again. For two years she'd been hearing this.

She knew, because everybody did, that under certain Civil Defense emergencies, the people of Hartford were meant to evacuate to Vermont, passing sort of right through Stockton on the way. That was one of her father's concerns.

18

The other scenario was a little less specific. In that one, the city people just got completely fed up with who-knows-what—the cost of living, housing, heat or the lack of it, unemployment, politics, cops, who knows?—and went, like, berserk. It'd be more or less like it had been when the barbarians knocked over the Roman Empire, except that these barbarians were already *here*. Harold Ayer had read the family a letter that was in the *Courant* one morning, where it pointed out how much this country was like Rome, before it fell. According to the letter writer, the Romans had had abortion and something called a secular society. Devon had asked his father what that meant, and he'd said he *thought* it meant real sick, like with pornography and all that.

When Harold Ayer talked about a "they" that would start pouring out of Hartford, he wasn't thinking of the Governor, the members of the State Legislature, and all the lesser bureaucrats, or even the mobs down at Aetna and Connecticut General. Foolishly, he wasn't at all afraid of them. He meant black people, plus maybe some of the white kids from the university and the motorcycle gangs, and the ones you'd see on TV lying on the sidewalk two days before a rock concert.

It wasn't that he held a person's skin color against him; he'd had a buddy in the service who was black, and wasn't he taking his wife to Puerto Rico? "Hey," he'd told the kids more than once, "everybody's people, just like everybody else. They pull their pants down one leg at a time, you know." He'd chuckle when he said that, to let them know *he* knew he was making a joke.

12. Woman's Work

By the time the meal was over, Harold Ayer had realized—
had understood—his daughter was upset. Well, the fact of
the matter was, *he* was upset, too. It wasn't the sort of thing
a girl should have to think about, and he hoped it'd never
come down to her having to do anything more than quartermaster duties up there. But it was like back in pioneer
days, you might say, when women had their woman's work
to do but they *could* damn well pick up a musket or a
tomahawk and blow an Indian into the happy hunting ground,
if they had to. You could bet Mrs. Daniel Boone could
shoot almost as good as a man, and her daughters, too.

Harold Ayer shook his head. "I'm sorry, sugar," he said,
"but these are crazy times." Before he pushed his chair back,
he slipped a hand into his pants pocket and got out his
money clip, keeping it under the table. He slid a five out
of it—no, a *ten*—and then, as he got up, he stuck that bill
right under his plate, while she wasn't looking.

"Me 'n' Devon are gonna have a little catch, before the
Red Sox game comes on," he told his wife. "We'll get our
dessert when we come in." The boy got up and followed
him. Toby'd find the money when she cleared off the table,

before she and Flo did the dishes. That'd make her feel a little better about going up to the Institute, he bet.

There were, at that time, exactly thirty-eight days until the beginning of the Teen Survival Session at the Francis Marion Institute.

13. Francis Marion

Francis Marion, the "Swamp Fox," really messed up the British and the Tories during the American Revolution, mostly in South Carolina. Every time the British or the Tories would think they had him trapped, but good, he'd disappear into the swamps with his men, only to pop up miles away and make some more trouble.

There aren't any definite records on this, but it is believed by some that he, rather than Mrs. Marion, did the dinner dishes at the plantation when the dishwasher wasn't working.

The dishwasher, of course, was a slave.

14. The North County Gun Club

Before the Francis Marion Institute was called that, it was the North County Gun Club, owned and operated for several generations by some gentlemen from Greenwich, Stockton, and New Canaan mostly, who used to go up there to shoot birds.

There were some wild birds on the property—a rather marshy fifty acres with a pond—but most of the birds that got shot were raised in cages by the North County Gun Club's gamekeeper. Members would call ahead when they felt the need to do a little shooting, and the gamekeeper would take out a bunch of pheasants, or whatever, and plant them in the various thickets and hedgerows, not too far from the clubhouse. Before he'd plant them, he'd put them in a burlap sack and whirl them around his head a few times, so the birds would be good and dizzy, and stay put for a while. Sometimes a member would just about have to kick those birds in the tail to get the darn things to fly.

Rodman Plummer's father had been a member, before he moved down to Captiva, and Rodman Plummer himself was on the Steering Committee, at the time that the property was sold.

What had happened was that times had changed. Northern Connecticut was a great deal more settled and built up than it once had been, and one didn't have the same sense of "getting away" on a trip to the club. Then, too, it seemed to be a fact that people—men—now worked much... *differently* than they used to. Taking an entire Tuesday, say, to shoot a bird or two—it simply didn't look right anymore. Nowadays, if an executive took time away from the office during the day, it'd be just an hour or so, and he'd probably be seeing his psychiatrist, or be getting laid by his girl friend. Either at the advice of the psychiatrist, or as fodder for future visits.

Birds are just not as popular as they used to be, compared to shrinks and girl friends.

In England, it can get a little confusing: a man's "bird" *is* his girl friend, over there.

15. The Francis Marion Institute

At the time that the North County Gun Club put its fifty acres on the market, the Francis Marion Institute was already a large, if nameless, gleam in the eventual buyers' eyes. So what if none of them had ever heard of Francis Marion? Or ever thought they'd join an Institute? It usually happens that way: something is conceived before it's named—although not everything that's conceived gets named. Some people bemoan that fact, and not all of them are manufacturers of personalized costume jewelry.

The buyers, in this case, were nine men, all of whom owned a Jeep or a Scout or a Bronco, or some other American-made four-wheel-drive vehicle. They were members of a larger organization called the Stockton Off-Road Ramblers, and they had spent many a Miller-time talking about the possibility of owning some property where they could do and have some things they thought they ought (or just would like) to do and have. They had a great deal more on their minds than four-wheel-driving.

When they told the sellers what they wanted with the property, the sellers were delighted. Archie Cobden, Edgar Ransome, and Rodman Plummer found—believed—that Ricky Renko, Bill Bartowiak, and Harold Ayer (who spoke for half a dozen colleagues in the purchase) had all their heads screwed on exactly right. They were, the former Gunners agreed, the sort of people that a person knows, at once, that he can trust.

First of all, they had all been in the service—not Vietnam, Korea. They all had families for whom they wanted more than *they* had had, while growing up. They were informal, easygoing, unpretentious: "Call me Ricky, Mister Cobden," Ricky Renko'd said. "Everybody calls me that," he said. They were clearly the sort of men who might have played around some, growing up, but who would have married virgins in the end; in other words, they had "horse sense."

At least that's what Cobden and Plummer and Ransome had inferred, from talking to the other three.

"I don't know," Harold Ayer said, when the conversation touched on the second-class status of America's military establishment, and the need for many more than the present stockpile of nine thousand nuclear warheads. He always said those words when he was going to tell you something he was goddamn certain of. He pulled his lower lip for emphasis. "I don't know, but it seems to me that a country that could send a rocket to the moon ought to have been able to fly a few helicopters over an empty desert in Eye-ran."

"If it was me," Ricky Renko added, "you would have seen that B-1 and that MX and your neuron bomb or whatever they call it built a long time ago. It's like I said to my wife. The Russians are the same as our kids: if they think they can get away with it, they sure as hell are gonna try. Everybody's looking for an edge. Dog eat dog."

Bill Bartowiak nodded. "That's human nature," he opined.

Archie Cobden, Edgar Ransome, and Rodman Plummer almost jumped up and down with excitement, in the face of wisdom like that.

They realized that what these men—Ayer, Renko, Bartowiak, and company—were proposing to do was nothing more or less than become a kind of . . . *militia*. They wanted to prepare themselves and their families for the legitimate and *very* Constitutional defense of life, liberty, and property in the state of Connecticut. And they wanted to turn that old gun-club property into a sort of training and survival center. Wonderful! It was Archie Cobden, as a matter of fact, who suggested the name "The Francis Marion Institute." He'd been a history major at Princeton, and so knew things about the Swamp Fox.

Rodman Plummer, who was Kenyon College '55, did voice some small concerns about the project.

"Doesn't all this smack, a bit, of vigilantism?" he inquired of his friends. For a while, in college, he'd been dated, mated, and indoctrinated by a wicked, wild-haired girl from Antioch, whom he still had dreams about, sometimes. "We have the State Police, after all, and the Guard—plus all the local cops and sheriffs. Seems to me that this sort of private army routine sounds awfully . . . *Latin American,* somehow."

"Bullshit," said Dr. Edgar Ransome (who'd gone to Dartmouth). "It isn't that at all. These guys are vigilant, not vigilantes. All they're thinking of is taking care of Number One. That, and maybe bringing up their girl friends for a little romance in the country. What you might call a few Swamp Focks," he said, and laughed most heartily, his big broad orthopedist's face all pink and shiny. "Christ, Rod, what they want to do with the club is no different than that setup of Archie's in the Adirondacks. How many cases of Chivas is it, Arch?" He turned back to Plummer. "You ever see that cave he's got, the old tin mine, or whatever the hell it was? Put some gals in there and you'd have every college sophomore's dream of heaven on earth. And lay in a case of fresh oysters and I wouldn't think it was too bad, either." Dr. Edgar brayed some more.

And so the deal was struck, and bit by bit the necessary buildings and equipment that made up the Francis Marion Institute were bought, built, buried, and bastioned. By the spring of 1982, it had been in service for more than a year.

Most of the local people were convinced that the property had become a CIA training area. Here are the clues that

27

brought the locals to that conclusion, in addition to the sound of small-arms fire:

1. All the people, including women and kids, who were seen entering or leaving the property, or who were known to reside there for certain periods of time, were extraordinarily ordinary-looking. They looked, in the words of one local person, "just like you or me." Everybody knew that CIA agents were selected, in part, for their ability to blend into a crowd.
   a. Exception: There *were* a few women who went in and out (fast) who were not so ordinary-looking. Oh, no, good buddy. More your Mata Hari type, if you know what I mean.
   b. Addendum: The local person who'd said the people in the Institute looked "just like you or me" *was* a CIA agent who, knowing that the Institute people *weren't*, was trying to make the Russians think they *were*.
2. The work on the property—building, electrical, and so forth—was all done by people brought in from the outside, presumably with special skills and high security clearances.
3. A goodly number of the vehicles entering the property had "America—Love It or Leave It" bumper stickers.
4. Whoever heard of a four-wheel-drive club that strung barbed wire all through the woods, near the perimeter of a fifty-acre piece of land?
5. And then had an electrified chain-link fence inside of that?
6. With signs on it, like:
   This fence is intermittently and massively electrified. If you touch it when it is "on," you will almost certainly be killed, and your death will be presumed to be a suicide.

16. Driving

"So before he goes out to throw the ball around with Devon, he shoves a ten-dollar bill under his plate, like he's at a fucking restaurant," Toby said.

Zachary smiled and kept on driving. His mental movie house was showing a short—a cartoon, actually—about a restaurant where customers (dogs and pigs and cats dressed up like people) could order different kinds of sexual encounters from a huge, perfumed menu, much of it in French.

"I know it's his way of saying he's sorry," Toby said, "but it makes me furious anyway. What he is, is goddamn stubborn, that's what *he* is. Once he gets an idea between his ears, you're not going to get it out with anything short of a lobotomy."

"Well, I'm not so sure that'd get it either," Zack replied. "If it's right between the ears, that is. I think you do a lobotomy more up here." He tapped his head beside his forehead.

Toby swung a foot up under her fanny and half turned to face him. "You are *such* a know-it-all," she said. "You big, fat Scudsy, you." According to her, people who went to Stockton Country Day were "Scudsies"; she attended Oliver Wolcott High.

29

She grabbed him just below the ribs, above his belt, and pinched. "Aha!" she cried. "My calipers discern an extra inch of flab, young Scuds. For your penance: fifty extra sit-ups, five Hail Marys, and no hot fudge for a week." She fished the ten-dollar bill out of her pants pocket. "And I was buying, too."

"You shouldn't touch me when I'm driving," Zack said. He had driven from his school to hers and picked her up, as usual. She had asked to be taken to the Mall, and he was happy to oblige. But he didn't like her joshing him about being fat. He really wasn't. There was a full-length mirror set into the back of his bathroom door. Since he'd met her, he'd lost three and a half pounds, and you could see the effects of the push-ups and the sit-ups he'd been doing, especially when he had just the desk lamp on, and the light sort of glanced off his torso. She had never really seen his present body yet, along with every other woman in the world.

"You're right," she said, "I shouldn't. It could be really dangerous. Like in the book what happened to Garp's wife's boyfriend. Oh, except he wasn't *driving*, was he? It was *Garp* that was driving. He was just parked." She laughed. "You *might* say."

Zack made a face. "That scene was so gross," he said. And then he thought he'd better add, "What happened to the little boy and all."

At this point, he didn't have the slightest idea if any of the girls that *he* knew would ever do the sort of thing that Garp's wife was doing in that scene, before the accident. Or, put it this way, any of the girls that he might ever go out with. Or even Toby, say. She *did* go to the high school, but she was also a Catholic. Yet she had read that scene, and Garp's wife was a college professor, which made it— that sort of sex—a lot more respectable, you might say.

It was quite a bit of a turn-on to be almost talking about stuff like that with Toby, he realized.

He turned in to the Mall.

17. Raccoons

The Spring Valley Mall was actually in Oakwood, the next town over from Stockton. The Mall had taken a long time to build, because of all the springs in the valley; they'd had to pour a lot more concrete than they'd originally planned. Nowadays, the water for the Town of Oakwood came from the reservoir system, upstate.

Where the Plummers lived, up on Catamount Hill, in Stockton, there were still some of the same kind of old white oaks that Oakwood got its name from, originally. But there were no big trees in Oakwood anymore; it was mostly residential. Since the forties, all the wooded land had given way to street after street of new middle-income homes. The little streets had names like Bayberry Lane and Foxhollow Drive.

Some people on Honeysuckle Terrace were furious when raccoons started knocking over garbage cans and eating meals of pizza crusts and hardened Beefaroni, but others, although they complained, were actually sort of tickled by the need to take precautions. A third group put out food for the raccoons and wondered where they lived; these were mostly children, and old men.

The raccoons, oddly enough, lived in the drainage system

that the engineers had worked out under the Spring Valley Mall to keep the springs from undermining all the stores and that whole huge parking area. The tunnels were the nearest thing to a big hollow tree in all of Oakwood.

The raccoons were the only living things in town who drank unchlorinated and unfluoridated water for free. In the Grand National Supermarket, up in the Mall, it was ninety-nine cents a gallon, seventy-nine on special.

18. Outlines

Looked at from above, the Mall was shaped like a huge staple, with parking in between the pointy parts. There were lots of arrows painted on the blacktopped parking lot, and lots of painted slots that you were meant to park your car in.

Some people stayed between the lines, and went the ways the arrows pointed; others did the opposite. Both kinds of people thought the other ones were jerks and losers.

Zack neatly parked the Rabbit far from all the stores; other than a stolen van, which was also squarely in a slot, there weren't any cars near his. He tried to lead a hassle-free existence, and—face it—he had not been driving long. Parents didn't like for things to "happen" to their cars, never mind whose fault it was, so why not play it on the safe side? Besides, this way it always was a cinch to find the car. And people ought to walk more, anyway.

Toby took Zack's hand and didn't ask him why he parked out there; she thought she knew the reason. They were heading for the Four-Way Pharmacy.

"Anyway," he said to her, "can't your mother get you out of it? Going in July, I mean."

"Of course she could," said Toby. "But I don't think she

will. She knows the Institute's absurd, but still she doesn't think it'd do me any harm to go on up there for a month. See, the thing is that *she's* going to go herself, which has to mean it isn't all bad, right? And on top of that, being a nurse and all, I guess she thinks it'd be healthy for me to be outdoors all the time. *And* away from certain evil influences—not you—*and* the heat, et cetera, et cetera. Plus, most of all, she knows what a pigheaded paranoid my father is. If I didn't go, that's all she'd hear, all summer."

Zack chewed on that. "The question always is," he said, "how far you ought to go to make your parents happy. If you do everything they say, right down the line, you really give them a completely distorted idea of their own importance. *And* have an incredibly stupid, crappy time yourself. So what you have to aim for is to do just enough so they know you love them and all that—at least when you basically *do* love them, like we do, right?—but still not let them run your life for you."

"Exactly," Toby said. "But the problem is deciding where you're going to draw the line. I took karate, right? That was his idea. Of course. I'm taking first aid now—which I basically wanted to do anyway, but he doesn't have to know that. Doesn't that seem like enough? It does to me."

A compact Toyota pickup roared across the parking lot in their direction; arrows on the blacktop didn't mean a friggin' thing to that macho little package of a truck. Its driver was Toby's classmate Rod Renko; he was sippin' on a Heineken's. His passenger was Merribeth Scarpa, who was one of Toby's best friends and drove her crazy; she had a Sunkist orange soda.

"Hi, Tobe! Hi, Zipper!" Merribeth squealed as they shot by. Rod raised his beer to them, and eyebrows.

"He's a jerk," said Toby, waving at the desert sunset painted on the truck's rear window. She couldn't see her, but she knew that Merribeth was looking back at them and waving.

Zack grunted. Toby had called him Zip or Zipper for a while, on account of his initials, but then she had decided that the nickname didn't fit him right. Merribeth was not discouraged; she thought that it was "cute." The second time he'd met her, Merribeth had told Zack she thought she'd like him to be the father of her fourth child. She was planning to have exactly eight children, all by different fathers, each of whom had something great about them, like looks, musical ability, brains, or money—qualities that maybe would make the world a better place, Merribeth said.

"You know this is all your fault," Toby said to him, as she started toward the drugstore, once again. "If your father and *his* friends hadn't sold that swamp to my father and *his* friends, I wouldn't be in this mess right now."

They were going single-file now, between two rows of cars, with Toby in the lead. Zack was mulling something over. She was wearing tight cord Levi's, tan. He didn't want to say a thing before he'd thought it through—then, later, have to take it back. She had on underpants, all right. Was he in good enough shape for a place like that? He'd had a friend, Jim Brett, who'd gone to Outward Bound; now that was really tough, Jim said. They were the bikini type of underpants she wore. But hadn't Jim also said that he thought a guy from SCD was in much better shape than a guy from public high school? There wasn't any outline of her bra, because she had a down-filled vest on. His parents wouldn't mind—his dad might even really go for it. She wore a bra to school, but not at other times. He'd never known her in the summer, yet.

"Well, if you decide to go, I'm going, too," he told the shape in front of him.

Toby turned her head and looked at him.

19. Rocking Horse

Outside the Four-Way Pharmacy, there was a rocking horse.
It was pretty big for a rocking horse, more the size of the
horses on a carousel. Children would sit on its molded
saddle, and their mommies would put twenty-five cents in
the slot, and the horse—which had a big steel piece coming
out of its belly into a big metal box with a motor in it—
would rock for exactly a minute and a half.

The horse was brown and made of an incredibly durable
man-made material. The chemists who put together that
material didn't have rocking horses in mind, just durability.

"This stuff ought to last forever," they said, on the day
that they created it. And with that, they took the rest of the
afternoon off.

"Forever" isn't exactly a scientific word, and there was
already stuff around that'd last longer than that material.
Some nuclear wastes, for instance.

20. Oke

As Zack and Toby approached the door of the Four-Way Pharmacy, old Oke was sitting, rocking, on the rocking horse.

"Hi, Oke," Toby said to him. Toby had a special sort of "Hi," unique with her, Zack thought. It was wrapped a different way and had a silver bow, with spangles.

Oke smiled his tiny little smile and tipped his cap to her. He always wore a red-and-black-checked visor cap, except in summertime. The rest of his late-April outfit was an old Chesterfield coat over blue-and-white-striped overalls, with black galoshes buckled partway up, and those brown cotton gloves. Oke was just a little man, exactly five foot two, with a pointed nose and round glasses and very clean-shaved cheeks, and such a small mouth you expected to hear him whistling. No one knew how old he was, any more than anyone knew his real name, but he had to be over sixty. One person said he was ninety-three.

It annoyed some folks not to know his name, so they started the rumor that he was a direct descendant of Oliver Wolcott and John Haynes, two very big names in the history of early Connecticut. That would account for the Chesterfield, and his good manners. A lot of people got to be certain that his name was Hubert Wolcott Haynes, and that he had a small fortune on deposit in the Bank of Oakwood. But whenever anyone asked him, directly, what his name was, he'd shake his head and say, "Oh, my. Just call me Oke." Everybody did, even people like Toby, who'd never been introduced.

Oke had first showed up in Oakwood right after World War II; he wasn't young-looking even then. He'd bought an old high-ceilinged house in the oldest part of town, right near the village green, and every day of the week except Sunday, he'd appear on the bandstand of the green, at nine A.M., and noon, and five P.M. Standing right where the bandmaster stood at concerts, but looking out instead of in, he'd give a talk that lasted maybe twenty minutes. It didn't seem to matter to him whether anyone listened or not, and once the people found out that he always talked on the same general subjects, hardly anyone ever bothered to come.

What Oke talked about was how terrible war was, how utterly *unacceptable;* he said he had hated killing Japanese people and seeing his friends killed by other Japanese people, and he said that he was sure that Japanese, in their heart of hearts, felt the same way about Americans. He also talked about visiting Hiroshima and Nagasaki, right after the war ended, and how incredibly unacceptable *that* scene was. Oke spoke quietly, but he was *telling* people, not asking them to believe him or trying to convince them. It was like getting the news that seven times eight is not fifty-five.

At first, most people more or less agreed with Oke. No fewer than five young men from Oakwood had been killed in the war, and a lot of others had survived it. None of the ones who'd been anywhere near combat would admit that they'd had even a remotely good time, and they were the only ones whose opinions counted for anything. They nodded when they spoke of Oke, and said, "He must have had it really rough, poor guy."

But after about ten years, the general consensus was that Oke was crazy. He'd kept on with his three-a-days when the Korean War started, and some people hadn't appreciated that at all: it was bad enough having friends and relatives over there, and obviously there were going to be wars whether Oke liked it or not. They wished he'd just shut up. In neighboring towns, Oakwood began to be referred to as "the place with that crazy guy on the green."

It was probably lucky for Oke that people thought he was extremely rich.

By the time ten years passed, and the Vietnam War came along, Oke had been known to be crazy for a long, long time, but some of the young people took to coming to his talks anyway, when the weather was fine. They would sometimes make a great show of agreeing with what he said, by shouting "Right on!" and "Say it, man!" and "Hell, no, we won't go!" The townspeople didn't go for that at all. It was barely all right for Oke to carry on the way he did: he was crazy. But those kids ought to know better. "These sure are crazy times," a lot of people said.

When the Spring Valley Mall was opened, in 1970, Oke moved his base of operations there. He'd take the bus out every morning and give his talks, three times a day, on the sidewalk in front of one of the big stores. He never had a large enough audience to block the sidewalk, so that was okay. In between times, he'd either take the bus back to Oakwood, or buy some food or a handkerchief, or ride the rocking horse, or stand at the automatic teller that the Bank of Oakwood had installed out there, chatting with the computer. He'd withdraw a few dollars from his checking account and put it into savings, or maybe vice versa—stuff like that. Whenever someone else wanted to use the machine, he'd quickly tell it that he didn't want to continue with his transaction. He never held anyone up. On Saturdays, if there was a comedy at Cinema 1 or 2 or 3, he'd go to the bargain matinee. When they showed previews of a war or violence picture, he would hiss.

A while after Oke moved his routine to the Mall—after the end of the Vietnam War, in fact—he also changed his basic speech, or speeches. You could say that he abandoned them completely. It was as if Oke had been transformed into the most average person in the world.

Whatever the majority—or even a decent percentage—of the people in and around Oakwood thought, he said. As their opinions changed, his did, too. For instance: although he'd acted extremely upset at the time, by now Oke said that Watergate was "pretty much water over the dam."

The people who shopped at the Spring Valley Mall were not at all pleased to hear their opinions coming out of the mouth of a man who was known to be crazy. A lot of the time, it seemed as if Oke would say something just as they were starting to think it, which had to make them wonder if they were right or not. It could be very upsetting to hear a lunatic say, "Why shouldn't an actor make as good a President as a peanut farmer?" just the morning after you'd said the same thing to your wife.

Not everyone agreed with Oke, of course, anymore than they did when he gave the same old peace speeches, day after day, but somehow it was easier to *disagree* with his up-to-the-minute commentaries than with his sadness over Hiroshima. Gradually, people started to holler back at Oke when, passing by a speech of his, they'd overhear a controversial view.

It was amazing how many authorities on the Bible, the U.S. Constitution, and the theory and practice of communism just happened to shop at the Spring Valley Mall.

Oke never responded to his critics during his speech times, and if one or more tried to get him into an argument when he had finished speaking, he'd simply start reciting one of several texts that he seemed to have committed to memory: a New England Telephone Company radio commercial ("the knowledge business"), the correct wording of the proposed Equal Rights Amendment, or a recipe for Beef Bourguignon.

Some people were mildly interested in the third of these, but others mostly muttered as they walked away.

"Crazy son of a bitch," they'd say.

21. Shopping

Toby had come to the Four-Way Pharmacy to buy a hair-brush, and some aspirin and shampoo; she knew she could get each of those items cheaper at the Four-Way than anywhere else.

She was not interested in six-packs of cola, paper plates, outdoor furniture, stationery, lamps, canned tuna fish, bumper-pool tables, popcorn poppers, or pantsuits, which were also on sale at the pharmacy. And none of those items reminded her of other things that she wanted. When Toby was a little girl, her mother had taught her to look people in the eye, and keep herself clean, and make sure her letters fell in the mailbox, but she had never taught her recreational shopping.

You want to hear about "disadvantaged"? You want to hear "deprived"? Get this.

She'd never, in her entire life, been hustled into Bloomingdale's to see if decorator towels could make a difference in that dreary little downstairs powder room. She had never been taught the importance of a Dollar Daze, or been driven into the Exit Only opening of a shopping mall in a gut-shot '58 Impala by a woman wearing pink plastic curlers. She'd never walked down endless aisles until her legs had turned to stumps, having to pee, whining, getting hit and crying and being promised either candy or something to really cry about. She'd never been taught to say *"This* is nice" or "Will you look at this junk?" and want—oh, terribly—the first and—just a little bit—the second.

Instead of "shopping," she'd just go and buy things that she needed when she needed them, and then spend the rest of the time reading books or exercising or painting pictures or trying to figure out just what the hell was going on. No wonder she drove Merribeth Scarpa crazy, too.

Merribeth blamed it on Toby's mother's being a nurse and not having time for her, when she was growing up.

22. Organismic Truth

Periodically, all the managers of all the Four-Way Pharmacies would get a letter from their main office in Perth Amboy which told them to shift all the merchandise in the store around. There would be diagrams, too, ordering Dr. Scholl to get up against the left-hand wall, and Mr. Coffee to move into the center, next to cameras.

Such a letter would always arrive on a Friday, and would inform the store manager that the changes had to be in place by Monday morning. The managers involved, most of whom were dark, single men with moustaches, insisted that the letters only—and invariably—came when they had finally succeeded in lining up a long weekend at the shore (if summer) or on the slopes (if winter) with a girl so uninhibited that they'd actually felt constrained to make out their wills the day before, a Thursday.

The idea, according to the main office, was to force every customer who thought she knew what she wanted to search for whatever it was. In the course of that search, the main office knew, she (and even he) couldn't help but find some other things she also had to have.

Because of this policy, Toby couldn't walk right up to hairbrushes.

"Damn!" she said to Zack. "They've shifted everything around. The brushes used to be right here." She was looking at instant coffee. "But, anyway. As I was saying... What's happened is that Daddy and that original group have taken all these others in. A lot of them aren't even from around here—their kids don't go to my school—and some of them—well, let's be kind—*appear* to be a little weird." She twisted up her mouth, connoting weirdness.

"They had a sort of open house up there, last fall"—she tried to make a tic-tac-toe field on his chamois shirt front, with a finger—"and I went, and here were these men—and some kids and women, too—running around in these camouflage suits, with pearl-handled pistols and knives in their boots. I kid you not. Some of them even had their faces painted." He rolled his eyes; she slapped him on the shoulder. "I don't mean like *that*," she said.

She craned her neck around. The new signs saying what was in which aisle were suspended from the ceiling in the middle of the aisle and written in letters that caught the glare from the lighting in such a way as to render them unreadable, except at point-blank range. "Over this way, maybe," Toby said. She started across the store.

"Yeah, but... well," he said. "The main thing is, how do *you* feel about it? About my going up there. When you do, that is." He wanted to be sure she understood.

Toby knew she felt a lot of ways. Zack had told her about The Egg, so she knew *his* father was sort of paranoid, too. That was comforting, in a way. But she kind of doubted that Zack had ever gone one-on-one with a fourteen-karat bigot like Rod Renko, or an ex-Marine drill instructor like Mr. Bartowiak, or a maybe-I'm-not-acting Crazy like one of those painted-face numbers. It'd probably be a lot better for her to tell him no and just go by herself. She was pretty sure that she could deal with it up there, whatever it turned out to be, but he was such a good, clean, sheltered little Scudsy.

"If you want to come, come," she said to him. "I'd like that."

She started down another aisle. Suddenly, she felt furious, and her eyes were burning. "But don't blame me if you hate everybody up there—including me." She sort of threw that over a shoulder at him.

He couldn't really see her, and there was Muzak in the store, so he only heard the words and not the anger.

"Yay! It's settled, then," he said, coming up alongside her and holding out his hand as they walked. "Shake," he said.

She started to, and then at the last moment made a fist and jerked it up and back. "Sucker!" she cried, and forced a big guffaw that sounded like a snarl.

And then she looked at his face.

"I'm sorry, Zacker," she said. "I really am." She'd stopped and faced him; they were close.

Zachary Izak Plummer was not a genius, or real experienced with girls, but he'd been allowed to feel things, growing up, and also to believe that certain kinds of feelings were the truth.

"Organismic" truth is what that's called: those clear and undiluted messages we get sometimes, that aren't from our minds but from our beings. They are things we know because we are, and not because we grew up in Skowhegan, Maine, the middle child of rich Tasmanian dwarfs.

Zack got a message, then, that had to do with Toby. It didn't come to him in words, nor did he feel that there was something that he had to say. He knew, just knew, that she was good.

And so he kissed her.

It was their first kiss, and hers as much as his, for sure. And it put them right in the path of a gentleman who wanted to get at laxatives.

"Would you *mind?*" he said, his voice dripping with disgust and embarrassment, as he shoved the well-clasped couple right across the aisle.

"Hey—watch it, will you?" yelped a junior high school boy who'd been sauntering along trying to get up the nerve to steal a box of condoms from the display on that side of the aisle. Toby's Frye had caught him right across the Puma.

Before they'd shifted everything around, they'd had the phonograph records right across from the condoms. During that time, a lot more Trojans left the Mall in bookbags and backpacks than Greeks came into Troy in wooden horses, ever.

But that's another kind of truth, historical.

23. Changes

By the time Toby and Zack came out of the Four-Way Pharmacy, the world—this earth—had made about a two percent rotation on its axis. That was one change that had taken place since they'd gone in the store. Another was that Toby, by assuming legal ownership of a wood-backed hairbrush, a plastic bottle containing many chemicals that added up to "shampoo," and a hundred aspirin tablets in a child-proof container, had suffered an eighty-three percent reduction in her liquid assets. Like the first one, this was clearly a quantifiable change.

The one in Zack was not. It was not only unquantifiable; it was also, to a certain type of person, indescribable, or "bullshit." Dr. Edgar Ransome would be such a type of person—Rodman Plummer's gunning pal?—but the poet John Keats was not. When he wrote about the feelings of "stout Cortez," when he saw the Pacific Ocean, he might have been writing about Zachary. And when the physicist Archimedes ran down the street in his bathrobe shouting "Eureka," he was changed in much the same way Zack had been. Unlike Cortez and Archimedes, Plummer couldn't have told you what it was he'd discovered, but if you've

47

guessed "love," there's no reason to slide your paper into the middle of the pile.

Love is felt, as much as feeling; love is sunshine in a mirrored room. Wasn't it the psychologist Erich Fromm who pointed out that you can't love the Pacific Ocean until you love yourself?

Outside the pharmacy, another change had taken place. Whereas before Oke was sitting on the rocking horse, more or less ignored by passersby, now he was the center of some ten or twelve attentions. They all were people, all of them were male but two. Being certain of their ages would have been a bit more difficult, even for a tavern owner. Most witnesses probably would have said sixteen to eighteen, although in fact the youngest girl was fourteen and the oldest boy twenty-four.

Most of these kids would have said that they were "kidding around" with Oke. Other examples of kidding around would be pushing over gravestones or any rape committed by a friend.

24. Bird in the Hand

What those kids were actually doing was feeding quarters into the rocking horse, keeping it going. And by pushing against the horse's base, at either end, with the soles of their boots, they were making it rock harder. It was pretty clear that the old man wouldn't be able to get off that moving horse without risking quite a fall. With the toes of his galoshes jammed in the stirrups, his brown-gloved hands clutching the rubber reins, and the visor of his cap pulled low over his spectacles, the little fellow looked like an eccentric geriatric jockey on a runaway.

The group around him found the situation humorous. They laughed and urged him on to greater speed. They asked him how he liked the ride, and made a lot of urban cowboy sounds. They also, in the manner of their elders, asked him questions about, and offered rebuttals to, the things that he'd been saying in his talks.

And when they ran out of issues, there was always the good old standard to fall back on: "You crazy old bastard. What the hell do you know, anyway?"

Zack, seeing some of this, quick-turned to Toby. "Wait here. I'm going to get the car."

"You mean . . ." she asked, her eyebrows up. This didn't seem, to her, his type of scene. Emphatically un-Scudsy.

". . . get him out of here" was all she heard. He'd trotted off across the parking lot. He didn't have a plan, just an attitude. Plans are a lot more popular, and sensible, and flexible, and remunerative. Oh, yes—and safer. Attitudes are an endangered species.

With Zack gone, Toby analyzed the situation realistically. One-two-three. She was a veritable attitude preserve, but she tried to never let the beasts stray out and trample down the one-two-threes. The first thing was to get the rocking horse stopped; the second was to help the old man down from it; the third was to get out of there. In that order. While Zack was getting set up for number three . . .

Ten quiet steps and she was in and of the mob.

She saw the mechanical horse begin to slow. An arm in a blue-jean jacket reached out casually; a quarter headed for the slot.

Toby raised one straightened, stiffened hand, and hinged it at the elbow. And when she whipped it down, she got her weight behind the blow, as well, and aimed it not just *at* the elbow of the boy, but *through* it.

The quarter Frisbeed through the air and bounced along the sidewalk. The boy let out a holler. "Ooo-ow-aw! Gah! Muh fuggin' arm!" he might have said. He took it in his other hand and, making noises still, began to pirouette, jumping in a clumsy circle, head thrown back.

He got the other sharks' attention; at last, an active victim.

"Lookit that," they cried, and laughed. It was a girl that had hit him, after all. "Hey, Louis, whacha doin'? Dancin'?" No one kept an eye on Oke.

Toby stretched her weapon out, but now it was palm up: the helping hand. "It's okay, Oke," she said. "Come on. You come with me."

The old man scrambled off the horse's back and let her lead him down across the sidewalk. Zack pulled up to the curb, and Toby opened the door, pushed the seat forward, and helped Oke into the back. Then she jumped in herself and slammed and locked the door.

Eleven heads (or maybe nine) had turned to watch them pull away. Maybe they'd missed the Rabbit, but Toby flipped them the Bird.

25. The Sam N. Dreyfus Flaw

"It used to be I had one song to sing." Oke said that brightly, looking like a little bird himself. "Too-ra-loo-ra-loo-ra," he sang, in a thin, old man's falsetto. "I'd seen that war was bad and so I had to stop it. I'd seen the things an atom bomb could do. My plan was very simple. I'd start my talks in Oakwood, here, and when I got the people here convinced, I'd move on down the valley. You've got to start in somewhere, doncha know."

They were sitting in the kitchen of Oke's house, around a wooden table set before the big gas stove. Oke had asked them in for tea, and he seemed to be relishing the role of host: setting out the cups, putting cookies on a plate, and brewing up a pot of Morning Thunder. It was more as if he'd rescued them, instead of vice versa, and now was chattering away, so as to get their minds off what had happened.

"I used to like baseball," he explained. "Red Sox fan, I was. Before the war, the Red Sox had this pitcher that my father used to hate. His name was Ostermueller; first name, Fritz. 'That goldurn kraut,' my father used to say. But I'd stand up for him, and then away we'd go. Some arguments we used to have." Oke shook his head and laughed: a dry and unconvincing sound. "Oh, my," he said. "I used to *follow* baseball. But once I saw the war, I didn't care about the Sox at all, for the longest time. War was so much more important, doncha know. My father died when I was overseas. Yes, once I saw the war, I didn't give that baseball team the time of day. . . ." His eyes went far away, and he sipped tea, his little finger sticking right straight out.

They had entered the house by the kitchen door. It was a large, old-fashioned kitchen, with a rocking chair. Three doors opened off the room: one to the entrance hall of the house, one to a bathroom, and the third to the pantry, which connected to the former formal dining room. Starting in the pantry, Oke had made some changes, Zack and Toby saw. The way it looked to Toby was, he'd built himself an igloo out of newspapers.

For thirty-five years, Oke had been buying four daily papers, plus extras when available, like *Midnight, Grit,* and the *Enquirer.* He'd kept them all and tied them up in bundles one foot high by one foot deep by fifteen inches wide, and then he'd piled those bundles all around the dining room, a couple of feet from the walls. When he'd piled them six feet high, he'd run big planks across the top, and stacked more bundles over them. Eventually, he had at least a double thickness of newspaper bundles all around the room he'd made; he'd left a little hole on top for ventilation. And in the pantry, he'd made a tunnel out of bundled paper that you could crawl through to get to the larger room. Before he'd made the tunnel, he'd set up a bunk in there, and put in a lamp, and an upholstered chair, and some small wooden chests, for storing different things. It was a very cozy room, to say the least, and Oke enjoyed being in it, surrounded by thirty-five years of the world's history.

"You may have heard what happened with my war talks," Oke resumed. "People didn't go for them. But me, I wouldn't quit; I am a *stubborn* so-and-so. Twenty-five long years I kept it up, six days a week, three times a day. That's over twenty-three thousand talks I gave, which is a lot of talkin', doncha know. And if I didn't read the papers like I do, page by page and line by line—why, I might still be giving 'em."

Oke poured more tea in Toby's cup and pushed the plate of cookies nearer Zack.

"The piece was in the *National Enquirer*, if I'm not mistaken," said Oke. "The headline caught my eye at once, of course, given what my interest was, back then." He raised one hand and traced a banner in the air. "'Onward Christian Soldiers,' it said at the top of the page. I can see it still, today. And then, in smaller letters below that, it said, 'Arms Buildup, Wars, O.K. with God, says Rev.'"

Oke shook his head. "Well, what I was, was flabbergasted, I can tell you that. At first, I thought it had to be a joke, some sort of leg-pull, doncha know. I mean, here *I* was, talkin' for over twenty-five years about how war has got to be stopped, and along comes some *preacher,* for God's sake, saying it's all right. So, what I said to myself was: 'Oke, you'd better read this piece and read it good. 'Cause even if it ain't the truth, you might just find out why those people aren't coming to your talks.'" Now he nodded sagely, up and down.

"And you can bet I did," he said. "There had to be a reason, doncha know, and, well-sir, there it was in black and white. This Reverend Dreyfus had figured out some things that I'd been blind to, all along, and the figuring he did just changed my life, is all. It's pretty slick," Oke said. His eyes were bright with recollection; he stared off at a corner of the ceiling.

"What he said was, first of all, that everybody *knew* that war is awful, and they always have; God put that knowledge in us at creation time." His eyes swung back to Zack and Toby. "Well, soon's I read *that,* it clicked with me. Right there'd be reason enough for people not to come to hear my talks: who'd want to go and hear a feller say the sun is gonna rise tomorrow, or the leaves fall off the trees, come next October? No one, that's who, Mister No-body. But this bird Dreyfus, he had more to say than that, you bet he did. He said the only reason people *ever* fight a war is that they think that if they do, they'll get themselves some peace and quiet after it. People *love* peace, the Reverend Dreyfus said, 'cause that's the way God made them, in His image. They love it so much, as a matter of fact, that they'll do anything to get it or keep it, including fighting a war. And because that's so"—Oke's voice was rising, now—"they also know that wars are going to happen, and that there's nothing anyone can do about stopping them!

"Well, when I read that," Oke said, "you can bet I felt like some kind of a fool. My heart just kinda sank. But then I looked at what he said again, and I felt better. A kind of certainty came over me, an almost holy sort of feeling. I felt I was transformed with understanding, more or less like I'd been chosen. Of course people didn't come to my talks! They knew, just like this feller said—and now, well, I knew, too: God put something into all of us, just like he said, to remind us that we aren't perfect and we aren't God. And *that* means it's nothing more or less than natural and normal for us to want to build up our armies and our nuclear stockpiles and fight wars. In order to get peace, people make war. And this is why earth is something less than heaven, doncha know. Earth is a place where people make war— that's the big thing wrong with it. The paper said folks were starting to call this the Sam N. Dreyfus Flaw, after this reverend that discovered it.

"The rest of the article talked about how people, knowing that war is the worst thing that could ever happen to them, always manage to convince themselves that it isn't going to happen *now*, or happen to *them*. They more or less try to pretend that this thing—the Sam N. Dreyfus Flaw— doesn't even exist." Oke's voice was back to normal, con- versational, matter-of-fact. "It's too awful to think about. Imagine this: everybody that's ever lived *could* have been killed in a war, and everybody who's living now might be. It's too much to think about, doncha know." Oke shook his head again. "Those people were right not to come to my talks. I wouldn't have either."

Toby put her foot on top of Zack's, and when he looked at her, she switched her eyes toward the door.

Zack laid a hand down on her knee, but underneath the table: the just-a-moment touch.

"Well, I can sort of see all that," Zack said, "but how come you have that bomb shelter in there, if you don't think about war anymore?" His thumb jerked toward the former dining room.

"Bomb shelter?" Oke said. He laughed. "You think that there's a shelter?" His eyes sparkled. "Well, I guess that you could call it that. But from the cold, not bombs. What you're looking at in there is *insulation*, boy, about the best there is. You try to heat a house as old as this, with these high ceilings . . ." His gaze went up again, but then he shook himself. He pulled a pocket watch out of the chest part of his overalls; it was on a braided piece of leather. "Oh-oh," he said. "Fifteen minutes to my five o'clocker. I'm glad that you could come to tea, but now it's time to take me back. I hope it's not a lot of trouble . . . ?"

Zack looked at Toby. "Well, no—or what I mean is *sure*, we'll take you back up there," he said. "But what about those kids? They might be still around, you know."

"Kids?" said Oke. He wrinkled up his brow, as if he'd heard an unfamiliar word, like "Callipygian." "What kids is that?" he asked.

56

26. The Month of May

If, by any chance, you'd arranged a meeting of all the world's leaders for a disarmament conference or, on a different scale, you'd invited Phyllis Schlafly and Bella Abzug to a popcorn lunch, you might want to consider starting off the session with some remarks about the month of May. Of the twelve, May is probably the most noncontroversial month, at least in the Northern Hemisphere. People who can't get together on May are pretty unlikely to agree on anything else, so I wouldn't waste my breath on them, old friend.

May is such a *juicy* month, *n'est-ce pas?*

The First of May,

when Zack was five years old, he was awakened by a nightmare, and he'd cried. His mother'd heard, and come to comfort him. Sitting on his bed, she'd left the door half open, and grown-up voices, coming from the living room, were very clear, when raised.

"Hey, hey, the first of May! Outdoor fucking starts today!" The voice, in all its heartiness, was Archie Cobden's. He'd drunk some gin, and gone to Princeton, in both that order and its opposite. When his alma mater gave him

57

younger sisters, he had raged: no more Cobden checks for Mother for a while.

"Outdoor *what?*" young Zack had asked *his* mother.

He could see that she was smiling, in the dimness. "Fucking," Belinda Plummer said.

"What does that mean?" he inquired.

"Making love," she said, in just a gentle whisper.

He didn't know what that meant either, but, yes, he did know love and how it sounded.

"Oh," he said, and fell asleep, entirely satisfied. In the morning, he remembered none of this, exactly.

Eleven Years After That,

Zack and Toby were lying on the small grassy slope that was the result of The Egg's being buried in his mother's back lawn and covered with rolls of thick, lush sod grass. They were talking about life after college, and merely kissing.

"I could see Colorado," Zack had said. "Or Maine. Those have always been my two favorite states, I guess." He wouldn't ever have admitted he liked Colorado because of its name and shape—just as he wanted to go to Yale because of its color, blue. He wasn't ashamed of his reasons, but he kept them from the public. Part of being smart was knowing what the world called "dumb."

Toby had pulled her shirt out of her jeans when they'd stretched out there. It was Saturday, so she didn't have a bra on, and she figured he was about ready to think it might be okay to touch her small breasts while they were kissing. Seemed that way to her.

That first kiss in the pharmacy had sent their relationship steaming off in a new, and as far as Toby was concerned unexpected, direction. It wasn't that she hadn't always found him attractive; it was more that she hated being such a typical high school junior, doing all the exact same stuff that everybody else was doing. She tried to insist on certain differences, at least.

"I don't want to be scared when we do it," she'd said to

him the week before. "A lot of girls are scared shitless. Or drunk. I don't want to be drunk, or even stoned. What I want is for it to be just another great thing in a series of great things. You know what I mean? It's probably got to be more of an event for a girl because—you know—being a virgin or not is such a *status* thing. But that's only one reason for taking our time." She'd hitched herself around on her car seat to face him squarely, the way she liked to do a lot, especially when she was saying something important, which was almost all the time. "I have this thing, this theory, about life: that people hurry too much, and don't really appreciate where they are, because they're in such a crazy rush to get on to the next place. I want to *taste* life, buddy." She licked her lips and rolled her eyes and tried to look lecherous, even if he was watching the road, not her. "Not just gulp it down like medicine. Oh, and speaking of medicine, I think that's one reason I'd like studying to be a doctor. I'll bet it really comes in stages, like karate: you've got to learn this before you move on to that. And I'll bet it never stops. I like that. There won't be any getting 'it' and that's the end."

That was the week before. Now she said, "I think you ought to live in Maine. At first, anyway. That's near Boston, and Boston's just crawling with med schools. Harvard's there, of course, and Tufts, and B.U. Maybe I'll go to one of them—that's if I don't stay in state and go to Uconn. That'd be a lot cheaper. Of course, the truth of the matter is I probably won't get accepted anywhere except the Carvel College of Ice Creamology." She was lying on her back with her knees up and her head on his arm. He smelled of Right Guard and spearmint gum, and the sun was on his face and hair. She thought he smelled like a *man*.

"Don't be stupid," he said. "Of course you will. I keep forgetting you have four *more* years, though, after we graduate." He'd noticed that it gave him a fantastic feeling to talk about the future as if they were a couple, as if this major thing was set, between them, and all they had to do was fill in little details, like what color bathroom. Talking that way made the future a lot less scary, both for him and in terms of *it;* it was much easier to believe there was going to be a future when he put Toby into the picture. By himself, he wasn't any more confident than his father was.

"Oh, yes," she said. "And if I do get in, and I do get through, there's still a year of internship and at least two years of residency after that. That's when you really learn to be a doctor, I guess, and you work all those grotesque hours. I'll hardly ever see you. But at least I'll be getting paid."

"Would you think of having a kid in there, somewhere?" he asked. He didn't put a "we" in that one, though of course he meant with him. But he couldn't quite imagine himself as a father; cripes, his *father* was a father. *He* hadn't even done it, yet. Also, a "we" in a question like that sounded either married or like some sort of half-assed proposal. It was one thing to talk about being with someone, but marriage was a different story. His *parents,* for example, were married. Or the Montagues. For sure.

"I don't think so." She rolled a little toward him and ran her fingers through his very straight brown hair. And then another time. "I think that I'm afraid to." She laughed at his expression. "Oh, I don't mean for *me,*" she said. "For the kid. Maybe I've been listening to my father too much."

Zack nodded. "Maybe I have, too," he said. But he felt relieved.

"I think I can stand whatever happens to me," Toby said. "And in a weird way, I'm even kind of optimistic about my life. But I don't know about anyone else's, except maybe yours. All I know is I don't think I could stand feeling responsible for whatever might happen to a kid of mine. You know—because of the world situation or something. But get this, if you want to hear something weird. If I could get a guarantee that nothing would happen until the kid was eighteen or twenty or something, that'd be okay. Then it'd be his funeral, like my dad says. He'd be on his own, or *she* would be. Most likely, I'd probably have a girl. But

60

having something happen to a little kid of mine . . ." She tightened up her lips and shook her head.

Zack had flopped over all the way onto his side to look at her. Underneath his ear, he thought he could hear The Egg's various heartbeats, all in their turn inspired by the electrical umbilical that was, for the time being, working off his house's current.

"I know what you mean," he said. "Taking your own chances is one thing." He shrugged. It was phenomenally easy to feel brave on a Saturday afternoon in May on Catamount Hill, with the sun shining warmly and the earth-smell full of promises. And here a girl—he slid his arms around her, and her face came close to his—beyond belief, without a bra and skin like silk, and not at all alarmed and maybe even pleased by things that happened in the course of kissing.

"Nice manners," she said a moment later, maybe two, and gave him just a touch, a pat, down there. He swallowed, moved his open mouth, and got a hand, a very gentle one, onto her chest, and pretty soon he groaned and ground the front of his corduroys into the front of hers, feeling, at the same time, powerful and shy.

Archie Cobden would have recognized the symptom, anyway.

Two Nights Later, in Another State,
the Reverend Sam N. Dreyfus, TV's "Parson of Preparedness," was putting the final touches on a letter when he heard the back door open, almost stealthily, he thought.

"Sylvie?" he called out.

There wasn't any sound at all for a slow count of five. Then a board creaked, and a girl's voice answered.

"Yes, Daddy."

"What time do *you* have, Sylvie?" Reverend Dreyfus gently asked.

"I couldn't help it, Daddy," said the girl. "I know it's twenty after, but what happened was that Becky had to go and pick her mother up at bowling, and the league she's in

61

had started late, and so we had to wait on her till they were done. There wasn't any other way to get home sooner, I promise you. You can call Missus Randall if you want to. She'll tell you the exact same thing."

"You go upstairs and wait on me in your room," he said, not loudly that time, either. "The thing you've got to understand is nine o'clock means nine o'clock, and you don't *get* yourself to places where you can't control what happens. That's a particularly impo'tant lesson for a young woman to learn," he said. "An'"—softly, softly, softly—"*you* are going to learn it."

He heard her footsteps going up the stairs, and he turned back to the letter on his desk. His latest project was a zinger: to start a network of "survival centers" all around the state, as a counterforce to all those so-called women's health places where girls could go and get abortions—uncontrolled and undetected, you might say. The centers that he planned would counsel pregnant girls ("girls in a family way," as he thought of them) in a family-oriented manner and would help them to involve their parents and their boyfriends' parents in the birth of their babies and their proper rearing. He thought that the births themselves could take place right at the centers, under the most modern, hygienic medical conditions, and at modest fees; it would be no trouble attracting volunteer physicians, he felt sure—he would ask them, himself. Other volunteers—you could call them "social workers"—would monitor the competition, these women's health places, not to keep girls from going in to them— oh, my, no—but just to identify the clients, so as to be sure that *their* families could be involved, too, if they cared to be.

When Sam Dreyfus stood up, he was sweating more than the warmth of a pleasant May evening could account for. Moving quietly and lightly for a man of his girth, he exited his study and started up the stairs. His wife would hear and maybe be upset, but in the end he knew that she'd agree that he knew best. A man's children didn't stop being children just because they'd got to high school.

He didn't notice that his mouth was dry as he knocked on his daughter's door and opened it.

Meanwhile, Back in Connecticut,

Merribeth Scarpa had an altogether different kind of problem. Her parents usually didn't notice if she was in the house or not; she'd gotten "it" over with at thirteen; and she'd already decided she was going to have eight kids— right? She was pretty sure that by the time they got around to having another big war, they'd have worked out an antidote, or whatever you want to call it, for all that radiation jazz. Her "problem"—as she said to Toby a few days into May—was not in figuring out what she wanted to do and doing it, but in getting a little cooperation out of her immediate surroundings.

Specifically: When, just to be a good kid, she'd stay out late with Rod Renko, she wouldn't study. And when she didn't study, she'd flunk the test they'd always spring next day, and then, because she'd feel real bad she'd flunked the test, she'd want to get a little drunk that night and just forget about it.

Well, usually she didn't drink, because she knew she had to stay alert to fight off, and sometimes something-else off, Rod, in case he didn't have a condom on him, which was often. Merribeth *loved* Rod and planned to have her first baby with him—he was just a fabulous bass player— but not until she'd graduated high school.

"The thing is," she told Toby, "that Rod just can't *stand* condoms. It probably has something to do with him being a musician, and being so incredibly sensitive and tuned in to everything, but condoms just almost ruin it for him, he says. So if I'm drunk, I get to feeling sorry for him and think oh what the hell, this once won't probably matter. . . ."

"That is *such* bullshit," Toby said. "About condoms. My mother says that men just don't like to be bothered and boys are too embarrassed or too cheap to buy them. It's so much easier to just shove all the responsibility on the girl. Yeah, and *in* her. I'll tell you this much: whenever Zack and I do it, it isn't going to be just one person's responsibility."

"Oh, sure, 'going to be,'" said Merribeth. "You're such a kidder, Tobe. But, anyway. You're right. What I've got to do is get up the guts to go somewhere and get fitted for a diaphragm. But I'm just so scared of being spotted and having my parents find out. Can you imagine my mother? But even Rod agrees with what you're saying, sort of. I mean, he always says if I get into any trouble, he'd go down with me to the clinic and do whatever had to be done. Money, anything. He'd take care of the entire thing."

"Oh, sure," said Toby. "I can just see him now, sitting bravely in the waiting room, getting his jollies from *Personal Health*, while you're inside with the doctor. The entire thing? Only one of you gets to take your pants off, Merri. And it won't be Rod, I guarantee you. He's much too *sensitive* for that."

27. Mayday

Oke didn't hear them breaking in. The first he knew that
they were there was when they brought the tunnel down
and blocked him in his paper fortress. After that, he heard
the sounds they made as they were throwing stuff around
the kitchen, and elsewhere in the house.

One of the things that someone threw across the kitchen
was the saucer on the table that another person, just before,
had put his latest Camel in.

That made the worst part just an accident.

There were, that early evening, thirty-three days before
the start of the Teen Survival Session at the Francis Marion
Institute.

28. Rooftop

Because Oke's old house was in the oldest part of town, right near the village green, it also sat upon a ridge that could be seen from Hartford.

On the night it burned, a lot of the people who were slated to leave Hartford in the event of a Civil Defense emergency would have been able to see the glow on the ridge from the roofs of their buildings, had they happened to be up there, at the time.

A man named Albert Reeves was up on the roof of his building with his wife and his wife's sister and her husband and their two Dobermans. The people were all sitting on nice folding chairs from Caldor's, and they were all drinking a Budweiser and listening to the music on Albert Reeves's portable radio; the dogs were just listening to the music and smelling about 1,001 different smells and thinking about who they knew that might be fun to take a bite out of, sometime.

All of a sudden, Albert Reeves noticed the glow from Oke's house burning up on the ridge, and he said that, oh-oh, it looked like maybe the Russians were bombing Oakwood. Then he picked up his radio and made a big fuss out of getting the pointer switched around to the part of the dial where he said the CD stations were, or used to be.

Of course he didn't get a thing, and so he put the music back and said he guessed that everything was still all right.

That got a laugh from everybody there, except for the dogs, who already had all the respect they needed.

29. *De Mortuis . . .*

There were stories in all the local papers about Oke's house burning down, and of course a lot of people who lived on the village green, or close to it, had actually gone to the fire and gotten in the way of the people who were trying to put it out. The merchants out at the Spring Valley Mall heard about it the next day, and when any ignorant customer happened to ask them what had happened to Oke—as quite a number did, over the next few weeks—they'd shake their heads and say he hadn't had a chance, poor devil.

"I never seen him smoking," said Mr. Edwin Purvis, of Purvis Brothers Jewelers. "But who knows what he might have done in there? I unnerstand the house was fulla paper. Chockablock, they say. Can you imagine that? Can you imagine what a firetrap that old place was? Burned him to a cinder, so I understand."

Mr. Purvis understood wrong, of course, as lots of other people knew. Bundled paper smolders, burns reluctantly. Before the fire engines ever reached the scene, the house itself was up in flames, beyond control—the wood parts of the house, that is: the walls, and second floor, and roof. And when they'd burned and tumbled down, and gotten soaked and soaked again with water, Oke's inner room remained intact, a small, black, steaming, sodden igloo, draped with charred wood rafters. When firemen broke into it, they found Oke quite unburned and lying on his bed, a victim of the smoke and lack of air. He'd had the time to take a red bandanna handkerchief and fold it catty-cornered, and tie it tight around his face, below his eyes. Beyond that, he was wearing a perfect child-size replica of a Boston Red Sox baseball uniform, except that his shoes had harmless rubber spikes on them.

The firemen got him in a body bag and took him out of there. And although, later on, they sometimes spoke of Oke among themselves, none of them ever told another soul that he'd been dressed that way.

30. ... Nil Nisi Bonum

Toby talked Zack into going to Oke's funeral. Like everyone else, she assumed that the fire had been an "act of God," as people sometimes call disasters that can't be blamed on someone else, or a pile of oily rags. Zack had never been to a funeral before, but from what he'd imagined, and seen on television, he didn't think it would be his kind of thing.

The president of the Bank of Oakwood had made the arrangements for the burial. Oke's will had specified a graveside service only; "short and simple" was his rather vague instruction. He hadn't thought to mention what he was, religion-wise, so the Catholic priest had met at the Oakwood Diner with the Unitarian, Methodist, and Presbyterian ministers, two days after the fire. They tossed fingers, and the Presbyterian minister won, or lost, depending on how you look at it, and the runner-up, the priest, got to pay for their coffees. The other two were awfully good losers.

It turned out that Oke's name wasn't Haynes, or Wolcott, or even Hubert; it was plain and simple Arthur O'Keefe. His reason for choosing Oakwood as his postwar place of residence was (he'd told the banker) that he'd spent a night there as a boy, while on a summer trip with his parents.

He'd told the banker that he "fell in love with Oakwood" then, but he didn't tell him why. In fact, the reason was the huge dessert they'd served him at the Oak Tree Inn—a Fudgy-Brownie's Split-Banana Sundae. Zack would have understood if he had known it, and certainly approved.

Oke wasn't really extremely rich, just very, very comfortable. His parents both had died during the war, while he was overseas, and when he finally got back to the States, Oke had invested his inheritance in his house in Oakwood and in one of the first companies to manufacture birth-control pills in a big way. At the time, he felt sure that his abolish-war campaign would be successful, and he thought that, lacking war, the world would have to employ other methods of keeping the population down. For reasons other than Oke's, the company did marvelously well, and the value of his stock skyrocketed. And because, amoebalike, the stock split quite a number of times in the course of some thirty-five years, at the time of Oke's death there was a portfolio of some ten thousand shares, valued at over half a million dollars, to be passed along to his heirs. Or *heir*, as it happened.

Oke had left the whole shebang to the Town of Oakwood Little League baseball program, and although a few parents promptly pulled their kids out of the league when they learned it was being financed with birth-control money ("a disgusting *mésalliance*," wrote one bilingual mother), others were plain delighted. In fact, over the next twenty years a substantial number of people were to buy homes in Oakwood just so their children would have the opportunity to play in the Arthur O'Keefe Stadium, and wear the immaculate double-knits and swing the new Louisville Sluggers that the program purchased yearly. Oakwood became perennial Connecticut state champions and, in 1988, defeated Tokyo, Japan, in the Little League World Series, in Williamsport, Pennsylvania.

If Oke had died a little closer to election time, chances are that at least one candidate for national office would have come to his funeral to celebrate their mutual devotion to peace, crazy or not. It wouldn't matter to politicians that Oke had gotten off the antiwar bandwagon; they could understand that kind of switcheroo. But as it was, it being May, the crowd at graveside was devoid of candidates. It was almost devoid of people. In addition to Toby and Zack, there were only Mr. Banigan, the commissioner of the Oakwood Little League; Mr. Arnold, the president of the Bank of Oakwood; and Mr. Bontempo, the bandmaster—plus, a little bit removed from the ceremony, the three fairly scruffy-looking guys who worked for the cemetery as gravediggers and caretakers.

The service went by the book, and it didn't take long. Toby did the only audible crying, though Zack had to mentally review his Spanish irregular verbs to keep from cracking up himself, when the minister recited the Twenty-third Psalm. After it was over, the minister and the three notables walked away together, leaving Oke's casket still held up on planks, above the grave.

Toby didn't feel great about the proceedings. She wished that there'd been more people, and a speech about what a nice little man Oke was, and how he'd been right to stand up against war, and how people really should have come to his talks and done as he said. She'd brought a yellow daffodil that she thought she'd be able to toss—perhaps just a trifle mysteriously—into the grave, on top of the casket, just before they shoveled the dirt in. But it was hard to tell just when the three men might get around to lowering the coffin into the cement-lined hole in the ground. They'd moved over near the head of the casket, all right, but then (it looked like) they'd lighted a joint and were passing it around their group, talking quietly as well and, from time to time, looking over at Toby and Zack.

"Well," Zack said to her, "I guess that's it." The gravediggers didn't look hostile, particularly—more like waiters at a first-class restaurant, when closing time has passed. Except for their hair, perhaps, and the way they were dressed.

"I don't know," Toby said. "I'd like to know if they're going to bury him now, or what. I just want to be sure it's done *right*." She shook her head, knowing that that was a ridiculous thing to say. What did she know about "right"? "To heck with it," she said. "Let's go." And she walked away from the grave, holding herself around the upper arms, like a person in the cold.

Zack walked beside her, paying a lot of attention to the surface of the path. There were other people strolling around the cemetery, and some of them were talking in normal tones, as if they were in a park or something. He only saw a couple of kids their age, though, and they looked uncomfortable, too. He was glad to get in the car when they reached it; he didn't feel anywhere near as relieved as he thought he would.

Back at the gravesite, the workmen had lowered Oke's casket into the cement vault that had already been placed in the grave, and now the three of them were sitting tailor-fashion on the ground beside the hole. Two of them had taken daisies out of the arrangement of spring flowers that the bank had ordered and were holding them in their laps. The third one had a guitar in his hands.

"'How many roads must a man walk down...'" the gravedigger sang. His voice was soft and steady in the sunlit afternoon.

31. After Math

A lot of people, speaking of themselves or others, have been
known to use the expression "worth more dead than alive."
They're usually talking in dollar terms, and when referring
to themselves, they laugh a little, so you know they aren't
serious.

Nobody said it about Oke. Nobody talked about him very
much at all. But a goodly number of people thought about
him: about his not being around anymore, and about the
number of years he'd put into speaking about peace and
against war, and how at the end he'd talked just like they
did. It was too darned ridiculous to say out loud to anyone,
but they *missed* Oke.

Toby felt sad for several days after Oke's funeral, and
then one night, in her bedroom at home, she lighted a candle
and burned a stick of incense and drank two plastic bathroom
tumblers full of wine and listened to her Joan Baez records,
and cried. Merribeth had gotten her the wine, from Rod,
and it was lousy, but okay.

The next day she had to start the careful reviewing she
always did for finals. She hadn't forgotten Oke, but she'd
put him in a comfortable place. It was all right to go on
with life; she felt a little older.

Zack supposed that the way he was feeling had something to do with *his* finals, which started much sooner than hers. He didn't like the math he was taking, advanced algebra, and although he knew he was going to pass it all right, it was a constant, heavy downer in his days. He told himself that the exam would mean the end of math, for him; he wouldn't have to take it senior year. It was his last exam and after it was over he could just slip into a summer frame of mind and feel better. But his depression continued. Just telling himself these things wasn't enough, apparently. Francis Marion would be no picnic, he brooded, and he'd have to worry about college applications in the fall. He and Toby weren't looking for a real country club; all they wanted was a prestigious college that they could both get into, and also have a good time.

But finally the exams came, and when the math was over, he felt a lot better. He really did.

The day he took that math exam, there were some twenty-seven days before the beginning of the Teen Survival Session at the Francis Marion Institute.

32. A Real Country Club

If human beings look and feel their best in June—as Toby had suggested with regard to Zack's conception—so does the Catamount Hill Country Club. Oh, I know some picky-picky people will insist that country clubs don't feel—have feelings. They shouldn't be so sure. A good country club attracts a lot of compliments, as well as some abuse, and kidding. It isn't always easy for a club to keep its balance, its perspective. You've heard some country clubs described as "snobbish," haven't you? Well, that's a feeling, isn't it?

In any case, there can't be any argument at all about the way *this* club was looking on that Saturday in early June when Zack and Toby met his parents there, for lunch. "Gaw-jus"—Rodman Plummer said the word that way—was not an overstatement, dear old friend. When Zack turned in the driveway, by the "Members Only" sign, Toby put it differently: "Ummm, *boy!*"

Then, leg tucked up and head aswivel, she went on, "Why can't the Institute look more like this? That's all *I'd* like to know. I mean, if I could spend July right here..."

The driveway wandered prettily, the golf course on its left, a grassy slope with rhododendrons set in pachysandra islands on the right. You didn't see a building for the longest time. The golf course itself took up about a hundred and fifty acres. It used to be a farm that people worked on, fifteen-hour days, the year round. But when the family got offered what'd take them thirty years to earn from it, in one lump sum, they sold. You can't blame folks for liking money more than cows and corn and apples, can you? Uh—so long as there are plenty of cows and corn and apples, that is.

"You want to hear something?" Toby rattled on. "If the people ever start pouring out of Hartford—that's what my father always says, I must have told you, right?—I think I'd rather come up here than Francis Marion. No kidding. I mean, why would anyone pour up this road? There's nothing on a golf course but a bunch of holes." She watched a foursome walking up a fairway. The men had lime-green and lemon-yellow slacks on, the women wore short white skirts with apples and bananas printed on them. "That doesn't apply to your parents, of course." She gave his arm a soothing pat.

"Don't *touch* me," Zack replied. "But I guess you're right: this place is *damn* secure." He used his most aristocratic fake-o accent. "There *is* a 'Members Only' sign, as plain as day."

Toby sighed. "I mean it," she said. "I think this'd be a much better place to learn survival at. We could run on the golf course in the early morning—wouldn't that be neat?—and do a lot of swimming in the pool . . ."

"Yeah, and you could work on your reflexes, dodging all the horny college guys," Zack said. He had reached that point in high school life where "college guys" equate with "Mongol hordes," at least as far as girl friends are concerned. "And we both might maybe get some older members to give us courses in crawling through tax loopholes."

"Or—um—how about swinging through the jungle of antitrust laws, or finding the way around the clean-air regulations without a compass? How to make your pile in spite of anything the government can do," Toby said. "You know something? I think that this is an idea that's found its time.

Is that the way you say it? I bet the members here know a lot more about staying alive in the 1980s than those riflery instructors up at FMI."

"Well, yes and no," Zack said. "In some ways, they're a little retarded. Practicing with clubs, instead of guns, for instance. But on the other hand, with their technology, they can stab you in the back without even *touching* a knife."

The clubhouse was a large, rambling building, cedar-shingled and green-shuttered. They parked off to one side, in a lot full of crunchy white gravel that was sectioned off by railroad ties.

"My parents said they'd meet us by the pool," Zack said. "They thought they'd be through with their round by twelve-thirty or one. There'll be a buffet out there." He looked at his watch. "It's almost twelve-thirty now. We don't have to swim if we don't want to. That was just my mother's idea. In case they were late or something."

He was more or less of two minds about the swimming, himself. On the one hand, Toby's body in that polka-dot bikini—never before observed in these latitudes—spelled prestige for him with a capital P. But how would he like her being ogled by those college perverts? He remembered when he first saw her in that outfit—he'd been standing in the shallow end of the pool at home—he could swear the water all around him had come to a rolling boil.

"Listen," Toby said. "If you think I'm going to miss *anything* on the menu up here, you're crazy." She held up her little canvas beach bag, white with red stripes. "Where's the Cinderella section, Prince?"

As it worked out, any college lad who tried to throw some moves at Toby would have had to go through Rodman Plummer first, as well as Zack. His father and mother had arrived at the pool just moments after Zack and Toby did; Rodman Plummer had met Toby before, but not when she was so . . . outstanding. He quickly understood that his son's apparent interest in survival was not an idle or unfounded whim. Who wouldn't want to stay alive with a . . . ah, mmm, yes, he thought. It was kinda too bad (he thought some more) that she wasn't . . . well, more their kind, you know? But that was being silly and old-fashioned, he quick-told himself. He wasn't his father, after all, and the world was a far, far different place than it once was. Why, a big majority of the kids in the Ivy colleges these days had come from public high school.

To Belinda Plummer, Toby's body came as no surprise. She'd seen her at the pool at home, and anyway, she'd known that Toby would be fit; that would make sense to her, be worth it. It was Belinda's first experience in sharing her son with another female person, and she was interested in her own reaction to it. Instead of feeling threatened or endangered, she felt good. She knew that Toby *knew*. "Never mind *what*," she would have said, had Rodman Plummer asked her. Belinda could see that Toby was better than Zack, but only in that woman's way of being better, in which there didn't (therefore) have to be a *less*. Zack would grow into Toby, and she would want him to. He would dare to be himself with her, and not be role-bound, all aggression and defenses. Sometimes Belinda Plummer thought that she loved Toby better than Zack did, though never better than he would. She just hoped—and thought—he was smart enough to know how lucky he was. Toby would never tell him, and neither would she.

Looking at Toby now, in her polka-dot bikini, Belinda Plummer, for the first time, found herself wanting a grandchild.

"I guess it's changed a lot," Toby was saying to Rodman Plummer, whose attentiveness she found "boyish," rather than "disgusting." She was eating—what else?—a club sandwich and drinking a double-thick chocolate shake. "Though of course I never saw it in the old days. I mean, before it got to be the Francis Marion Institute," she corrected herself. "I just assume it's changed. The tunnels are all new, aren't they?"

"Tunnels?" Rodman Plummer said. "Oh, my gosh, yes." He was thinking a second Finlandia on the rocks might be in order; this was something of a special occasion, after all. "Yes, they're new, all right," he said. "As far as I know, anyway, and I guess I would have known. The lodge had a cellar, of course—I was down there once, looking at, well, the place we kept our wine—but I don't remember any tunnels. Albert?" He raised his glass and eyebrows and shook the former just a little. The waiter nodded with a sort of humble semi-smile that worked quite well for him, around checks-giving.

"Well," said Toby, "nowadays they've got a whole bunch. Some of them, they use for storing stuff, but they also connect most of the buildings. And of course they'd be used for shelters, in case of . . ." She shook her head and made a face. *"You* know." She wondered if their waiter lived in Hartford; he seemed pretty cool and suburban.

Belinda Plummer made a face of her own, but her husband nodded, looking grown-up boyish now. "Sure," he said. "And the old lodge itself—is that still the dining room?"

"Yes," Toby said, "and it's also for general meetings, and whatever social life goes on. Then *it's* connected to these four new dorms they've made: a big one for the men, and another big one for the women and little kids, plus two smaller ones for the teens—that's us, I guess—boys in one, girls in the other."

Belinda raised her eyebrows as the waiter put down her husband's drink. Sheer coincidence. "You mean families don't live together at the Institute?" she asked.

"As best I understand," Toby answered, "they do and they don't. All around the perimeter of the property, they've got these cottages. I don't know how many there are—like, ten or fifteen? And anyway, families sort of rotate out of the dorms and into them—and then back again—for different periods of time. The idea being you'd get something out of both kinds of experience." She took a long, creamy swig of her milkshake, and then licked her upper lip. It was definitely the richest, thickest milkshake she had ever had.

"Of course, all that's sort of theoretical," she went on,

when no one spoke. Zack's mother really seemed interested, and she now spoke mainly to her; his father looked a little stunned, or maybe blasted. "I mean, that's what'd happen if everyone went up there at the same time. Obviously, that's never happened yet. What happens now is different smaller groups go up for different special deals. Like this July thing is for kids our age. I guess about a third of them'll be kids from families that belong to the Institute, and the rest—like the Zacker—will be 'guests.' Daddy says a lot of *them* are kids whose families may be thinking of setting up an institute of their own."

"Ah-hah," said Rodman Plummer, nodding, looking pleased. "I'm not at all surprised to hear that. I mean it. When you think of the number of countries with the capability of blowing us all sky-high . . ."

"Or vice versa," Belinda said.

"No one's safe nowadays," Zack chimed in, solemnly, "except the Callipygians."

Toby started to smile, then checked the senior Plummers, first. Belinda grinned at her and said, quite plonkingly, "That's true. The thought of anyone doing anything to Callipygia is . . . is just *unbareable*."

"No country could afford to," Rodman Plummer added, pounding his fist on the table, but not noisily, "and that's the bottom line."

Toby cracked up.

That afternoon was only twenty-three full days before the Teen Survival Session started.

33. Members Only

There was another club—another kind of club—in down-town Stockton, near the City Hall. The older Plummers certainly had seen it, driving by; they'd noticed it was called the Game Room. Zack and Toby were familiar with the place, and also with the games, but didn't happen to indulge, at least not steadily. They both described themselves as "social players" and tried to make a little joke of it.

The regulars were serious—well, most of them, except for guys like Frogger. They didn't socialize with one an-other, they just played. Their place was always very dim; a lot of the light came from the machines themselves, and in a very little while they'd learn to recognize the sounds the new machines would make—the way they would the voices of their friends. Or whatever.

The Zacks and Tobys didn't interest them at all—the sorts of kids their parents held up as examples all the time. Kids like Zack and Toby had *their* clubs and places where they had it all their way—like school, as one for-instance. They didn't have to have the Game Room, too.

That's what Asteroids thought. He was second best in the whole place. In another arcade he would have been the best, away from Pac-Man, but he liked the Game Room better than the places in the Mall. It had a certain atmosphere. For a while, he told himself it was like comparing apples and oranges, him and Pac-Man, and in a way it was. But still. His game was a classic, the only '79 left in the place. He'd been fourteen when he'd started playing, and he'd worked at it. Things didn't usually come that easy for him; he had to practice, practice, practice. You could always get better with practice. That Pac-Man was like a natural, a genius, though. All you had to do was *look* at him. Asteroids wore a cutoff gray T-shirt, so in addition to his biceps and forearms you could see the double muscle columns of his lower back. His old eight-inch Dunhams were laced just halfway up, and the laces wound around the boots, and tied; his hair was curly blond and his hands were very fast. ROTATE RIGHT—FIRE—THRUST—ROTATE LEFT—FIRE. When he finished the game, his last for the day, there came a printout on the screen: his score was the highest ever made on that machine. Would he—please—initial it, so it would be recorded and displayed as his? But Asteroids walked out, his face expressionless. All the top-ten scores were his; he never put them up. What'd it mean? Doing it was all that mattered. Making all that space gah-*baj*, he thought.

Space Invaders was a girl. She would rather have been Pac-Man—not Pac-*Girl*—because she actually liked the game better than her own, but that was hopeless, face it. She played the game sometimes, if he wasn't there, and she was good, but "good" didn't mean a thing around that game. He was simply awesome. Space Invaders didn't know that Pac-Man used to steal glances across the room at her ass, while she was playing. She wore tight and faded jeans, with a lot of perfectly sewn patches on them, some in shapes, like a heart. She had a mop of curly hair, like Asteroids', but much longer and darker, even before the rinse, and where his was off his forehead, kinda like Art Garfunkel's, hers was all around her face, reducing it to lips and cheeks and dark-lined eyes. Asteroids thought she was a woman of mystery and he didn't dare speak to her. She thought she was ugly and told herself he was a fag, anyway.

Frogger was almost always high on something. He giggled all the time, and muttered to himself; his frogs had modest life expectancies. The cars and trucks and logs and turtles knocked those little suckers off before he knew it. Frogger'd go "Aieee!" whenever that'd happen, and he'd laugh. Jumping on the girl frog drove him wild; that wasn't any lady frog to help across the street, to him. "They're doin' it!" Frogger would yell, and Ellington, the guy who made change and Windexed the games' screens would come over and tell him to put a cork in it or take a stroll.

Pac-Man was about the most casual player you could possibly imagine. He was never casual doing any other thing, in any other place, but he was casual doing his game. He was that good. Pac-Man was fat with an overbite, and a perpetually glistening lower lip; he had plastic-rimmed glasses with dirty tape wound around one temple; his hair had a terrible cowlick, in the back. But playing his game he was a Gretzky or a Valenzuela. Just as the greatest matadors work closest to the bull, so did he control his piece: the smallest step away from danger. He seemed to know the routes his enemies would follow. People started watching him, at first because he was so jerky-looking, and the game looked pretty easy when he did it. Then he'd offer them a turn, and step away, and they found out. "That's pretty *good*," he'd always say, and smile, when they were done, but they'd just throw a nod and miss his eyes and hurry off. Pac-Man was probably all right, but things were dicey enough without people thinking you were a friend of his.

Defender never spoke to anyone or looked at anyone. Defender was older, maybe thirty-five or forty-five, some age like that. What he looked like was a Dallas Cowboy offensive guard who'd been transistorized to maybe five-ten, 175. He had a short crewcut and a good jut-jaw, and was sort of chesty-gutsy down the front. Before he took a quarter out of the breast pocket of his fitted blue shirt with the white piping, he'd flex his shoulders a couple of times and set his feet nice and wide apart. And then he'd *go*, his

spaceship streaking left to right, movin' up and down, kickin'
shit out of everything else in the sky. Defender took no
prisoners, my friend. He just plain e-*rased* them sonsa-
bitches.

34. Say Hello to Old J.B.

At 7:33 P.M. on June 15, in the basement all-purpose room of the Church of the Assumption, Mr. Bill Bartowiak, ex-gyrene, head usher at the nine o'clock Mass on Sundays, founding member and current President of the Francis Marion Institute, looked down at eighty-odd teenagers and their parents. Included in the group were Harold Ayer and Zack and Toby, plus Rod Renko and his dad, with Merribeth; no one else from Stockton Country Day.

Coming to the end of quite a glowing introduction, Bill Bartowiak said this:

"Folks, say hello to my old friend and First Division buddy, now Director-designate of the Teen Survival Session at the Francis Marion Institute, former Sergeant Jewell B. Fairchild, better known as old J.B.!"

The man beside him (rising to his feet) had both a brush cut and a western shirt; his chest was slipping slightly. Turned out he had a southern accent, which he'd picked up, along with a disease, in the months he'd spent at Parris Island.

* * *

Two hours later, driving home, Harold Ayer asked his passengers what they'd thought of their Director, and his talk.

"I don't know," Zack said. "I guess he's all right. He seemed to be in real good shape." As his father said, you could always find a positive thing to say about a person, if you tried.

Toby made a throat sound of disgust.

"I think he's a sexist moron," she proclaimed.

It was then two weeks, two days, before the Teen Survival Session started.

35. Bedrooms

"How come you're still awake?" said Florence Ayer, undressing in the dark. "The Sox go into extra innings?" She'd worked the four-to-midnight shift, up at the hospital.

Harold Ayer could never figure out how his wife always knew whether he was awake or asleep. That was probably because he'd never heard himself sleep. "No, no," he said. "They lost in regulation. Every ball the Yankees hit was off the wall, I swear." He sighed. "I just couldn't get to sleep."

"So, how'd the meeting go?" she asked.

"Okay. It didn't last real long. Zack came over, and the three of us went." He paused. "Bill's friend was there. The guy that's heading up the program? You knew that, I guess. He's been caretaker up there awhile. He gave a little talk."

"Well, how was he?" Florence asked. "Did you like what he said? What did Zack and Toby think?"

"She didn't seem too crazy about him," Harold said. "You know how she is. I thought he was all right." Another pause. "Hey, *you* know Bill. You know the kind of guy *he* is. Any buddy of his—hey, you *gotta* know he's going to be all right."

It being dark, she didn't bother with a nod. He seemed to think she knew a lot, that night.

Belinda Plummer was wearing only an old blue oxford shirt of her husband's, unbuttoned, and was sitting on the fronts of his thighs with her long, strong legs, folded at the knee, on either side of him. Perhaps he'd given her the shirt off his back—which was flat on their king-sized bed—because he didn't have one on just then, or anything else, either.

"Was that the door?" she asked. She slipped off the bed in one athletic glide, beginning to button her shirt; she went to the window to look out. Sure enough, Zack's car was in the circle, just out front.

Rodman Plummer groaned and pulled the covers up. Zack sometimes knocked and came on into their room, if he saw their light on, and it wasn't very late.

They heard his footsteps trudging up the stairs, but then they turned and went on down the hall to where his room was. In a moment, Carly Simon sang.

"I wonder how the meeting went," Belinda said. She shook her head. "You know, except for being with Toby, I think he's going to hate that place."

"Well," said Rodman Plummer, a little testily, "maybe he will and maybe he won't. But it can't do him any harm to be with some different kinds of kids, and rough it for a little while. It's only a month, after all." They'd had more or less the same conversation a number of times before. "Now, will you just get your whatsis back on over here?"

Bill Bartowiak's wife, Mary, was standing in front of the bathroom mirror, flossing her teeth. She turned and looked into the bedroom; he was sitting on the end of their bed in his undershorts, taking off his socks and handling his large, white feet as if they had some secrets to reveal.

"You know," she said, "I can't remember your even *mentioning* J.B., when we were down at Bragg."

"Well, that's because I didn't know him then," he said.

"He joined the outfit in Korea. I must've written you about him. It was after Marducci got the hepatitis, or whatever it was. Remember? He did real good with us; Farrell used to talk about him all the time. Wild man, he said, not afraid of nothing. He'd been a D.I. at Parris Island and got sick of it, I guess."

"Oh," she said. "So you actually didn't know him all that well. I mean, from the way you were talking tonight, it sounded like him and you . . ."

"Ah." He waved a hand, more at the floor than her. "You gotta say that kind of stuff. Build the guy up a little. J.B.'s all right. I've had some good talks with the guy."

His wife had the floss deep into her upper-rights. "Aw 'idn 'ike 'im," came from her. She took her hands away from her mouth. "What was he doing in Hartford when you ran into him, anyway? You know where he was working at? I mean, how come he's so *available?*"

"Crissakes, Mary," Bill Bartowiak said. "He'd been laid off down in Danbury—all right? He was staying with his sister for a few days and looking for something up here. And we needed a caretaker up at the Institute anyway, right? What's the matter with you, for gosh sakes? You barely met the guy."

"Call it woman's intuition," Mary Bartowiak said. She was back looking at the mirror. "I'll tell you one thing, though. You can forget Ricky going up there, as long as that creep's in charge." She got her toothbrush off the rack.

"Who knows where any of us'll be, by then," her husband answered gloomily. Rick was only seven, after all.

36. Bobo Bodine

The only weapon that Bobo Bodine was showing, as he stood by the gate in the chain-link fence, on the private road that led into the Institute, was his Gerber Mark II Survival Knife. It was a present from Willis Rensselaer, who'd used *his* with the Special Forces in Vietnam, and who'd known the first-time he saw the weapon that his old prep school history teacher *and* Outward Bound instructor would go completely apeshit over one. It had a six-and-three-quarter-inch blade, razor-sharp on both sides, with a special serrated section near the hilt that could take you right through heavy bone and gristle. The black armor-hide handle was easy to keep hold of, even when you'd think it might be slippery, with stuff.

Rutherford Bodine didn't look much like a Bobo, except for his clothes, maybe, which were green fatigues, and a visored cap. He'd hated the name when he'd first gotten it, at GCD. His mother'd called him Fordie, and his father and his teachers Ford, but on the baseball field a teammate, his first baseman, started in with Bo. "Hey, Bo, chuck it in there, babe. You can do it, Bo-babe."

"Bobo" followed easily, and stuck. Now, at forty-four, he kind of loved it.

Yes, he was forty-four, but could have passed for thirty-two, he knew, no sweat. He had a full head of curly black hair that, though it looked a little rumpled and informal, was in fact as neatly trimmed as his black beard, with full moustache. He had a strong and slightly hawkish nose, and perfect white teeth that often flashed, at different times, in sentences. He looked intelligent, and because he taught at the same prep school that he'd gone to as a boy, and had access to the files, he knew that his IQ was 142—and he had gotten *no* demerits in four years. In another era—the Age of Chivalry, let's say—his looks would have been perfect for the king's brother, or one of the more ambitious dukes.

When Belinda Plummer slid the Volvo up against his thighs, almost, he smiled and touched the green cloth visor of his cap.

"Good—lovely—after*noon*," he drawled, and smiled again. He thought he'd known Belinda Plummer and her Volvo all his life, but he was wrong, of course.

"Hullo," she said. "I bring you able persons, three. One man- and two woman-jacks: Ayer, C., Scarpa, M.B., Plummer, Z. How about a guinea for the lot?" She thought she might know Bobo, too—that smile and "after*noon*"—but she was just as wrong.

"Give ye twenty shillings, not a farthing more," he said, and stuck his hand up by the window. "Rutherford Bodine," he said. "But better known as Bobo." Flash. "One of the instructors." Flash.

"Done," Belinda Plummer said, and shook his hand. Her grip was a surprise. "Where d'you want the bodies dumped? As you can see, I've drugged them to the eyeballs and beyond, but when they come around . . ." She didn't say *her* name, he noticed.

Merribeth and Toby thought that he was handsome, and so they simply sat, and smiled, and stared. Zack was, most of all, surprised, but also—face it—pleased, *relieved*. Rutherford Bodine was not a total stranger, not a Jewell B. Fairchild.

"No more than half a mile," said Bobo. Flash. "Building on the left, the big main lodge. Mr. Fairchild's piping everyone on board himself." Flash. "Good to see you, kids." A look for each of them, and flash, flash, flash.

Belinda shifted gears and nodded, smiled, and fed the Volvo gas. She'd finally taken all of Bobo in. Why on earth a foot-long knife, with scabbard thong tied around his upper thigh? Was there some sugarcane along the fence she hadn't noticed? Or was it . . .

"Jeezus," Merribeth Scarpa muttered, as they drove. "Didja see the pig-sticker on that guy?"

The Teen Survival Session had begun.

37. "Plus, for the ladies..."

Belinda Plummer didn't hang around. She didn't want to
have to catch Zack's eye, not after being ma'amed by Fairchild—"up one side and down the other" she later said to
Rodman, who just grinned. Zack had told his mother this
and that about J.B., and so she hadn't been surprised by
all the cheerful folksiness. The thing that bothered her was
being sure that she was getting bullshitted, but good—that
underneath he probably disliked her, just because... She
felt like saying something unexpected to the guy, like "Never
mahnd the sugar-tit, le's rassle." Old J.B. and Bobo Bodine
had met at a pistol range outside of Stamford, but because
Belinda Plummer didn't know that, she couldn't figure out
what in the hell the two of them were doing at the Institute
together. She spent a lot of the drive home asking herself
if maybe she wasn't reading too much into too little. Or not
enough, you might say.

As Toby had remarked to Rodman Plummer, the main
lodge was pretty much unchanged from gun-club days. It
was big and rustic, but not rough: stained shingles, with
white trim around the windows, and a splendid covered
porch that ran the building's length and looked out on the

graveled circle of the drive, shaded by enormous maple trees. Inside the circle was a grassy space, a flagpole, and a cannon. Also, a small wooden platform two feet high and eight-by-eight-feet square. The cages that they'd used to keep the pheasants in were nestled in the rhododendrons, down by one end of the porch, and outside the circle of the drive. They were made of bolted, painted two-by-fours, a forest green, and heavy mesh—the kind you see on windows in an inner-city school.

Although the North County Gun Club had been a bird-shooting organization, a number of members (at their wives' suggestive ultimatums) had donated heads and horns of other animals, to put up on the walls, and most of these had been included in the selling price, along with all the furniture. "Thrown in" would be another way of putting it. And so that meant when Toby, Zack, and Merribeth were greeted by J.B., they were also stared upon—but glassily—by white-tailed deer and moose and elk, and one poor lesser kudu.

The near half of the room was organized for sitting; the chairs and couches all were big upholstered things, the kind a member could sink into with a sigh, before he went a-wassailing. Some were leather, some were sort of velveteen; the tables tended to be oak; the standing lamps had mellow parchment shades. The fireplace was huge, of course, and made of smooth, round fieldstones, bound by grayish mortar. Past a barricade of oak-armed sofas was the dining half-a-hall: round hardwood tables, heavy armless chairs with leather seats and ladder backs. One table, in the middle, sat upon a platform made of new pine boards; it had only four chairs, whereas all the other ones had six. And also, unlike all the others, it wasn't piled chest-high with stacks of shirts and pants and socks and underwear, and so on.

"There's your leisure suits," said old J.B., with a gesture. "Every size and all the colors that you spell like olive green. Two shirts, two pants, three handkerchiefs, three pairs of socks, three sets of skivvies, and a jacket and a cap. Plus, for the ladies, three brazeers, and you make dadgum sure you wear 'em, hear?"

Zack realized he should have guessed that they'd be wearing uniforms.

38. Missus Fairchild

Barracks B (for boys) and G (for girls) were shaped a bit like loaves of bread, or modern, plastic-covered greenhouses; in other words, their roofline was an arch, a semicircle. Outside, they were corrugated metal, painted swirling browns and greens, for camouflage, and both of them were loosely draped with wide-mouth mesh, made out of heavy rope. To private pilots, flying over them, they looked like beached and netted Quonset huts.

Missus Rita Fairchild was in charge of Barracks G, as Merribeth and Toby soon found out. Jewell B. Fairchild might have been a diamond in the rough, but Mrs. F. was nothing but a dame.

"Hello, I'm Missus Fairchild," Missus Fairchild said to them, when they came reeling in, with duffel bags. She'd risen from a folding chair, where she'd been sitting, reading. Reading books was one of her great pleasures, as she often said. *The Sea Dog and the Strumpet* was a good one, full of sword- and foreplay.

Missus Fairchild never wore a uniform; olive green was not her color and shooting a machine gun not her thing. She was a Mother (Dave took after her—an independent boy who lived in Hamden, nowadays) and a Woman, short and starting—barely starting—to get squat. Now she wore a warm-up suit, in powder-blue velour, with white silk ribbon down the outside of the legs and arms, from foot to waist and wrist to collar. Her running shoes were gleaming white, with clean tan waffle soles and curving aqua emblems on the sides. She'd seen to it her breasts looked firm and confident, like the pointed rubber bumper guards on certain older Cadillacs.

Missus Fairchild wore her rinsed blond hair in waves, at shoulder length, and curtaining one eye. Her face was white, and blemish-free, but pouched with little flattened mounds of fat, and sectioned off by lines.

"Scarpa? You're the upper over there," she said. She had a clipboard and a list she'd made, in bright-red ink. "Ayer? Let's see. You're right there underneath her, as it happens." She made two check marks on her list. Ayer and Scarpa were checked in.

Originally, old J.B. had strongly opposed the inclusion of girls in the Teen Survival Session, and so had his wife, but they'd been overruled by the Institute's Board of Directors. Rita Fairchild planned to make the best of it. She would, on the one hand, make it crystal-clear she disapproved of girls in uniform, with weapons—calling them by their last names would help to get that thought across, she felt. But (on the other hand) she'd also use the time to teach them what it meant to be a Woman. There'd be no sluts or dykes in Barracks G (for girls).

"Boys are not allowed inside this barracks, ever," Missus Fairchild said. Her nails were long and shiny, perfect pink, the color of her lips, which glistened, too. "We aren't going to have no hanky-panky, crystal-clear?" She nodded her agreement with herself. "What you do outside is their responsibility—my husband and the other men are here to give you certain kinds of training—but here and in the lodge we look and act and talk like ladies." She smiled as *she'd* been trained to do, when she was selling Mary Kay. "Men, they have their skills and usefulness, but women set the standards. Let's be crystal-clear on that. A woman in a uniform is still a woman, first." She smiled again. "So you just put yours on and get back over to the lodge, and kind of keep an eye on things. All the clothes are stacked by size, but two-to-one the boys'll get them all mixed up, unfolded, thrown around. One of you can keep that straightened up, and the other can maybe make some coffee for the folks. Keep a pot of coffee on the stove, and you're halfway to the good side of J.B."

The girls were putting on their olive-drab brassieres; two nice little sets of jugs on them, so Missus Fairchild thought.

39. Willis Rensselaer

When Zack saw Merribeth and Toby leave the lodge dining place, with duffel bags, he felt a little bit the way he'd felt the day his mother left his kindergarten room, and he had had to stay. Well, one thing he was glad of was that he hadn't felt that way *before* the girls had left, like when Belinda Plummer had. That was progress, anyway. Mama's boy grows up: gets into girls. Well, kind of. In a sense. You know.

Zack put his uniform inside *his* duffel bag and headed out the door toward Barracks B (for boys). He knew there was a tunnel going there, but for the moment he preferred fresh air and open spaces. He didn't really feel that bad. Like Rutherford Bodine, he knew he had credentials, and not just what they called (at Stockton Country Day) "an enviable record." *That* meant points for student government and grades and sports and yearbook editing, plus the new college-admissions biggie, Social Services, which was putting energy into some major national concern, like polluted streams, or inner-city kids, or even alternative energy.

But, over and above all that, he "got along." With—if you can believe it—everyone.

Although this fact had always been a fact, Zack had never

noticed it until a friend of his (well, wasn't everyone?) named Terry Bradford said to him, "You get along with everyone, you know that?" They'd just been standing talking to a man named Raymond Kempton, who was the head custodian at Stockton. Kempton was a tall, aloof, aristocratic-looking black man, who'd played at Norwalk High with Calvin Murphy, everybody thought. He was going to Western Connecticut, nights, and he didn't have time to buddy-up to faculty and students *and* do all his homework, and his job. But still, he always had a word, a smile, for Zack. As in: "Hey, Zacharee, how many Yalies does it take to change a person's mind?" What Raymond Kempton perceived about Zack was that Zack actually cared how Raymond Kempton was, and who he was, and what he thought. And not "as a black," or "as a college student," or "as an employee of Stockton Country Day." Just as a guy. Zack paid attention; that was something that he *did;* he really paid attention to a person. He didn't do it on purpose, or for a purpose, he just did it. He'd picked it up at home, that tendency, and you can guess from whom.

Overall, he was pretty much the kind of person Willis Rensselaer despised.

"Ho," said Willis Rensselaer, when Zack came into Barracks B. He'd been lounging on a lower bunk, chatting at Rod Renko, who was standing beside it, shifting his weight from one foot to the other, while he tried to think of a reason to leave and go somewhere else. Willis Rensselaer had already decided that Rod Renko was probably the dumbest cocksucker in the state of Connecticut, but what a build on the animal. He'd call him Peter Percheron, Willis Rensselaer decided; that would be amusing. Anything to lighten up the atmosphere a tad.

"And who do we got here?" he said to Zack, while reaching for the clipboard on the floor beside the bunk he was lying on.

"Well, I guess I'll..." Rod Renko rubbed his palms on the seams of his green fatigues. His T-shirt pulled real tight across his chest; his shoulders made the sleeves too short, those sleeves that barely fit around his massive upper arms. He turned and started for the door, which action brought him face to face with Zack.

"Hi," said Zack to him. "How you doing?"

"What's happening?" said Rod. He wasn't sure if he had met this kid before or not. He looked familiar. Sort of.

"Hi?" said Willis Rensselaer, pretending to be dumb. "Hi who? Who he? Ho-ho." He changed his voice to normal. "Let me guess." He ran a pencil down the list. "Plummer, Zachary. I bet that's it. You look like a Plummer, to me."

"Yes, sir," said Zack. He kept on going toward the bunk, guessing that the man—this youngish man—would soon get up, sit up, and offer him a hand. None of those events took place. Willis Rensselaer was propped up on one elbow. The eyebrow on his other side was also up.

If Willis Rensselaer looked cynical, and also like a wise guy, that was right. He was. And advertised. There wasn't much that he believed, and the one thing that he knew for sure was he could kill you if he wanted to. His age was twenty-eight, his occupation racing driver...or *investments*, better make that.

Both his parents had been rich, and he became extremely rich himself, the day they died, near Saratoga Springs— the Adirondack Northway—the victims of a drunken guy from Unionville, Pennsylvania, who'd merely lost a bundle on a jumper, at the track. Willis, who was ten, and also in the car, was almost killed himself, but many months and operations later he was fine, except for having only half a face that moved. Looked at from the front, the left side of Willis Rensselaer's face was set into a single, unchangeable expression, a kind of minor grimace, the sort of thing that goes with the electric bill, or gas. When he was first at boarding school, he got the nickname "Smiley," and shortly after, Bobo for a teacher, then a friend. Bo had got him into this, this Francis Marion affair, against his better judgment. He'd never liked kids, even when he'd been one. Especially then, as a matter of fact. Kids were Stateside Charlies: treacherous and all the same.

102

"I am Mister Rensselaer," he said to Zack, "and I do magic tricks. Like turning Plummers into butchers."

Then he laughed with half his face and now that Zack had stopped expecting it, stood up and grabbed his hand and squeezed the fingers hard, and ground the knuckles into one another.

"Hey," said Zack. The pain had made him clench the other fist. His eyes got wide and angry.

"*Comme ça,*" said Willis, letting go, and smiling, on the south side, anyway.

40. Eating

By nightfall, every kid on both the clipboards had checked in: eighteen boys, or one per bunk in Barracks B, but just a dozen girls. They gathered in the big main lodge for supper, and the first official meeting of the group.

The food was just a little late. What happened was the monster can that held tomato sauce "with meat" wouldn't fit under the cutting edge of the kind of electric can opener that they had, so Missus Fairchild had had to send one of the girls to find J.B. and borrow his pocket knife, which had about fourteen different tools on it, including a scalpel for meatball surgery. When they'd got the knife, it took them about a quarter of an hour to figure out which "thin-gumabob" was the can opener, and another to get it to work, in the course of which Doris Mullady got a pretty deep cut on her thumb. At one point Zack had wandered in the kitchen wondering, out loud, if he could help. But Missus Fairchild shooed him out at once. "What do you suppose is the matter with *him?*" she asked the girls, when he had gone.

The meal, when it appeared, was spaghetti, with the sauce, which Missus Fairchild had "jazzed up" (as she put it to the girls) with half a bottle of Gallo Hearty Burgundy, two good shakes of dried oregano, and three of Kraft grated

Parmesan and Romano cheese. "Makes all the difference in the world," she told them. Each table also got half a loaf of supermarket white bread, inverted on a dinner plate, and a plastic container of soft margarine. Toby wondered out loud if maybe they shouldn't bake their own bread, using whole-wheat flour they had ground themselves. Missus Fairchild shrugged and said why bother, it was just a filler, anyway. In point of fact, she'd never seen flour ground or bread baked from scratch in her entire forty-two years. What the hell was the point of living in the twentieth century if you didn't take advantage of it? was what she always said.

Willis Rensselaer, sitting with the Fairchilds and Bobo Bodine at the raised head table in the middle of the dining area, plucked a piece of the white bread from the pile as if it were a tissue and pretended to blow his nose in it.

"Dear Christ, Rita," he said. "You don't expect us to survive on *this*, I hope." He crumpled the bread into a ball and tossed it on the table by his plate.

Missus Fairchild snuck a glance at old J.B., but he was feeding stolidly, as usual, hunched forward, with his eyes down on his plate. His huge quadraphonic AM-FM cassette radio was parked on the table in front of him, tuned at low volume to the Sam N. Dreyfus Hour of Decency. He'd told her that these fellows that he'd hired were a couple of real gents.

Gents, my ass, she thought, which was unfair to Bobo, who'd only sat and smiled.

41. Meeting

After the meal was over—there were canned fruit cups and chocolate-chip cookies for dessert—and the tables cleared, and the dishes washed and put away (Missus Fairchild made a point of seeing to it that the boys "pitched in" and carried out the heavy trays), it was time to have the first official meeting of the group. The boys had milled around the living-room end of the lodge, waiting for the girls to get done in the kitchen, and Zack had used the time to introduce himself to maybe half a dozen guys he hadn't met before. He was getting the idea that his fellow survivalists were a mixture of goof-offs, music buffs, sex maniacs, druggies, drivers-of-fast-cars and -parents-up-the-wall, and sociopathic killers. Or, in other words, pretty much like the kids at SCD (except for the sociopaths), take away a little on the verbal and a lot in the bank. He'd spotted one kid who didn't seem to want to have anything to do with him, specifically, and two or three who didn't look as if they were in anywhere near the kind of shape it took to survive survival training. Rod Renko had gotten his mind around the fact that Zack was "Toby's friend," and they'd been standing talking Dukes of Hazzard-ish, when they were joined by Merribeth and Toby, looking frizzy-haired and red-of-face, respectively.

"Jeez-Mareez," said Merribeth, "that place is a real steam bath, that kitchen. If it wasn't for the bra, I'd feel like I been in a wet-T-shirt contest." She pulled her olive-green T-shirt away from her front, and shook it a time or two. "That dishwasher they got?" she said to Rod. "I bet it was here when his grandfather owned the place, or whatever." She jerked a thumb at Zack.

Toby's color had as much to do with mood as heat, apparently. "I can't believe this." She was fuming, but she didn't raise her voice, Zack noticed. "Except for 'lifting heavy trays,' it's Women Only in the kitchen? *We're* going to be the goddamn help up here, you know that? Missus Fairchild said"—she made her voice real snappy—"that *that's* because there's certain training things that aren't right for girls to do, and this just makes it even." She clenched her teeth and fists and made a bottled screaming sound. "I said he was a sexist moron, didn't I?" she said to Zack.

Her answer was a piercing whistle blast from down the room.

"A'right now, people, listen up. How about we hustle over here and come to order? Drop one end on a chair and stuff a sock in the other, okay? It's time for *business*, now."

The Hour of Decency was over, and Jewell B. Fairchild was about to give them the who-when-what-why-how of the next four weeks of their lives.

He began with introductions. It turned out that the training staff would consist of himself and two others. With only thirty trainees, a staff of three would be "ah-deal," J.B. informed them. "That comes out to one trainer for every ten recruits," he said, which caused Toby to pantomime the actions of a person using a pocket calculator, just below the table's edge—then nod in solemn agreement.

The trainers would be himself, Mister Rutherford Bodine (who half rose in his chair, and smiled around the room), and Mister Willis Rensselaer (who kept on looking at the tabletop and flicked a quick salute at nothing). And the fourth member of the staff would be his wife, Missus Fairchild, who'd bunk in at Barracks G, and also serve as Quartermaster General, in charge of meals and all supplies, excepting weapons. Missus Fairchild, he informed them, would "keep us all in line" and make sure we don't forget "our P's and Q's." Missus Fairchild stood straight up and smiled and raised one hand, bending her arm into a right angle at the elbow, the way she'd seen Mrs. Reagan do.

The training they would get, J.B. went on, could be thought of as being divided into four categories. The first of these was just about the most important, and a part of all the others. As such, it would be the responsibility not only of all the trainers, but also of each and every trainee, as well. What he was talking about was Physical Conditioning, he told them. There were groans, but of the "good sport" sort, Zack thought.

"If a man's going to survive, he's got to be in what I call a superior physical condition. He's got to be hard, and he's got to be lean." J.B. slapped his hand on his shirtfront, just above the belt. "'Cause unless he's *hard* and unless he's *lean,* it's just that much harder for a man to be *mean.*" He led, and therefore got, the chuckle that he wanted. "Which I'm here to tell you what a lot of the rest of your trainin' is going to be about." He looked delighted. "Bein' mean," he said, just to be sure the dimmest bulbs were glowing.

J.B. explained that everyone in camp, except for Missus F., would fall out for Cals in front of the lodge at five A.M. each morning, and when they were loosened up, they'd take an easy little run. Later in most days, there'd be some other runs, wearing different levels of equipment, and traversing different terrains—including a special "challenge" course, devised by Mister Bo Bodine himself, who said it beat the ones at Outward Bound all hollow. J.B. said they had to learn to run good not just because (he checked an index card he'd palmed) "the guy who fights and runs away will live to fight another day," but also because you ran to *get to* a fight a lot of times, to get there (peeking) "fustest with the mostest." So starting in the morning, they would run their you-know-whats off. And were there any questions about *that?*

Doris Mullady, the girl who'd cut her hand opening the tomato sauce, had a question. She wanted to know if this was one of the things the girls didn't have to do, 'cause she'd noticed J.B. had only said "man" and "guy" and "he," all the time he was speaking.

J.B. smiled, a big wide tight one. "Indeed they do, little miss, indeed they do," he said. "What the word 'man' happens to mean, as I been using it, is everybody that isn't an animal, which certainly takes care of you girls." A lot of the guys laughed at that one. "But while we're on the subject of girls and running, let me tell you this. I don't want to see no jiggle-jangle-jiggle out at Cals, and when you're out there running. You understand what I'm saying? It's up to every man in an outfit to wear the proper equipment appropriate for their sex at all times. And you boys'll know what I mean by that, too—right? Nobody wants to run their you-know-whats off *really,* do they now?"

That got a big loud hee-haw from a number of the guys, but underneath it Toby felt a tension start to build, a mounting lack of ease, already. J.B., smiling broadly, just moved on to Teeth.

Teeth, J.B. wanted them to know, were an important— *real* important—part of any survival situation. If a man in combat had bad teeth, he wasn't going to be worth "diddly-squat," he told them. Not that it came up too often where you actually had to bite the enemy, but the thing was you couldn't fight worth a lick with a toothache going on, and the exact same thing applied to the whole matter of survival in general, did they follow that? A survivalist kept his teeth and gums in an A-number-one physical condition at all times, with checkups every two–three months, at least ("Think like every checkup just might be your last") and brushing after every meal, no matter what or where. Why (he told them) he'd heard of troops that didn't have no drinking water use you-know-what to brush their teeth with. Now, those were some crack troops (yes, he was there to tell them).

So, he concluded, for the next four weeks they'd be expected to take care of their bodies like never before in their entire lives, which "when you think about it," he said in tones of revelation, "is what the game of survival just happens to be all about.

"Which brings us," old J.B. went on, and rubbed his hands together, "to what you'd call the more pacific skills we're going to teach up here"—Zack looked at Toby— "which is namely Wilderness Survival, Firearms Training, and Unarmed Combat, by which we mean fighting with anything that don't go 'bang.' So, without further adyoo, I'm going to present the first of your resident expert instructors to tell you a little bit about Wilderness Survival, Mister Bodine."

Bobo stood up and looked around the room, and smiled.

"First of all," he said, "just call me Bobo."

You could feel the room relax, and so it stayed while Bobo told them things that he had planned, in an easy cultured voice that made it sound like fun, and even not too difficult, to stay alive forever in a postdisaster wilderness: building shelters, making fires, foraging for food, disposing of their wastes ("without embarrassment or odor"). When he had finished, everybody clapped, and he responded with another set of smiles.

Mister Rensselaer did not suggest that anybody call him Will or Willis. He said that the best he could hope to do in the little time available was to show them how they could use their bare hands and their knives ("both as an extra finger, sharp and terrifying," and mounted on a rifle, as a bayonet) "to make live meat into dead meat," or to "render it impotent and in pain." There wouldn't be enough time for a lot of practice on refinements, or to get into such esoterica as darts or bows and arrows, or strangling with wire. Too bad, he said, but "that's the way the cupcake disappears, my dears." With which he sat down suddenly, in silence, winking, with his active eye, at Bobo.

After that, old J.B. on the 9mm pistol and various kinds of rifles was a bit of an anticlimax, Zack remarked to Toby, later on.

"When he told us that some .30-30 shells are 'blunt and slow,' I actually thought of marshmallows," he said.

42. Night Sounds—1

Just as Archie Cobden, Rodman Plummer's friend, had seen to it that there'd be Chivas Regal in his hand, if he survived whatever horrors were unleashed upon the world that he'd grown up in and made it to his Adirondack cave, so too had fourteen of the eighteen boys in Barracks B been moved to slip a little this or that to drink or smoke or drop into their survival-training luggage.

Which meant that at 9:05 in Barracks B, five minutes after the lights went out, the air was full of busy-searching sounds, followed by the scratch of matches, and the squeals of corks pulled slowly out of bottle necks, and the tiny crack a twist-off top will make at the moment that its airtight seal is broken. By 9:10, the room was fragrant with the smell of burning hemp, and peppermint, and certain of the sorts of fruits produced by Farmer Boone and Mr. Boston, Senior.

Zack had also thought of bringing up a flask, and then decided not to—better play it safe. He and Toby had discussed it just a little, the role that he would play at FMI; she seemed to be concerned.

He'd told her, "Listen, what I plan to do is blend right in the woodwork, be a little Zachameleon. I'm going to keep such a low profile that I could walk stark-naked on a glass-topped coffee table, and no one'd notice me."

"You wanta bet?" she'd said, and licked her lips to see if she could make him blush. Of course he did, but still he planned to be as inconspicuous as possible.

The trouble is that when you "get along with everyone" (Terry Bradford), even a "fourteen-karat bigot" (Toby Ayer) like Rod Renko will find he gets along with *you*, and even likes you. So Rod, on this first night, along with Frank and Duke and Ernie (friends of his from school), assembled by Zack's upper bunk, with Rod's fifth of peppermint schnapps, and Ernie's pint of muscatel, and Duke's big spliff of Housatonic Valley Gold and Lucky Strike tobacco. Zack simply lay in bed and helped himself to minuscule amounts of each and paid to every one of them his natural attention.

Below him, in the lower, Arthur Barrett looked at Rod's and Duke's and Frank's and Ernie's knees and thought about how dread-ful all this was. He had a soft, fat body and bad vision and an overbite, but no real friends and no real life, except in the dim arcade his father'd vowed to get him out of "just so he would know it's summertime."

In the living room of Cottage 1, two hundred feet away, Willis Rensselaer had started to adjust the knobs that made his electronic "ears" pick up the sounds of Barracks B at night.

"I could hear a roach expire over there," he said to Bobo, with a crooked smile.

"And probably you will," said Bobo, getting up, and interested.

43. Night Sounds—2

In Barracks G, the dozen girls (some eight of whom, including Merribeth and Toby, were also in possession of some ways to change their moods) were wondering if Missus Fairchild was ever going to take a hint from *The Sea Dog and the Strumpet* and close the book, turn out the light, and put her bod to bed.

Merribeth had learned from Rod that all the bunks in Barracks B were taken up by kids, so they—the boys—would be unsupervised at night. So what that meant to her was when (not if) she found a way to find her way on out of Barracks G, without her chaperone's awareness or (for sure) consent, there would be a party, of some sort, most every night. If she could start by stuffing lots of clothes inside her bunk, she thought, and, yes, her pillow, too . . .

Merribeth had never been away to summer camp. Her parents didn't care enough to notice much of anything. So all of this (old stuff) was new to her. Teen survival just might be a blast and a half, she thought.

Toby knew that probably, tomorrow night, she'd be asleep by 9:02, and thankful for the chance to be. She knew she was in halfway decent shape, but still. Any day that starts with Cals at five A.M. is bound to kind of tire out a girl.

But now, that night, she lay there in her bunk and curled her lip in every known direction and degree. What *was* she, ten years old, that she was ordered into bed at such-and-such a time, with Matron making sure she did as she was told, and washing down her soft-core pulp with drafts of Diet Dr. Pepper?

And also, there was something else. She'd seen a kid that night, at supper, a kid whose name she hadn't known, but she had recognized, for sure. And vice-surely-versa.

He'd been one of the ones who'd done that stuff to Oke, when Oke was on the hobby horse. And when he'd seen her looking at him from across the dining room, he'd kind of more or less freaked out. The spaghetti that he'd started toward his mouth had slithered off his fork, but he had never stopped the fork. He'd stuck it in his mouth completely bare, and when he took it out, he chewed.

His name, she later on found out, was Louis Ledbetter.

"Hey, Tobe." Merribeth looked funny, upside down, her curly hair *above* her face, not hanging to her shoulders. "What do you think'd happen if I lighted up a jay?" Merribeth wasn't much of a whisperer.

"All right, pipe down over there," said Missus Fairchild promptly, from across the room. She spoke much louder than Merribeth had. "We don't want any talking, after lights. Let's show a little consideration, girls. There's people trying to sleep, you know."

Someone whistled softly: "'Lullaby, and goodnight...'" and Doris Mullady giggled.

44. Louis Ledbetter

Louis Ledbetter had long hair and wore blue jeans, back in Oakwood. He listened to a lot of music and did a certain amount of dope, and claimed to be against all wars. He didn't like cops in general, or a lot of laws, and he said all politicians were crooks. Louis Ledbetter repeated the same few things over and over, just the way cops and politicians often do, and the people he hung out with would nod and say "yeah," and repeat the things *they* said a few times, too. None of them thought about anything, not because they couldn't but because they didn't see any point in it. It was too confusing and a pain in the ass, besides. This way was better.

It's guys like Louis Ledbetter that commit a lot of what the laws they don't like call "manslaughter." "I never meant..." they say, and mean it, but it's done and what's-her-name (or his) is dead. Anyone who's hit another person with a stick or rock or fist, or driven fast or funny, is a candidate.

Oke's death had been an accident: tragic, horrible, unexpected, and unplanned. When Louis Ledbetter put down his cigarette in the saucer on Oke's kitchen table, he'd had no idea that Jasper James was going to throw that saucer up against the wall—and Jasper James had never seen the cigarette. But because Louis Ledbetter was the sort of person that he was, he had to feel that no one in the world would possibly believe the truth about this matter: he'd forgotten all about the cigarette, till later. He was that way, too. And because he was this sort of person, he was sure that he was in bad trouble, as perhaps he should have been. The idea that he could (or even *must*) forgive himself, and start to think, was much too odd and unexpected for his static, made-up mind.

What Louis wondered now was whether Zack and Toby had actually followed him to the Francis Marion Institute, or whether it was just an incredible piece of bad luck, like a coincidence, or whatever you want to call it. It had probably been a mistake on his part to go over to the cemetery and let them spot him there. What he'd wanted to see was whether there were a lot of cops around, plus maybe to show—just in case that bullshit of his mother's turned out to be right, *you* know—that he wasn't a *totally* bad guy, and was sorry it happened, and crap like that.

For all he knew, the old man might have been one of their grandfathers. And maybe one of their fathers was a cop. If one of them was a cop's kid, they'd have probably put two and two together (the action at the Mall, plus the cemetery bit) and *known* that he had helped to trash the old man's house. And also, they'd probably have ways of finding out who he was, after they'd seen him at the cemetery, and once they knew who he was, it'd have been a cinch to follow him to this Teen Survival Session that his old man had stuck him into.

But what were they planning now? So far, all they'd done was look at him; neither one had spoken to him or, far as he could tell, spoken to any of the teachers about him. This Mister Rensselaer, in fact, didn't seem too crazy about the Plummer kid, for openers; in fact, the person he seemed to like—at least a little bit—was *him*. That was amazing. Teachers, as a rule, thought he was a piece of shit, and vice versa.

45. Night Sounds—3

J.B. Fairchild was sitting up in bed in Cottage 2. He had the cottage to himself, and he hadn't any clothes on. Underneath the covers, he had bent his legs; he leaned an open magazine against his knees.

He turned a page. There was an ad with a rich-looking man holding on to a good-looking woman, and the ad told him that when a man felt good about his condom, he felt good about himself. That made sense to old J.B. He had stockpiled condoms at the Institute, a lot of different brands and styles. Not for now, of course, for later. If you had to, you could build your own shelter and grow your own food, but there was no way in the apple-knockin' world that you could make your own rubbers.

J.B. turned another page. There were two girls in a meadow full of flowers, and they were both buck-naked, real cute girls. That was the way it might turn out to be, after whatever happened, happened. People would have to start from scratch, and build a new world, a world that wouldn't have the same old rules and hang-ups that you had today. J.B. could see himself in such a world. He could imagine him making it, surviving—him and, like, some kids, some girls from Barracks G, let's say, and for somebody to talk to, maybe Bill Bartowiak, a guy like that. Not Rutherford Bodine or Willis Rensselaer. Not Rita, either. Poor Rita. She'd be at work in downtown Hartford, probably; she'd never make it out.

He turned another page. Holy shit, will you look at that? Those girls were *wild*—there wasn't anything they wouldn't do, he'd bet! That's the way it'd be. Not like Rita, now, no way. Like this, like this, like this, like this, like this, like this, like this.

A regular tattoo, in Cottage 2.

46. Five A.M.

To almost all of the trainees at the Francis Marion Institute's Teen Survival Session, the words "five A. M." had, up until this point in their lives, only been used in sentences that began with: "And I didn't fucking get home until..."

When you stayed out until five A. M., the chances were that you'd gotten really shit-faced earlier in the evening, and maybe even passed out awhile, and then finally come around into good enough shape to get yourself home, somehow. Five A.M. was *late*, not early; it was the end of a long, long night, and not the beginning of the morning.

Even your parents didn't get up at five A.M.

47. Stretching It

"Now, tuck that left leg up, and streh-heh-hetch straight forward on the other side—that's it—and hold it while I count off one one-thousandth, two one-thousandths, three one-thousandths, four..." crooned Rutherford Bodine.

"Don't bounce it, please. That's beautiful," he said.

Bobo'd gotten up at 4:30 and brushed his teeth, of course—the first of five such close-ups in a normal Bobo day. After that, he'd showered, doing side and forward body bends, and pulling up his knees, swaying in the comfort of his early-morning spray, by Water Pik. At 5:08 he was standing, Newly Balanced, on the platform near the cannon in the circle by the lodge, clapping his hands together and beaming almost blindingly at the thirty dazed and sleep-deprived survivalists in front of him. By 5:20, he'd coaxed them through a half a dozen stretches; he had another ten or so to go.

He was about as happy as he ever got, sprawled out on that platform on a lovely summer morning, teaching kids some stuff they really ought to know.

The people spaced in rows of six in front of him were, nonetheless, in lesser states of ecstasy. They'd all been kids for long enough to be a little skeptical. If every grown-up knew exactly what they ought to know and do, why wasn't every grown-up rich, or anyway successful? Or even happy, come to think of it.

Besides, the grass that they were sitting on, with one leg stretched and one leg tucked, was soaking wet. There'd been a lot of groaning when they'd first gone down on it, but Bobo'd only laughed and told them it'd help to wake them up—think of it like throwing water on their face, he said. Some girls giggled back at him, but Toby'd only narrowed up her eyes suspiciously. Running in wet shorts and underpants (as they would shortly do) was no-one-who-knew-anything's idea of fun, and Bobo seemed to know a great deal more than nothing, so she thought.

Willis Rensselaer and J.B. Fairchild were also on the platform, but in back of Bobo. Willis was the only person there not dressed in the survival-session outfit: shorts and matching T-shirt, in olive green. He wore a runner's top, all white and partly mesh; his shorts were silk, or nylon maybe, very light and brilliant red, not only short and wide, but deeply vented on the sides. Willis Rensselaer was very limber, and his legs were very smooth. Underneath, he had on tight bikini briefs, white nylon ones, as everyone could see. He hadn't shaved his legs, but it looked as if he had, except if you were right up close to him, where you could see their few, light, silky hairs. He didn't have much body fat, either, and his arms and legs were clearly ridged with muscle.

The basic running course—the "track," as old J.B. referred to it—began beside the driveway. From there, it snaked its way, for five full miles, around a wooded portion of the property, and in the end returned to where it started. It was more or less one John Deere tractor wide: part up, part down, part dirt, part grass, part rock, part roots, part puddles when it rained. They'd stuck in colored stakes on either side of it, a quarter mile apart.

When the stretching was over, the running would begin, with Bobo and Willis taking the boys around the track in one direction, while old J.B. accompanied the girls in the other. That meant that somewhere on the course they'd meet, and have the chance to "check each other out," said Bobo with a wink and (yes, of course) a smile.

J.B. had decided that whenever the girls trained separately from the boys, it'd be a good idea if he, a married man, was in charge of them. He'd be more accustomed (he told the other two) to "a gal's moods, the way they carry on sometimes," and he had winked himself. Then, too (he'd told himself but no one else), the gals'd be a lot more disposed to mention any personal problems of a physical nature they might have to a married person, such as himself, rather than to a single guy. Plus, of course (he tried to not even think about this), there was the small uncertainty in his mind as to whether he would altogether trust those two around a bunch of teenage quiff. Or the even worse suspicion that he really *could*. Bobo seemed like a regular sort of gent, but Willis, now ... you couldn't really tell with him, the way he talked, and all. He'd heard a lot of guys who'd been in 'Nam had come back home a little bit ... peculiar, you might say.

"Listen up now, gals," said old J.B. to his dozen stretched-out adolescent charges. "I'm gonna set the pace from in back of the pack. Everybody stays in front of me—you got it?—running altogether in a bunch. I don't want to see no sprinters or no stragglers," he said, "and that's the truth."

Just lots of legs and asses will be fine, he might have added, without stretching it, at all.

48. Handling Women

I'd really love to tell you that Jewell B. Fairchild's original reason for not wanting any girls at the Francis Marion Institute's Teen Survival Session had been that he realized he'd never had a bona fide conversation with a female human being in his life, or even read a book by one, and hence knew nothing about that style and shape of creature whatsoever. I'd also like to be able to say that nationalism has nothing to do with war, and that there's no earthly reason for people not to have all the kids they feel like having.

But even if I told you stuff like that, the J.B. Fairchilds of this world and the politicians and the other heavy breathers—*breeders* make that, sorry—wouldn't (still) believe me for a moment, so why bother?

The fact of the matter is that old J.B. thought he was "an authority, when it comes to women," and *that's* what made him very much of two minds about the idea of starting out around a five-mile track, running, with a dozen teenage girls, at 5:38 A.M.

Here's the way he looked at it.

On the one hand, girls just weren't built right for running; everyone knew that who'd ever watched one trying to catch a bus. Also, there was this: a woman didn't want too many

124

muscles. Muscles didn't go with being "feminine"; muscles went with "masculine." So if a woman had a lot of muscles, you could draw your own conclusion. What would probably be right for females would be a little light jogging, interspersed with walking. That'd "tone them up." Being such an authority on women, J.B. knew expressions like that. He learned them from Rita. She learned them from *Cosmopolitan* magazine. Learning and doing are, as you've noticed, two entirely different things.

But, on the other hand, this *was* survival training and, as Rutherford Bodine had said, in training for survival you had to take people *past* their expectations of themselves, past the point they thought they had to stop.

"The last part of a drill," Bodine had said to Willis and himself, "will be the only part that really counts. The two push-ups that he just guts out, when he thinks he can't do any more, the quarter miles he runs *beyond* his goal. Those are the ones that put the muscle on a boy—both on his body, friends, and on his will." He smiled at old J.B. "I shit you not, Commander; I'm talking scientific facts. Stuff they've proven out at KIOSK." Willis raised the brow that could be raised. "Kansas Institute of Sociometric Kinesiology," Bobo said. "Our function is to make our students go beyond their limits, get them to believe they haven't any, really. Survival, *in extremis*, may come down to, simply, that." His voice got slower, deeper. "At times, they'll think we're being cruel to them, I'd guess, when we're really being very, very kind."

Well, that made sense to old J.B. This *was* survival training, not just weight control, and there wasn't any point in arguing with scientific facts. Besides, Bobo was as sharp as a tack, a college grad, and a hell of a pistol shot, to boot.

So when, after less than a quarter of a mile, it seemed to him that the pack of girls in front of him had slowed down to what was little more than a quick-step, he remembered what Bobo'd said, and he started to exhort them both with words and (trotting/wheeling back and forth, like a Sheltie with a bunch of Highland sheep) flat-handed contact with their wet behinds. Not very hard. And only certain ones, at that.

Toby kept herself well out of range of this activity, moving from the middle of the pack—the *unobtrusive* middle, as she thought of it—to almost at the front. She knew that she could run a five-mile course with ease, in forty minutes or even less, but she couldn't see the point in doing so, up there. She didn't want to star, but to survive.

Merribeth was not in Toby's kind of shape, nor was that one of her ambitions. Shape, to her, was something that you had a real nice one of, or not; you got it by good luck, and dieting sometimes, not exercise, and she had sure been lucky. J.B. didn't miss that fact, and so he didn't miss what Missus Fairchild's current book would call her "saucy backside," either.

"Hey," she said, and rubbed it. "Cut it out. That *hurt.*" She took a swipe at old J.B., who sprang away, quite coltishly. Merribeth might never make a dean's list in her life, but if she ever started in on deans, no problem.

Now, she dropped all pretense of a trot, and as she walked, she tossed her head and said, *"Some* people, I just happened to notice, got to do *their* stretching exercises on a nice, dry platform, so's they don't hafta try to run with sopping wet shorts on. Oh, no, not the *instructors*. It's all right if the kids get all sortsa *chafing*, and like that. Who cares about the kids? Set the girls down in a bunch of puddles, if you hafta—let them all catch their death and whatever. But let's be sure the *instructors* are okay. Just so long as *they* survive."

That zinged J.B., but good. Pushing people beyond their limits was one thing, but here was a girl talking about a personal problem of a physical nature, wasn't it? It could be even worse for a girl, running in wet shorts, he wasn't exactly sure. Rita had never mentioned that fact, in the course of their marriage, but then he couldn't remember a single time that Rita had ever run in wet shorts. Maybe that was why she never had, because it was really awful, doing that, for girls.

"Okay," he said, "supposin' that we all just walk awhile, okay? Maybe when we catch our breath and—uh—dry off a little, we can try a little jog again." He ran one hand across his crewcut and he smiled at all of them.

"One thing's for sure," he said. "It sure is a nice day."

He got some nods, and even parts of smiles, for that. If you knew women, you knew how to handle 'em. No question about it.

49. HUP

When he was teaching, Bobo didn't use a "lesson plan."
Lesson plans were "public school," and Bobo liked his
flexibility, those little side trips off the (oh-so) beaten path
that gifted teachers often took, when student questions
showed that there was need for them.

That didn't mean, however, that he approached a unit
"cold." Oh, no, indeed—not ever. Never. No. A part of
competence was this: anticipation. Only rookie teachers got
surprised. So, in the case of running, at the Teen Survival
Session, he and Willis had their strategies agreed upon,
down pat. From the opening gun.

They started off with Willis in the lead, to set the pace,
then eighteen boys, then Bobo. As soon as Zack saw Willis
floating down the rustic track, he knew that they (or some
of them, at least) were in for lots and lots of trouble.

That spring, Zack had been a substitute outfielder on the
Stockton Country Day School varsity baseball team. He
wasn't much of a hitter, and his arm was less than great,
but he could cover ground in the field, and catch the ball,
and run the bases pretty well, and he was always cheerful
about his role, which was late-inning defense and pinch-
running, plus lots of chatter on the bench. Voluntarily, he'd

done extra running during the season, so as to keep his legs in the very best of shape, and after the season was over, he'd kept on running even harder and longer, more or less in anticipation of this very moment. It wasn't that he wanted to outshine the other kids at the Francis Marion Institute Teen Survival Session. Far from it.

50. *Au Contraire*

Zack had already grasped the first rule for preparing yourself to be inconspicuous, which is:

YOU CAN ALWAYS GO SLOWER (ACT DUMB-ER, LOOK UGLIER) THAN YOU ACTUALLY ARE, BUT NOT THE OTHER WAY AROUND.

51. TWO

Willis Rensselaer was striding: long, smooth legs and real short shorts, no socks. A pack of eager hounds came after him, a group of four—no, five. No, six. Zack, hanging back as number seven, saw that maybe three of those were runners, lean and limber guys whose feet came down real lightly on the ground; the other ones were athletes, or thought they were, or wanted to impress somebody. Zack knew that he could run maybe *one* mile at the pace Willis Rensselaer was going. Maybe. If this was the speed they expected you to run, for five miles, at the Francis Marion Institute, it was going to be a very long four weeks, with very few survivors. He threw a glance behind him. Great good Lord. Forget four weeks; there were people there who might not make it through the morning.

Zack was well past the first quarter-mile stake when he heard the whistle blow behind him. Three short blasts meant "stop," and those were three short blasts. He stopped. Again, he heard the whistle: three more shorts, and now, from up ahead of him, an echo. One, two, three. Zack hadn't moved. Then, from the rear again, a single long one: tweeet. One long blast meant "come." Zack turned and trotted toward the rear. Low profiles always did as they were told.

When he got back to the quarter-mile stake, Bobo and eleven of the group were there already, and Willis and the six who'd been ahead of him arrived a moment later, all together, prancing.

"What's the story here?" asked Willis, continuing to jog in place. Not even out of breath. Not even sweating.

He must have been kidding, Zack thought. A *Weekly Reader* story wouldn't be more clear or obvious: some members of their group were just about to die.

Bobo had perceived this, anyway, it seemed. He didn't look delighted, either.

"Correct me if I'm wrong," said Bobo. "I have heard— I think from Mister Fairchild, though I wouldn't swear to that—that everyone was told, not once but twice, that they should start to get in shape *before* they came on up here. One time at a meeting, and before that in a letter, is that right? I didn't see the letter, and I wasn't at the meeting." Bobo sounded rational, and calm, and fair. ("I like to feel I'm *scrupulously* fair," he often told his colleagues, at his school.) "But I'm pretty sure that Mister Fairchild told me that. What's *your* recollection, Swezey?"

"Uh," this round-faced kid with lousy skin replied. "Yeah. Think so. Something like that." Swezey was, as Mr. Slagle, soccer coach at SCD, would put it, "sucking wind."

"Well, it looks to me as if you, and quite a number of other people, just decided to ignore what Mister Fairchild said to you, and wrote you in a letter. It looks to me as if certain people here just didn't care enough about themselves, or this group, or about the *principle* of survival, to follow what seems to me to be a perfectly reasonable suggestion." Bobo's voice had gotten quieter as he spoke, but now he turned his chin and volume up and seemed to ask the trees some questions.

"So what if these people couldn't participate in parts of the program? So what if they threw the schedule completely out of whack? So what if they got in the way of other people's training for survival?" He looked down at the group.

"Well, the chances are they may not even care," he said,

"but here's a partial answer to those questions, anyway: So, other people are going to have to help them.

"This place is nothing but the world in microcosm," Bobo said. "All over the country, people are deciding that they don't want to work. They could get jobs, the jobs are there, but they don't want them. And the rest of us end up supporting them. Out there"—he waved a hand—"they call it welfare. Here"—he dropped his voice again—"I think it's just a goddamn shame.

"I need some volunteers," said Bobo, brisk again. "People who've done their running and reported in shape, and who'd be willing to help the people who couldn't or wouldn't be bothered." He looked around the group; some heads were up, and others hanging.

Zack waited just a careful second, till he saw that all the ones who'd been ahead of him had volunteered, and some of those behind. It was extremely obvious to him that there were a fair number of kids in the group who even if they'd started twelve-hour-a-day workouts when they'd gotten Fairchild's letter, and then stepped it up to eighteen after the meeting in the church, *still* wouldn't have been able to run five miles at any sort of pace. But his father had given him a piece of advice, one time, that seemed to apply in this situation.

52. Rodman Plummer's Advice

"When the inmates take over the asylum, the smartest thing to do is cross your eyes and piss down the stairwell."

53. THREE

Soon, Bobo had the whole thing organized. Five pairs of guys like Zack, in shape, would help one weaker one, apiece; that would leave three in-betweens, to go it on their own. Zack had his doubts that there *were* ten of them in any sort of shape, but in any case he and Ernie (friend of Rod) were put with Arthur Barrett, from the bunk right under Zack. Rod and Frank would help their other friend, the skinny kid named Duke, who smoked two packs of Kools a day, at home, and who'd never (even) walk inside a Burger King, if he could get his Whopper at the drive-up window. Willis watched this all shape up; he looked as if he smelled, at least, an open sewer.

They started off again. Willis, still, was first, followed by the in-betweens. Then, five sets of three abreast, then Bobo.

Zack saw at once there would be problems. Even when Arthur was going his fastest—which he probably wouldn't be able to keep up for more than a hundred yards—he wasn't going quite as fast as Willis was, even at his present, more retarded, pace. What he and Ernie would have to do was grab Arthur under the arms, from both sides, and by taking a certain amount of his weight off the ground, make it

135

possible for him to move his legs a little faster. In other words, they pretty much had to carry the kid, while staying at about an eight-minute-mile pace themselves, and looking out for roots and rocks on this uneven stretch of ground. And the trouble with *that* was that it was really pretty hard to run at normal speed and balance when you had one arm engaged in lifting the rough equivalent of, say, a dead hyena.

They tried it, anyway. So did the groups ahead of them and after; it seemed like the only thing to do, just then, as new as everybody was. It was terrible, but they tried it.

Arthur was muttering, "Geez, I'm sorry, you guys. I really am."

And Ernie was muttering, "Shut the fuck up, will you?" while Zack was trying to count, "One-two, one-two, one-two," kind of like in a three-legged race, when all of a sudden Bobo started in on *them*.

"All right, let's move it, *Plummer*," Bobo said. He'd slid ahead of the three triads behind them, and now he went on past *them*, too. He was moving lightly, easily, running almost sideways when he spoke.

"What's the matter with you, Fazio?" he snarled at Ernie, next. "*Push* it, will you, man?"

When he turned away, it sounded very much as if he said, "No *wonder* this country's in trouble."

Zack could feel it happening: he started to get pissed. Pissed at Bobo, first, for being so unfair, and pissed at Arthur, next, and maybe even more, for making him get into this. He'd been doing fine, no problem; *he* had been in shape.

He could hear Bobo yelling at Rod and Frank, now, asking them what they thought this was. He sounded utterly disgusted and let-down.

And then the kid in front of him tripped over the root.

Later on, Zack told Toby that it probably would have looked funny—a movie of this chain-reaction tumble.

When the kid in front of Zack—who was one of the athletes—tripped, and started to lose his balance, he yanked on the arm of the load he'd been dragging, who, being a

136

spaz anyway, went completely out of control, lurching into the original tripper, and guaranteeing that they'd both go down.

As that began to happen, the third member of their group tried to slam on the brakes and more or less leap over their legs as they fell, but that (as you might guess) only sent him slamming into the group behind them: Zack and Ernie and Arthur.

Zack, seeing this guy coming, had tried to counter the force by pushing Arthur to the right, which made him nick the guy and then bang into Ernie. And by that time Zack's feet had tangled with the two fallen bodies in front of him, and he was starting down himself. Arthur, reeling back from hitting Ernie, spun around and actually fell over Zack; Ernie had bounced away from Arthur, staggered a couple of steps, tried to jump over the writhing mass in front of him, but didn't make it. Which brings us to the moment that the three guys right behind them got involved, and Bobo, safely off the trail of course, was letting go three short ones on his whistle.

When Willis and the three kids running by themselves got back, they found that only Bobo was on his feet. The other fifteen people were sitting or lying on the path, a few of them trying to make the best of things, and the others wondering aloud if "it" was broken, or using the language of the streets, or both.

Bobo looked at Willis, as if the others weren't there. "I give up," he said. "This isn't going to work. Not that it really works anywhere in the country. They ruin it for everyone."

Willis said, "I remember what you told us about the Plains Indians, back in US-10. How they'd simply leave the ones who couldn't keep up, the sick and the crips and the old ones. It isn't fair to have the worst and weakest set the pace. In 'Nam, we had the same trouble with wounded, sometimes. There, we'd leave it up to the wounded guy himself, a lot of times. 'Full-service' or 'self-service'—he could have his choice. If he couldn't talk or move, he'd have to take 'full-service.' No one wanted to be captured in those days, thank you very much."

Bobo smiled a thoughtful one. "I'm glad that you remembered that," he said. "About the Indians, I mean. And I can understand about Vietnam. But here we've got a different situation. We've got to—somehow—wing it. Come up with something new. A way of being fair to everyone."

"Well, I've got a suggestion," said Willis. Zack was amazed how totally the two of them continued to ignore the eighteen of the rest of them. He'd heard that people treated slaves like that, in years gone by, and maids, and also children. A low profile was one thing, but this was ridiculous.

"I think the only thing we *can* do," Willis said, "is divide them into two groups. The ones who are capable of completing this exercise in the form that we've planned it, who've cared enough about themselves and each other to report in halfway decent shape—we'll call them the Blue Group. I suggest that you go on with them, and finish up the running drill, exactly as expected. The others we can call . . . let's see . . . why not the A Group? A, of course, standing for asshole. That'll be our little secret." Willis smiled. "*I* will volunteer to be in charge of them," he said, "and they will simply do"—he sighed—"the best they can." He left the trail to rip a slender shoot from off a willow tree and strip it of its leaves. "I *guarantee* it."

54. FOUR

The girls were on one of their frequent "walking breaks"
when they passed Bobo and the Blue Group, coming from
the opposite direction, and really motoring along.

Toby saw that Zack was in the middle of the pack, where
he had planned to be, and she could tell that he was working
hard. But when he caught her eyes, he rolled his own and
stuck his tongue out, comically, so she knew he was all
right. Rod and Frank and Ernie, from her school, came after
Zack, and they looked really beat. When Merribeth called,
"Hi! Hi, Rod!" he didn't have the strength to even say her
name, it seemed.

"Shit" was all he said, in passing.

Doris Mullady laughed when the A Group came in view.
By then, the girls were jogging slowly, easily, with J.B.
going "Hup-two-three-four," happy in the rear of them,
again.

The A Group looked a lot like frantic ducks, their pace
a sort of tortured-looking scuttle. And, looking at their legs,
it seemed as if they must have gotten off the track someplace, and had to push their way through bramblebushes.

55. Rest Hour

Jewell B. Fairchild probably wouldn't have looked any more puzzled if Bobo had said, "I suppose that after lunch we'll have an *Agnus Dei* (or perhaps a *fille de joie*)," on the day the staff had first sat down to hammer out the Teen Survival schedule.

"'Rest hour'?" he'd asked, and slit his eyes and scratched his head, a bit above one ear. "And what in the hell is that?"

Bobo ordered his eyeballs to refrain from rolling around in his head—or from sneaking a glance at Willis, either. He commanded his tongue to be civil, as well.

"Well," he said, "it's sort of a space of time, after lunch, about sixty minutes long on the average, in which people more or less take it easy. Do anything they want, write letters, or whatever. Read. It's a time without any scheduled activities, you might say. Some people might lie down, take a nap, even."

J.B. thought that over. "Just like a rest period," he finally said.

"Exactly!" Bobo agreed. "What my teaching experience tells me is that the period after lunch is really the worn spot—a hole, really—in the warp and woof of a student's learning day. Everything goes through, then; nothing sticks.

The kids themselves are close to somnolent. A matter of digestion, so I'm told: most of their blood goes rushing to their stomachs."

"Which means it's *still* above their minds," said Willis nastily. Rest hour was fine with him; he'd grown up with the concept. Besides, it'd mean less time he'd have to hang around with kids.

J.B. assumed that all of what Bobo said meant he didn't like to teach school after chow. He wasn't sure what he felt, himself. They hadn't had any rest hour in the Marine Corps, and somehow the idea didn't seem to exactly square with *survival* training. Them people out of the city probably weren't about to hunker down and rest after their noonday meal, any more than a Russki missile launcher would. But these were only kids (he kept telling himself), and this Bobo fellow was the expert, as far as kids were concerned.

"Well, let's give her a try," he said.

Missus Rita Fairchild didn't mind in the least the idea of lying down after lunch and just closing her eyes for a minute or two. Not at all. Especially when she was waked up at five in the morning, day after day, as if she was some kind of farmerette, or something.

It never crossed her mind that her girls in Barracks G would use this free time to behave in an unladylike way with any of those boys in Barracks B. As far as Missus Fairchild was concerned, sex was strictly an afterdark activity, no matter how depraved a person was.

Ladies didn't use a word like "horny," even if they'd read it in a book, a time or two.

The very first rest hour, Toby took Zack on a tour of all the special secret places she'd discovered on her earlier visits to the Francis Marion Institute, when she'd made it her business to put as much pure space (and thicknesses of any opaque stuff) between her father and his buddies (on the one hand) and herself.

She began at the tree house, which was near the old

gamekeeper's cottage, by the head of the driveway. It was high up in a large old maple tree and was clearly the work of either a dutiful, safety-minded father/mother, or of one of those impossibly handy juveniles that a lot of us spend our childhoods being compared to. With the tree in full leaf, as it was, the house was all but invisible from the ground.

After that—and after some messy, muck-shoed marching through a lot of trackless woods (to Zack)—there was the narrow cellar hole, on the nice, solid island with the big spruce tree, in the middle of the marshiest section of the property, not too far from the pond. Toby'd roofed it over with some poles and plywood pieces and a tarp, and this was still in place, now covered with a layer of leaves. He said he'd slither under it another day, when they had brought a flashlight.

Their final stop was the abandoned skeet field, from the gun-club days, with its little padlocked storage house that Toby just happened to have the key to—it being the padlock that she'd put in place herself, a year or so before, when she'd discovered there was "neat stuff" in the cabin. She showed him; she had stored and stacked it in a closet. There were a bunch of cases of clay pigeons, like tiny, fragile Frisbees, plus box on box of brilliant plastic shotgun shells, a lot of six-packs (both beer and different-flavored sodas), and some jars of nuts and sour balls. Bonanza.

And all the while they toured, they talked.

56. Judgments

"I don't think J.B. is dangerous," Toby said. "Sexist, yes. Moronic, certainly. But I don't think he's dangerous. Those other two, I'm not so sure. Particularly Willis. He is *such* a creep. I can't stand him. Just looking at him makes my skin crawl. They ought to give him a bell, like in the old days with lepers." Toby raised an arm and flopped her hand around.

"Hmmm, yeah, well, I think I know what you mean," said Zack agreeably. "I guess being in Vietnam and everything . . ."

Given his tendency to get along with everyone, Zack was quite a bit slower than Toby when it came to putting people down. His getting along was founded, after all, on this genuine interest he had in people and on the honest attention that he paid to them, and that meant that he was (therefore) gotten along *with,* by all those other types. It is, unquestionably, a trifle harder to make heavy judgments on people who seem to like *you* a lot. I mean, come on, those people have good taste, *compadre.*

"I wouldn't care if he'd been on Juan Corona's farm," said Toby crudely. "I think the guy's a psychopath. At least a pervert of some sort. To do that to those kids! It isn't their fault if they're fat, or if they're weird or weenies, is it? I mean, not completely, anyway. And from what you tell me, Bobo's just as bad, almost. I've never completely trusted a teacher who acts like he wants to be my buddy. You know what I mean?"

"He *is* a little strange," said Zack. "All that stupid welfare stuff. But I can see what he means about a person having to learn to stretch himself—going past your limits, and all that. It's amazing how much more you *can* do than you think you can, at first."

Toby faced him then, and took him by the ears and did a little snakelike wriggle, up against his front. "And how much do you think *you* can do, big boy?" she asked him in a husky voice. "'Cause once I start, there's just no stoppin' me . . ."

"Boy," said Zack, and checked his watch, "you *would* get into this with only five minutes left in rest hour, wouldn't you? Pretty cagey, Tobe. If we don't get back in time for Wilderness Survival, you *know* Bobo'll give us to Willis to use as bayonet dummies."

"Oh, sure," said Toby. "Good excuse, Zackaboo. Why don't you just admit you don't want to stretch yourself"— she licked her lips—"with little bitty me?"

And turned and ran off through the woods, a-cackling.

57. Talking to the VoystrComp

"A VoystrComp?" said Jewell B. Fairchild, with his nose all wrinkled up.

"Mmm-hmmm," said Bobo smoothly. "And you'll love it." He knew that J.B. was an old-fashioned guy, not the sort of man whose heart rejoiced at the sound of word combinations like "biofeedback monitoring device" and "analog computer," which was exactly what a voice-stress computer, or VoystrComp, *was*. J.B. *knew* his car started better *before* electronic ignition, in the days a handy guy could fix a clock, or a radio.

"The way it works, J.B., is on the same principle as those dog whistles?" said Bobo, lighting up a folksy and sincere one. "The kind you blow into, and people can't hear, but dogs can, because their ears are so much better? This thing is like the dog. Heh-heh," laughed Bobo, when he saw his colleague's face begin a frown. "By that I mean this little dingus here can pick up micro-tremors in a person's voice—like, sounds you couldn't notice with the naked ear. And what these tremors are is indications of how much stress a person is experiencing. You got it?" Bobo looked at J.B. closely. It really was exhausting, keeping his attention, making sure you didn't go too fast, or deep. "Look," he said. "We'll give you an example—like, a demonstration. I'll turn it on and we'll get Willis, here, to read these sentences I've typed. He's never seen a word of this before. Now, watch."

He whipped out the device, the VoystrComp. It looked kind of like one of those calculators that J.B. had always figured he didn't need one of (what in the hell *were* all those buttons with the funny squiggles on 'em?). But this one had just one control, a switch that Bobo turned from off to on.

Then he handed Willis a piece of paper, and Willis read this typewritten paragraph:

"I am an instructor at the Francis Marion Institute Teen Survival Session. It's located in North County, Connecticut, on fifty or so acres of mostly wooded land. I served with the Special Forces in Vietnam, and I am skilled in guerrilla-fighting techniques. I think a nuclear weapons freeze would be a fine idea, and I'm sure the military budget should be heavily slashed. I am very much concerned about the possibility of civil disorder in this country, and feel that when it comes, it will probably be communist-inspired. I love pistachio ice cream and think abstract modern painting is the greatest, but I also think there are kids enrolled in the program who don't belong here."

Willis Rensselaer read all that in a flat, toneless voice. Every sentence sounded the same, to old J.B. But when Willis said that crap about a nuclear freeze and cutting the military, the little amber light on the VoystrComp went off and the red one went on. And the same thing when he talked about pistachio ice cream and modern art. All the rest of the time, the amber light was on.

"Holy shit!" said old J.B. He might not be an engineer, but that didn't mean he was a dummy, either. "That thing's a goddamn lie detector!"

"Well, not *really*," Bobo said. "You couldn't *count* on it, for that. I mean, sometimes a person'll have these tremors in his voice talking about something he really believes in an extra lot—is superexcited about, you know what I mean?

But, in general, it *is* a handy gadget. I mean, we could use it to find out if there are things in the program the kids are feeling stressed about. I think we even might be able to define some problem areas before they got to be problems, if you follow me. Nip bad morale in the bud. I've used it a lot where I teach. It's just another educational tool, a piece of hardware, but one with a certain potential, I should say."

"Hell, yes," said J.B. Fairchild, bobbing his short haircut up and down. "I can see that. And, listen—you know who'd get a kick out of that? Rita. Anything that's got to do with . . . with *people*. And, *you* know, the *unknown*. Besides that, she's crazy about *science,* and all the new inventions." J.B. hoped he wasn't laying it on too thick. "D'you suppose that I could borrow it? Just overnight?" he asked casually.

"Sure," said Bobo, waving, smiling, generous. "Of course you can. You show her. And enjoy."

But well before Rita Fairchild ever set her eyes on VoystrComp (for a thirty-second demonstration: "You should see this piece of junk that Willis got," which ended all her interest, as he knew it would), old J.B. wrote out (in just plain pencil, thank you), and then read to it, the following:

"My name is Jewell B. Fairchild and I was born and raised in Conn and rite now Im Director of the Francis Marion Institute Teen Survival Sessian. I would'nt like to have sexial relations with any of the girls in Baracks G. When I was in the Marine Corps I served in Korea and got a Bronze Star. I beleive God wants us to gard the American way of life from it's enemys inside and outside the country, like diferent ones I don't have to name. My favorit meal is steak and french fried with apple pie and ice cream for desert and coffee after. If I do the rite things for my God and my country, itd be okay to have sexial relations with a girl other than Rita, particklerly if she was dead or didn't know it."

Afterward, he tore the paper up and flushed it down the toilet.

147

58. Letter

A couple of days later, Zack dashed off a letter to his parents that included the following paragraph:

"Toby thinks that at least two of the staff members are certifiable lunatics, and she may be right. I'd be more inclined to say 'a mite peculiar'—the way that old guy who rented boats up on Meddybemps Lake used to say, remember? It's mostly that the whole setup is so strange, the way these people think about what's going to happen in the country (probably), and how they see themselves as having this special sort of awareness that the average person doesn't have. I don't know if it's acute paranoia (Toby) or just some sort of ordinary, ignorant elitism (yours elitruly)."

He dropped the letter in the green wooden box in the main lodge living room, the one that had the words "Out-Going Mail" painted in white letters on its lid.

Bobo Bodine carried his old Royal portable with him everywhere he went; he never knew when he might get an idea for a new piece, and just want to sit right down and bang it out.

His "pieces" were scripts for a line of erotic cassettes produced by Lovesounds, Inc., on West 22nd Street, in

New York City. They were very hardcore stuff, making sure to leave absolutely nothing to the hearer's imagination, and repeating a lot of the same words over and over and over again. Bobo was the most versatile writer that Hymie Slaughter, president of Lovesounds, ever used. His stuff, at one time or another, included parts for actors who could do the voices of members of every known gender, between the ages of a few months and well into senility, and even the silence of . . . well, people slightly past that point, if you must know. All these came in various combinations, some so unexpected as to bring a gasp of amazement, even to and through the liver-colored lips of Hymie Slaughter.

Willis Rensselaer never used a typewriter. What he could do, though, and had been doing ever since his boarding school days, was an amazing job of copying people's handwriting. The way he'd do it was to turn the person's signature (let's say) *upside down*, and copy it that way, just as a design, rather than an actual word, made up of letters. It's pretty phenomenal how good a job he did that way.

"You want me to read Zack's letter to you?" Belinda Plummer asked her husband.

"A letter from Zack?" he said. "Yes, good."

"It isn't very long," she said, and started in to read. Near the end, it went:

"Toby and I can't get over how intelligent the staff members are. It isn't just that they know a lot about the stuff they're teaching—what they also seem to have are these extraordinary insights into the warp and woof of our society, and the places that it's starting to unravel."

"Warp and *what?*" asked Rodman Plummer slyly.

"Woof," Belinda answered.

"And a big bow-wow to *you,*" her husband said.

Rodman Plummer hadn't been aware that Zack knew words like "warp" and "woof." Another plus for SCD, he thought.

Belinda Plummer didn't even know her son could type.

59. Unarmed Combat

"Eyes, groin, neck, knee, nose," said Willis Rensselaer. He sounded somewhat distant, maybe bored.

"EYES, GROIN, NECK, KNEE, NOSE," the class repeated.

They were seated on the grass, beside the platform, in the circle by the lodge. Willis Rensselaer was standing, pointing to his body, different ways: eyes (with stiffened fingers), groin (a grab, with a pretended twist), neck (hand edge to the Adam's apple), knee (the other foot against the side of it), nose (palm heel underneath it). Today, he had a white silk scarf around his neck, a cutoff T-shirt, gray, that said "elaine's" in black and left his sculpted stomach bare, and green silk running shorts. Willis Rensselaer liked slidy stuff, on skin.

"Eyes, groin, neck, knee, nose," he said again, this time flicking out his scarf at one kid or another, aiming at the eyes, the groin, and so on.

"EYES, GROIN, NECK, KNEE, NOSE," they answered, all together.

"Okay," he said. "Now. Once you have your sweet spots memorized—that wasn't *too* hard, was it, Rod?—you have to know the different ways to play with them. Again, we'll start with nitties-gritty: kick, chop, twist, spear, gouge. You got it?" He held up his hands, like Zubin Mehta. Really. How could he be doing this?

"KICK, CHOP, TWIST, SPEAR, GOUGE!" They stayed right on the beat.

Toby was having just a little trouble with her face. The Stockton Y had always had a class in self-defense, and she had first enrolled in it when she was eight, along with Florence Ayer, her mother and a nurse, who often found herself in parking lots at night. They'd gone back for refreshers almost every year—she'd done it for her mother's sake—and then, four years ago, she'd started with karate. She always said that *that* was Harold Ayer's idea, and so it was, he thought. In fact, she'd had to leave the paper folded to the ad placed by the Kyong Kim Academy of Adapted Traditional Karate for four straight days, before he got it.

Master Kyong Kim was about as much like Willis Rensselaer as bean sprouts are like beefalo. Master Kim said things like "Form becomes emptiness, emptiness becomes form" and urged his students to perfect their characters. He would say "You must do each *kata* until the *kata* does itself" rather than "Practice that move until your tongues hang down to your ding-dongs."

Willis Rensselaer, in shorts and scarf and cutoff T-shirt, was prancing up and down in front of them: kicking, chopping, twisting, spearing, gouging at the air. It would have been ridiculous, she thought, except that he was serious. And what seemed almost worse to her was: so were certain kids. Kids should be above these kinds of things, these older-generation failures.

Toby kept her face impassive, just as Master Kim had taught her.

Willis urged them to their feet, so they could move together. "*Kick*—kick at his knee, that's right," he cried. "Now *chop*—aim at the old carotid arteries, just here and here." He pointed to the places, on his own lean neck. "And

151

twist—that should be *grab* and twist." He seized his crotch and seemed to give it half a turn, again.

"Of course..." He raised a hand to stop the exercise. "If the guy coming at you happens to be a gal, you don't use that one, no indeed. What you do..." Willis snapped into a fighting stance, hands stiff and up, with one leg forward, both knees bent. From there, he made a sudden leap and came down standing straight, his feet together, with one elbow crooked and offered to the side. "...is take her out to dinner." A lot of people laughed.

"Now, once again," said Willis, "but this time let me hear you shout with each attack, okay? I don't care what you say, but keep it short and sweet—one syllable. Oh, wait." He raised his hand, again. "Just so we can be sure— for Renko's sake—maybe Mister *Plummer* will give us an example. A one-syllable word. How about *commode*, Mister Plummer? Would that be a one-syllable word?"

"No, sir," said Zack. "It wouldn't."

"Well, how about *bidet?*" said Willis suddenly.

"No, sir," said Zack, and he was blushing, Toby saw.

"What is a *bidet*, anyway?" asked Willis Rensselaer. "Maybe certain members of the group don't know."

"I'm not exactly sure myself," said Zack.

"You're not? But you're a Plummer, aren't you?" Willis Rensselaer looked half puzzled. There was nervous laughter Zack plugged into.

"Well, aren't you?" Willis Rensselaer persisted, acting serious.

"Not the right kind, I guess," said Zack, with another little laugh. He sounded modest and regretful—cool—but Toby knew he hated this, the spotlight. He'd be trying to figure out how he could step away from it, why Willis had put him in it to begin with.

Toby looked at the other kids. Most of them had dropped their eyes, uncomfortable for Zack, embarrassed to be watching this. Good, she thought. But some of them were loving it, smiling, waiting, smelling blood—or nervous sweat, for sure. Louis Ledbetter's head was high, his eyes were sparkling; he ran them back and forth: Zack to Willis Rensselaer and back to Zack again. He even—Toby stared, incredulous—he even licked his lips.

"I guess you're not," said Willis Rensselaer at last, and shook his head, disgustedly. "So maybe you'll suggest another word, a word we *can* use, when we strike. A one-syllable word, Mister Plummer."

"Well, how about . . . 'hit'?" said Zack, a little weakly. He doubted that was gold-star country.

" 'Hit,' " repeated Willis Rensselaer. "Now *that's* original. Is 'hit' an anger word for you, peculiar bummer-Plummer? If you get angry, do you shout out 'hit'? Probably not. Even you might use a little stronger word, *n'est-ce pas?* Like—what? You tell him, Louis." He swung in a Led-betterly direction.

"Shit!" said Louis Ledbetter proudly, loudly. When Willis gave him half a smile, he pressed his luck. "Or fuck, or prick, or cunt, something like that."

"Prick?" said Willis. "Cunt? Louis, this is hitting, *hurting*, not ordering a meal." Louis and some others went hee-haw. "Oh, well," he added, losing interest, "hit-shit, punt-cunt—it doesn't make a hell of a lot of difference. Just yell *something*, will you? Now here we go again with . . . *kick*. . . ."

Willis was pretty bored, but he was making the best of things. The job was a bigger pain in the ass than he'd expected, even. He didn't give a shit if most of these kids survived the next ten minutes, let alone apocalypse. He wasn't crazy about unarmed combat anyway, as it happened. He much preferred a knife. People freaked to see their skin-tight wrappers torn, and leaking.

". . . which brings us, next, to counters," Willis Rensselaer informed them, shortly after. "Not *kitchen* counters, Renko," he continued, "but counter*moves*, the way you block attacks and even use them to advantage. Barrett, yes, and . . . *Plummer*. Come up here and face the class."

Arthur Barrett struggled to his feet. Some people laughed.

He had an odd-shaped body, fat, but not in any uniformly rounded, well-proportioned way. His legs were more like long and jointed flabby dunce caps, upside-down; his torso was a sack of grain, the stuff all settled in his hips and waist, and not much at the top. His hair grew out in clumps, where he had cowlicks; his underlip was always wet, it seemed, and he didn't have much chin.

Zack came after him.

"I hope you don't think I'm picking on you, Plummer," Willis said. "I wouldn't want you coming down with a case of acute paranoia. I just like talking to you. Call it ordinary, ignorant elitism or something—I don't know."

Toby knit her brow. Why had Z changed color, once again? Or was it her imagination, or a trick of light? People in a Rita Fairchild–favored novel "blanched"; Scudsies didn't blanch.

In the demonstration Willis organized, Zack was meant to start a kick, a chop, a twist, a spear, a gouge at Arthur. Arthur would react—deflect the blow, or otherwise defuse its force—using different movements Willis specified. The only trouble was that Arthur flinched.

"No," said Willis. "No, no, no, no, no. One may not flinch, fat Barrett. One *cannot* flinch, and also counter. Boldness, bulge-boy, boldness! Hold your ground and move!"

Arthur couldn't do it. No matter how he tried, it ended up the same; he couldn't do it. Willis screamed and raged and gave him "two for flinching." Arthur flinched from them. Every time Zack moved a hand or foot in his direction, he gave ground. At times, in fact, he cowered. The habits of a lifetime, and all that.

Finally, Willis Rensselaer had had it.

"Stop," he shrieked. "Enough. I cannot watch this any-more. Barrett, you are hopeless, less than human. You are chicken. Louis, Michael, Jerry. Put this chicken in its cage."

He pointed toward the lodge—but *toward* the lodge, not at it. Along the lodge's wall, just past the porch, were all those cages from the gun-club days: wooden-floored, with heavy mesh for top and sides, shielded by the rhododendrons. Each one was six feet square and six feet high—good-sized for grouse or pheasant or your standard barnyard fowl, not too great for Barrett, A.

But in he went, without complaint. People who have lived the sort of life that Arthur Barrett had are apt to almost lose the power of complaint. Call it the Law of Diminished Expectations; they *hope* for the best, but doubt that they deserve it. Louis Ledbetter and Michael Something and Jerry Whatever—three constant bitchers who absolutely planned to have their own Trans-Ams by eighteen, anyway—escorted him over to the cage, and Michael gave Arthur a good, hard shove on the shoulder once, perhaps to show everyone he was doing his job right, or hated chicken, I don't know. They put Arthur in the cage nearest the porch, and jammed a stick—in lieu of padlock—in the hasp.

When they'd returned and joined the group again, Willis waved Zack back into the crowd. "We need someone a little more nubile ... *mobile*, make that, sorry," he went on. "Honor us, Miss Ayer."

Toby rose. She hated getting close to Willis, but now, she guessed, she had to. She was pretty sure that he wouldn't be able to see her skin crawl, even though she just had shorts and a T-shirt on, but she could feel it happening, or *something* happening, right up her arms and legs, the backs of them. If she'd looked at Zack, she would have seen him "blanch" again.

"Now—yes—Miss Ayer," said Willis Rensselaer. He rubbed his hands together. "Suppose you punch me in the mouth. You wouldn't mind, I hope. I'm sure you wouldn't. Just pretend that I'm a mugger or a rapist or a ... certifiable lunatic, let's say. Okay? And I'm rushing at you, just wide open for a good shot in the mouth. Okay? All right—whenever you're ready."

Toby thought the best thing she could do was play along, conform to expectations, not make trouble. Be, in short, exactly what (or is that *who?*) her teachers always wanted

155

her to be: cooperative, a follower-of-all-directions-even-stu-pid-ones, and smart-but-nowhere-near-as-smart-as-they-were. She aimed a girlish right at Willis's half-smile.

The next thing she knew, Willis Rensselaer had (1) blocked the punch with his left forearm, hard, and stepped around her quickly, sliding both his hands beneath her armpits and behind her head, into a full nelson; then (2) using this, he lifted, turning her around so both their backs were to the group, at which point (3) he moved his hands onto her chest and gave her breasts a good hard squeeze before he (4) fell backward on his shoulders, carrying her along, and wrapped both legs around her legs in such a way he pulled them wide apart. By then he'd shifted to a left-arm choke hold, and his right was free.

"If she was a guy," said Willis, turning to the class, "I'd give him this." He lifted up one leg and aimed the heel toward Toby's crotch; his right hand had come down, hidden by the forearm around her throat, and was giving her left breast what she would later call "an oncologist's close-out special." "But in her case, I won't bother," he concluded.

Willis let her go, and Toby scrambled to her feet. She knew her face was red (a thing she couldn't help), but also it was blank, expressionless (she knew). In a second, she had let the anger go away. She had changed as the seasons change, without thought, as Master Kim had taught her to, and thought-less she was ready, empty.

Willis wasn't, though. Willis was cruisin', on a high. "And now, suppose I . . ." His hand reached out for Toby's arm, to put her into who-knows-what position.

The move that Toby used is called a leg sweep. It's really rather hard to do, and maybe not a true karate move at all; it only takes a person down and doesn't hurt him, other than whatever harm a fall might do. The sort of leg sweep Toby used is quite a showy thing, however, involving, as it does, a sudden spin, a pivot, and her right leg swinging backward in a sweeping, vicious arc, hitting Willis just below, behind, the knee. That leg leaped out from under him, just as Toby yanked against his reaching arm and threw him backward; it's fair to say he just took off and flew, and landed, sliding, on his green silk seat, about four feet away.

Toby, finishing the throw, did not relax, or laugh, or offer him a hand. Instead, she took her stance and waited, face expressionless, still empty. Some people in the crowd made this sound: "WO . . ." and one voice cackalaughed, but Toby didn't even hear it.

Willis Rensselaer was not the least afraid. He'd never been afraid of anything, at least not since the auto wreck, near Saratoga Springs. He was pretty sure that he could handle Toby—kill her if he had to; he had the strength and reach and knew enough techniques. But this was not the time to try, he thought.

And then he thought that what he meant—*of course*—was that he'd *never* want to go all out against this kid, this girl, this student at a Teen Survival Session. Oh, sure—she'd taken self-defense somewhere, and made him look a little silly, but after all, so what? She was a smart-ass, feisty bitch, but he had given her a first-class feel. Yes, first-class; too true. She'd have to act as if she'd hated it. In fact, he liked her to behave that way. There could be lots of fun for both of them in this.

He thought all that in just a second's time; his mind was trained to think, and not be empty, ever. Bobo'd been the first to really teach him that.

Willis Rensselaer tucked his knees into his chest and somersaulted backward. When his hands hit the ground behind his shoulders, he pushed hard and flipped his body up and back, and landed on his feet.

"As I was starting to say . . ." he told the class. He pantomimed the reach he'd made for Toby's arm before she threw him, but now from two or three yards away. He cleared his throat. "And now, suppose I get Miss Ayer to show you how she counters being reached for by a stranger. She calls the move a 'Cape Canaveral,' I think."

Almost everybody laughed with Willis, and people like Rod Renko agreed that although Mister Rensselaer was weird and a jerk-off, you had to say this much for him: he was a pretty good sport.

60. A Real Cute Saying

When Toby saw that Willis wasn't going to take it any farther, she relaxed. Emptiness filled up with thought again. She felt a little sick; she felt peculiar.

She had survived. The reason she'd survived was that she'd known—or maybe *been*—a throw that she had used on Willis Rensselaer.

But then she looked around at Zack and had another thought, a real peculiar one. The reason she'd survived was that she loved Zack Plummer so. And also Merribeth and poor fat Arthur Barrett, maybe even Rod, and others. This was a curious discovery to make, at the Teen Survival Session of the Francis Marion Institute.

"You cannot sharpen your sword on a velvet grindstone," Master Kim had often told her. Before, she'd always thought that was a real cute saying.

61. A Musing

"I'll bet he tore it up and flushed it down the toilet, don't you think?"

Zack said that to Toby, using gestures and a Willis-face. It was rest hour, and they had eeled off to the old skeet field and were sitting in the dappled shade, their backs against the little cabin's rough-sawn siding.

"Well, make that the *commode,*" she said.

"I mean, they wouldn't want my parents reading stuff like that," he said. "That I thought Will and Bobo ought to share a rubber room somewhere. Do you think?"

"Do I think *what?*" asked Toby with a frown. "*I'm* the one who said they're nuts, not you, you little . . . suck-butt. All you said was something about their being slightly strange. That's nothing. Kids in sixth grade wrote stuff worse than that on the blackboard, where I went to school. We had a teacher named Mrs. Pitcher, and one moron wrote 'Mrs. Pitcher's off the wall' on the board one day. Can you imagine that? So another kid put 'Mrs. Bitcher is a pore.' Now that was pretty clever, *I* think." She smiled and nodded, recollecting. Those were the good old days, in sixth grade, before you went to Stalag Junior High.

"But that's beside the point," she said. "The point is that

160

you said that *I* said that people on the staff were certifiable. They aren't going to like that. We know that Willis didn't like it, right? I can hardly wait till Bobo gets his shot at me."

"Look, Tobe," Zack said. He sighed. "I've said I'm really sorry, and I am. What can I do? Go tell them I'm a pathological liar and I made it all up to get even with you for taking my canned pear with cottage cheese at lunch on Tuesday? It honestly never occurred to me they might open our mail, for God's sake. Isn't that a federal offense, if you're not in prison or the army? Or the EPA?"

"It may be a federal offense," she said, "but I haven't seen a whole lot of postal inspectors skulking around the lodge, have you? Or any G-men on the pistol range. All it'd be is your word against Willis's, anyway, and you're not just a Plummer, you're a *minor*." She made the word sound less than insignificant; she made it sound perverted.

"Thanks a lot, Toby. Little Ayer-head. It's bad enough I have to take that stuff from Willis." Zack pushed against her shoulder. He loved to touch her, any way at all. She was the first girl he'd ever had more or less *permission* to touch, almost any way and any time he wanted to, and never have to worry. She had made that clear one day, with one small gesture, standing almost naked, in a bikini, by the pool. "It's yours," she'd said, and gestured at her body, head to toe. And she'd been serious. It didn't mean that she expected him to jump her, hump her, then, that very moment, or in fact that very month, or even summer. They might have talked in words like that, but not about each other. What they would do, eventually, was "making love." And, still, they hadn't. Yet. So far. What Toby's words and gestures meant—he thought—was that such things were possible. Anything was; what a feeling.

"Look," he said. "Get serious. We've got to figure out a way to make them think we've changed our minds, or something. Get them off our backs. It's only three weeks more."

Toby sat back up and tucked her knees. She wrapped

161

her arms around her shins, and leaned way back and shook her hair. "I don't know," she said. "The thing I'm wondering is if maybe we shouldn't just get the hell out of here, right now." She didn't want to tell him that it was a lot worse than she had expected it would be. And she couldn't tell him that even in spite of the letter, she was more afraid for him than for her. J.B. would probably take care of the girls, assuming he was still a factor all the way. "I honestly can't believe that people like my father and Mr. Bartowiak know what's going on up here. They can't. My father's an idiot, but he's not a sadist, or a...Nazi, for heaven's sakes. Putting kids in cages, whipping them around a track. That's unreal. And some of the kids are eating it up. That kid Louis. You know who that is?"

"Yeah," said Zack. "He's the one who doesn't talk to me."

"You don't recognize him, then, do you?" Toby said.

"Recognize him? From where?" Zack turned to look at her, his face scrunched up.

"From out at the Spring Valley Mall, when those kids were messing with Oke. He's the one I...you know, *chopped*. Right before we got Oke in the car."

"Oh—my—God," said Zack. He closed his eyes and let his head loll back, remembering. He is *such* a Scudsy, Toby thought; she loved him. "No *wonder* he's avoiding me. And I was blaming my Right Guard."

"And you know what else?" said Toby. "I wouldn't swear to it, but I think he was out at the cemetery, the day of Oke's funeral. Don't ask me why, but I'm pretty sure I saw him out there. Well, whatever his problem is, he really freaked when he saw me in the dining room, that first night. And almost ever since then he's become Willis's little errand boy. Like with Arthur, there. I mean, he's really getting off on that stuff."

"*Hunh*," said Zack. He nodded once. He's avoiding saying anything negative, as usual, Toby thought. "Well, well," he said, sounding something like his father, surely not on purpose. "But getting back to the letter, though.

What do you think of this idea? I'll write my parents another one and tell them you've changed your mind about the staff. Both of us have. That now we realize how sharp they are. And deep and on the ball." He laughed. "Sort of a cross between Einstein and Joan of Arc and Albert Schweitzer. Don't you figure that'd do the trick?"

Toby smiled and shook her head. "You know something, Plummer? You are the most optimistic, the most *naive* little Zackaboo I ever met in my entire life. Really. Do you actually think for a minute they'd believe that? For fifteen *seconds?* I can see it now." She held up a hand and ran it much as if along a banner, left to right. "'Dear Mom, I think that Christ's come down to earth again, in red silk running shorts this time.'" Toby swatted at the air. "Zackie, listen: Willis was *letting you know* he'd read your letter. He wanted *both of us* to squirm. That letter didn't get sent, and it didn't get gotten. Like you were saying a while ago, it got *flushed.* So there isn't any point in saying you changed your mind—if you say that, they'll just have to flush that letter, too." She threw up a hand again. "And as far as them believing you—Willis and Bobo—that's not going to happen now, no matter what you say."

"Hmmm," said Zack, this time, "you're probably right. I wonder if maybe I shouldn't just *call* my parents, then. Clue them in a bit about what's happening. Find out if they *did* get my letter, by any chance. See what they think about all this."

Toby realized that whether he'd admit it or not, Zack still thought his parents were in charge of . . . things. That they could somehow see to it that nothing too bad would ever happen to him. To both of them, probably. She imagined it'd be sort of a nice feeling to have. Sort of like watching the *Wizard of Oz*, on TV.

"Good luck with the phone," she said. "Merribeth wanted to call up her sister to get her to send up . . . something she'd forgotten, and J.B. said there weren't any outgoing calls allowed, except for in an emergency, because otherwise it wouldn't be like a real survival situation and kids'd spend all their time on the phone, and anyway, how would they 'evah' get the phone bill straightened out when all the kids'd be gone by the time it came? He went on and on. Merribeth said she felt like telling him it was her diaphragm she'd left behind and that it *was* an emergency, or might turn into one, and he wouldn't want that, now, would he? Just to see what he'd say."

Zack turned and looked at her and popped his eyes and jumped his eyebrows. "Golly, was it?" he inquired. "I thought you said she hadn't gotten one, and . . ."

Toby slapped him on the shoulder—phony outrage. "None of your *bizness*, Mister Nose. You're as bad as J.B., you know that? Him saying he hoped we girls'd 'feel entarly free' to come to him with any little problems we had, 'even of a personal and con-fee-denshal nature.' He is *such* a letch." She shook her head. "But anyway. What I was saying—maybe we should think about, you know, just sneaking out of here one day. Or maybe night. It wouldn't be too easy anytime. I *think* they keep the big gate locked, and it's the only one. And those are loops of that new kind of barbed wire on top of the fence. The stuff with the razor-sharp doohickies? I was here when they were putting it up, and Rod's father really cut himself. It isn't electrified, though; that's bullshit. What they wanted to do was freak the local lovers, so they put up all those signs saying the fence was juiced sometimes, but not others. That way, nobody'd know for sure, and wouldn't dare try."

"Well, don't you think," Zack said, "that if you wanted to you could just go to old J.B. and say you wanted out— that you were sick, or sick of doing this, or *something?* Don't you think he'd have to let you go?"

Toby shook her head again. "I just don't know," she said. "Remember when we signed the application? How he called it an 'enlistment,' four weeks long, no passes and no visitors? Our parents understood that, too. I'm afraid that if he knew we wanted out, it *might* be that much more impossible to get out, on our own."

"Wait a minute now," said Zack. "You're saying that

164

they've got us locked in here, and we can't make calls out, or leave. And they control the mail and have a fence around the place that maybe we can't climb. And besides that, that two of the staff members are psychopaths and the other one's like a jailer who's *also* got the hots for the female students." He sighed. "Tobe, that's just *too* crazy. How much do you really *know*, for sure? Yeah, Merri may have told you . . ."

And then he saw that she'd started to cry, and for perhaps two seconds the only thing he did was sit and gawk. Not because he was a jerk, a maladroit, afraid of (or turned off by) tears. He was just surprised, and so was she. Toby didn't cry—no, not the Tobe. She was much too tough, too calm, too all-together.

Zack put both his arms around her, and she laid her head down on his chest.

"Wuh-wuh-Willis felt me *up*," she sobbed. "He made me feel so *awful*. . . ."

"What?" said Zack. "You mean, like when he grabbed you then, and pulled you down . . . ?" Of course he hadn't known. He felt himself get furious. It seemed to be a different sort of fury than he'd ever known before.

Her head moved up and down, against him.

"He *hurt* me, first, when he just squeezed me. When he pulled me over backward. B-but the next part was worse. He had me in a choke hold—and then he got his legs around me. An' he took his time and did it, with his other hand. An' he was getting turned on, *too*."

She had no more planned to tell him this than fly to the moon. It just came out.

"I'd like to kill him," Zack began. And then he stopped.

It was like sometimes when he was playing the guitar, or writing a little poem, maybe even a haiku. And the thoughts and plans he had for it just went away, and he ended up having played or written something new and different, that surprised him altogether, but seemed right. He'd told his mother that this happened, once. "You've heard about the Muses," she had said, and smiled.

165

This time, he took hold of the bottom of Toby's T-shirt and pulled it up over her head, and off. And he undid the olive-drab bra and slipped it down her arms. He smiled and cupped her small breasts, each in turn, and kissed them. She stopped crying, and stretched and turned toward his body. They let themselves flop over on the grass.

62. Being Philosophical

Here is what a very smart Greek gentleman named Plato said, long before the first person ever asked the question "Cash or charge?":

> ...Are not all things which have opposites generated out of their opposites? I mean such things as good and evil, just and unjust—and there are innumerable other opposites which are generated out of opposites. I want to show that in all opposites there is of necessity a similar alternation....
>
> —Plato, *Phaedo*, B. Jowett translation

And he went on at some length to show that stuff went from hot to cold (as well as cold to hot), and whatever was fast speeded up from being slow (and vice versa). His real zinger was that (therefore) it must be true that just as you get to death from life (obviously), so must you be born from death—thereby proving that the soul was immortal. Neato!

Even if you didn't follow all that, you'll probably agree that before you are imprisoned you have to be free, and that if you find yourself in jail, it still may be possible to generate a little freedom out of that fact.

A very smart American gentleman named Willie "the Actor" Sutton proved that last fact quite a number of times, at a series of detention centers, lockups, county jails, and penitentiaries.

Zack and Toby hoped to do the same.

Out there at the skeet field, they had come to the realization that they were being held captive at the Francis Marion Institute, but, smart kids that they were, they were being quite philosophical about it.

63. Paying Attention

What with making and revising lesson plans, reading the students' mail, writing paragraphs for stress tests with the VoystrComp, and "overhearing" conversations inside Barracks B at night, Willis Rensselaer and Bobo didn't have a lot of time for themselves in the evenings. J.B. Fairchild, the Director, didn't know they were doing the reading and listening parts; they'd decided there was no reason to bother him with such trivia. And anyway (as Bobo once remarked), "Who knows what makes a turkey cluck?"

The number of cards and letters that the students wrote, and got, surprised them, but it really shouldn't have. With no touch-tones to pop, or decorator-colored Princesses to mainline with, the kids were up against it. Their choice was either write or give up friends, cold-turkey. So, groaning, they dug out the pads and envelopes their parents made them pack, which they had never, ever planned to use.

A lot of what they wrote was pretty gamy stuff, full of exclamation points and question marks, and words that everybody knows but some folks want to keep their kids from ever seeing. Most of what survival students wrote to other kids the censors (Bo and Willis) let go by, unchanged. They figured that the outside kids would never show the grossest stuff to any known adult. And who'd believe it, anyway?

"Why, I can hardly swallow *this*," said Bobo, reading, with a wink, a smile. "That some of the lads got up on Arthur's cage and pissed on him the other day."

"Agreed," said Willis, nodding. "Hey, if I hadn't let him out that night, and smelled him with my own two eyes..."

On the other hand, the things that outside kids claimed to be doing to each other (in the absence of their Instituted buddies) gave even Bobo cause for wonder—not to mention new ideas for his cassettes.

"Little liars," he maintained to Willis, but there was grudging admiration in his voice.

Anyway, between the letters, and the night sounds from the bug in Barracks B, and what they heard and overheard in daily conversation, it figured Bo and Willis could become a bit mixed up. Not about the facts they knew, but just about their sources. For example: they knew that Merribeth and Rod had found a tree house somewhere, and were using it for fun and (not exactly children's) games. *That* was in a letter she had written to a girl named Angela, outside. But how did Willis know—he asked himself—that Rod had leopard-printed jockey shorts and liked to give a Tarzan yell at certain magic moments? Had some kid said that, kidding Rod, in Unarmed Combat class? Or was it, still, a "confidential" item? He'd wanted Zack and Toby, just the two of them, to know he'd read that letter, but he didn't want the boys to know he had their barracks bugged. Louis told him stuff that happened in the barracks, and what people said in there, but Willis Rensselaer was much too old and wise to altogether trust the likes of Louis.

The way it turned out, Bo, not Willis, was the one who goofed.

Bobo, as it happened, was one of those teachers who like to call every kid they have in class by his absolutely most up-to-date nickname (no moss on Bobo's back, no sir). That meant it was almost like a reflex for him to call

Ernie Fazio "Luke," the very first thing one morning, just before the start of stretching exercises.

Well, the thing was, Zack, himself, had given Ernie that new name the night before, in Barracks B, calling him Luke Skywalker after Ernie had made this tremendous vertical leap to rescue some kid's Frisbee off a beam where it had landed. The name might not even have stuck, though, if Ernie's friend Duke hadn't overheard and said, "Hey, that's good. Duke"—pointing at himself—"Luke"—indicating Ernie—"Kook and Puke"—gesturing toward Rod and Frank, who had lately had an upset stomach, shouldn't wonder. "If we ain't the Four Stooges, right? Duke, Luke, Kook, and Puke." And, barracks humor being what it is, a lot of people laughed, and used the names. "Whaddaya say, Luke? Hey, Puke." Et cetera.

Probably no one else noticed this little slip-up of Bobo's, because afterward they were all calling Ernie Luke themselves; but Zack did. Bobo had known something he shouldn't have known, *couldn't* have known, and Zack knew that. Zack was now paying the sort of attention to Willis and Bobo that any intelligent captive pays to his captors.

The sort of attention that Odysseus paid to the Cyclops, for instance, or Hansel paid to the witch, or Willie "the Actor" Sutton paid to a lot of different guards.

Or Plato paid to Mrs. Plato, for all I know.

Zack located the bug four days later, inside the smoke detector, when he was all alone inside the building. A couple of nights before, a few kids had spent about ten minutes aiming pot and cigarette smoke at the detector, trying to set off the alarm, for kicks.

They never succeeded, even though Willis Rensselaer could hear the sound of each exhalation as clearly as if they'd been blowing in his ear, he said to Bobo.

64. Surviving in the Wilderness

Bobo Bodine had been part of the first wave of affluent Americans to get in on the wilderness-survival-as-a-way-to - build - character - in - your - sons - but - also - daughters - movement, back in the sixties. He had had a number of reasons for so doing, some of which were perfectly above board. He'd always liked the outdoors, for instance: the innocence/fragility of fawns, the rabbit's honest scream when taken by an owl. Then, too, he'd been well trained, by fishing guides along the Allagash, crack climbers in the Tetons, an Iroquois who went to Yale, at Camp Rocsoctomekin. Beyond that, he also took great pleasure in the sight of naked young women in a mountain stream that was also a long, long way from the nearest telephone that only he (for sure) could find their way to. It turned out that almost every trip he led—invariably co-ed—would have one student on it who was just like-wow ecstatic to experience the kind of interpersonal closeness, the totally natural but incredibly complex give-and-take, that can only be found in the forest primeval, and with a man who, quoting Ferlinghetti, can also snare and skin and stew a snowshoe, in a subtle, seasoned sauce. A *man*, that is—no high school/

college groper. A *partner*, but a leader and a teacher, bet-your-ass.

In other respects, Bobo had been no particular fan of the sixties; he was never that interested in civil rights or causes, other than his own, or saving the world as a thing to sink a lot of time or interest in. He went into boarding school teaching because he enjoyed making people squirm with impotent rage and simper with gratitude; he also liked to live in pleasant country settings, and go on lots of holidays.

He hadn't liked the seventies, as they unfolded, either. With more and more kids choosing to imitate their parents, and take a me-first attitude, it was harder to manipulate them than it used to be. Nowadays, you had to pick your spots (he grudgingly admitted to himself, back then); a lot of former leverage was missing. Kids were less afraid of being called bad sports, or cheaters, middle-class, or greasy grinds. The survival movement of the eighties, rooted as it was in abject fear, had certain possibilities, he thought. Which was (as you've assumed, I'm sure) the reason he had come to FMI.

At some time during every day up there, Bobo'd have a class or two in aspects of surviving in the wilds. He started with the basics, like learning how to walk.

"It's mostly simple common sense." Bobo smiled to the group. "Survival is the practice of caring for yourself, so when you're on the trail, you do exactly that. Everything you do is in your own best interest, right?"

They nodded, smiling, liking that idea; the seventies lived on.

"You're still a member of a close-knit team," he said, "and conscious of companions, but they're not who you're focused on, exactly. Now, look, I'll show you why. . . ."

At that point, he got some girl like Merribeth to walk in largish circles, while he followed her and repeated once again the importance of keeping a good six feet behind the person in front of you, *and* breathing in an easy, rhythmical way, *and* stepping over-not-on such obstacles as fallen trees and rocks in the path.

"Now," he said, "if, on the other hand, I got too . . . well, *involved* with my companion"—he came up beside Merribeth and put a hand around her waist, or sort of on the top of her ass—"before you know it, I start breathing in a different tempo"—he stuck out his tongue and panted, in a comic lustful style—"and having my attention occupied, pretty soon"—he stubbed his toe on a root and lurched forward—"I trip!

"And that"—he smiled some more—"takes it out of a guy." They laughed; he shook his head. "No, seriously," he said. "On a long hike, it's absolutely essential to conserve your energy in every way possible, and talking and stumbling and letting your breathing get out of synch can really drain you, over a full day of walking. I mean, who wants to be so pooped when they make camp that they can't even get their tent up?" asked Bobo, with his eyes atwirl, to laughter.

At still other lessons, Bobo taught them to dig a fire pit and lay a fire, and how and where to pitch those tents (always at a distance from that fire), and what a shit pit was and how to use it gracefully.

And also how to leave a campsite looking pretty much unmarked by human habitation.

"One good way to survive," he told them, nodding wisely in the style of gurus everywhere, "is to keep the other side from knowing you exist at all."

Another thing they learned from Bobo (Willis always helped with this) was stalking. Not fruits or nuts or wild asparagus, but "turkeys." That was the word they always used, in any case. Part of stalking, students learned, was camouflage, and Bobo taught them how to paint their faces and their hands, to blend in with the shadows. Willis stressed that they should stain their knifeblades, too, so there wouldn't be a glitter in the moonlight. "You want it in your hand before you ever see your turkey," Willis said, "so you can cut the gobble out of him real quick."

A final item in the Wilderness Survival curriculum was the learning of "proper expedition attitudes," which was mostly learning to beware of "gross survival habits." Bobo talked to them a lot about such things as Selfishness, and Blindness to Your Own Faults, and Stubbornness, and Hoarding.

"Survival companions," he told them, "must enjoy a special relationship with one another. It is absolutely vital"—he stressed this many times—"that each of us be able to put the needs of a survival companion ahead of the trivialities of our own selfish interests."

65. Voice Prints

Hip modern teacher that he was—or liked to appear to be—
Bobo wasn't about to exclude late-twentieth-century technology from his Wilderness Survival course; J.B. Fairchild
he was *not*, I'm here to tell you. And so it was in the context
of that class, though not exactly part of it, that kids met up
with VoystrComp.

Being also part of the computer age, they weren't in the
least bit bothered by the little box. Things with screens and
lights and buttons—these were "tools" to them, even as
they were to Bobo. Picks and shovels, axes, hoes, and rakes
were *artifacts*—still found in Third World countries and
perhaps in northern Maine, or Mississippi, they had heard.

Bobo's explanation, glib and quick, was that he wanted
"voice prints" for the files, for their "Survival Records."
He said he thought it would be great if kids, instead of
reading something from a book (how boring can you get?),
would start to offer input on the program, especially the
Wilderness Survival class. After all, he told them, this was
their survival training, not his own, and they must be the
ones to shape it, mold it, judge it. Everything they said
would stay in strictest confidence, he promised.

"If I hadn't been a teacher, I would have been a doctor,"

he explained to each of them. "Things told to me in confidence are as safe as nuclear wastes. No matter what you may have heard," he said.

The specific form of this "ongoing" evaluation was a question-and-answer session in which Bobo shaped (adjusted, I should say) the questions to the shape of the student, oftentimes. For instance, males were apt to get such stunners as: "To what extent do you feel that the program is meeting your needs and expectations?"

(Faced with language of that sort, Rod Renko answered, "Would you mind repeating that question, sir?" Either that, or "Huh?")

With girls, however, the questions often got a little more specific—*personal*, you might say. Consider this exchange with Merribeth. It took place after a few general warm-ups about the weather and the food.

Q. (softly): Do you feel close to any members of the staff?

A. Shuah.

Q. (gently): Do you have total confidence in that person?

A. Why not?

Q. (warmly): Are you conscious of the warm, personal interest of whoever it is?

A. Yeah.

Q. (coyly): Does this make you comfortable or uncomfortable?

A. Depends.

Q. (eager): On what?

A. Oh . . . *you* know.

The red light on the VoystrComp went on for the first answer, but not for any of the others. Bobo was sure that the stress in her voice was the product of a rush of heat and high excitement, rather than mendacity, however. He could tell. It almost always worked that way: they hardly dared believe that it was happening to *them*.

And he could hardly wait for their first overnight.

66. Capture the Flag

Bobo liked to take small groups on overnights. If there were only eight, or ten, or maybe twelve of them, he managed to manipulate—control—events much better, he believed—to stay on top of things, as the expression goes.

And that's the way he wanted it, on Merribeth's first overnight. A group of twelve, including him.

They came together in the afternoon, picking up the food and tinware that they'd need from Missus Fairchild's kitchen. Then off he led them, marching single-file, of course, and never on a trail, through willows, alders, stunted cedars, scratched by brambles, sucked by swamp. The way they went, the hike seemed twice as long as what it really was, and made them think that they were far from anywhere.

Once at the campsite, everyone got busy pitching tents and fetching wood and setting up the fireplace. After that they cooked and ate an early supper, did the washing up, and hung the next day's breakfast in a tree, safe from bears and porcupines (said Bobo).

With all that done, they organized what Bobo called the *pièce de résistance* (he chuckled when he used the French expression), the major highlight of their trip, and great survival training: a game of Capture the Flag. A game, he said, "of strategy and teamwork, thrust and counterthrust," and once again he chuckled.

So, first of all, they walked the boundaries of their "field," a twenty-acre piece of mostly woods and partly marshy ground. They chose the places where the flags would be, and set a midline running through their campsite. That made it time to choose up sides, but Bobo said that choosing-up was not "authentic."

"*Chance* is more survivalish," he said. "Like, going clockwise, we could just count off by twos." He smiled and looked at Doris Mullady. Between himself and Merribeth there were three other people.

"Huh?" said Doris Mullady. "How d'you mean?"

"You say 'One,'" said Bobo, patiently, "and the next person says 'Two', and the one after that says 'One' again—and so on. Then all the Ones are one team and all the Twos are the other. Okay?"

"Okay," said Doris. "I say 'One.'"

So of course the person on the wrong side of her smiled brightly and said, "Two."

"No, *clockwise*," Bobo said. "The *other* way." He wasn't sure if it would make a difference or not. "*You* say 'Two,'" he said to Swezey.

"What difference does it make?" asked Doris Mullady.

"Well, none," said Bobo. "Except that I said clockwise. The way a clock goes. It's a good thing to know."

"Two," said Swezey grudgingly, and so the count went on, and teams were made "by chance." Merribeth and Bobo both were Twos, with Swezey and three others.

"Okay," said Bobo, drawing breath. "So let's say the Ones'll defend the flag at that end and the Twos the one at this end. How about we allow a half an hour to get strategies in place and then we'll start. I'll blow one long blast on my whistle to start the game, and a bunch of double blasts'll mean that someone's won; it's over. Then we'll all come back to the campsite—right?—and talk about what-all we learned. Okay?"

180

Everybody shrugged or nodded and the two sides went in opposite directions.

Is there anyone in the world who doesn't know how to play Capture the Flag? Well, just in case, I'll tell you, briefly.

Imagine, say, a football field—half is "our" side, half is "theirs." Get tagged on foreign soil and you must go to "jail," a corner of each end zone, let's pretend. (You can be freed from jail by a teammate's touch, and if that happens, you both must take "free passage" back to your side, before you try for the flag again.) Flags are kept at spots agreed upon and known by all; they may not be tied down or hidden. A game is won when the opponent's flag is captured and brought home, without a tag. Players may assume specific roles—like "attackers," "defenders," "jail keepers," and "flag guards"—or not, depending on the mood and style of the team. Some players believe in elaborate plans, deceptions, feints, and ambuscades, where others just rely on speed, on taunts and insults, claims of cheating, and bad language.

Rutherford Bodine preferred (you guessed?) Type A, and so he skillfully made sure his teammates would insist upon it, and he would seem to merely go along with them.

"What say you?" he inquired of the other five. "You want to zip around and trust to luck, or should we work it out, some foxy kind of way? *You* say."

Of course *they* worked it out most foxily, exactly as he'd planned it, days before. He and Merribeth (Attackers 1 and 2) would hide themselves quite near the middle line. Swezey and the other three (Defenders 1 through 4) would form a tight circle around their flag and concentrate on taking captives. Once they'd gotten *two*—which gave them six-to-four superiority—they'd turn to the attack. Three erstwhile defenders now would serve as decoys, loudly sweeping down the left side of the field, and drawing the Ones' defenses to them. Then and only then would Bo and Merribeth emerge, to make one lightning pincer run. The way they

181

had it planned, there'd be one wimpy flag guard left to handle both of them: impossible.

"Right," said Bobo, nodding, when he had finished making it appear his team had made this plan. "I think I've got it straight. You got a watch there, Swezey?" The round-faced boy held up his wrist and showed he did. Bobo took the whistle from around his neck. "Suppose you give the starting blast—in seven minutes, isn't it?"

"But you said *you* were going to give it," Swezey said, while picking at his face.

Bobo smiled and winked. "What they don't know won't hurt 'em, pal. And anyway, *quelle différence?*" He chuckled.

Swezey took the lanyard and the whistle. Bobo pumped his hand, then suddenly embraced him.

"Good luck, Sweez," he said. He quickly hugged the other three and turned to Merribeth before reactions started. "We'd better go, good buddy."

67. An Unexpected and Unselfish Piece...

Of course, Bobo knew exactly where he was going. He'd cut the heart out of a dense willow thicket two days before, and even pulled the roots of the bushes that he'd cut, and scattered some dead leaves over the raw earth. In one pocket of his fatigue jacket he had a folded groundcloth, made of very dark green nylon.

"Maybe we can crawl in there—what say you?" he asked Merribeth, when they got to the spot.

She nodded, quite caught up in the game. They did so.

"Hey, this is a pretty fine spot," he said. "Look, I've got a sort of a tarp here. . . ." The woods were very shadowy, but far from wholly dark, and they could see just fine, between the willow stalks and branches.

"What a place!" said Merribeth. "This is really cool, you know it?"

Bobo put his head quite close to hers. "We maybe ought to start to whisper now," he softly said, "so we get used to it." He reached into another pocket, brought his hand out closed. "Three guesses what I've got in here, good buddy."

She shook her head. "I haven't got the vaguest. Really."

"Just to keep the bugs away," he breathed. He opened up his hand, and there was one rolled joint, plus matches.

"Sheesh," said Merribeth. She raised her brows. "You serious?"

He nodded, grinning boyishly, and lighted up, inhaled, and handed over. Time went back and forth until the whistle blasted from a ways away. Bobo pinched the roach and stuck it in his pocket. Her whispered "Some fine dope, *I'll* say" was a tickle in his ear.

The woods stayed quiet. Bobo slid a hand inside another pocket still. Now he had two tubes of greasepaint: one black, one dark, dark green.

"We ought to try to get a little more invisible," he said. "You know? I'll do your face, if you do mine—and each of us can do his hands." He waited, fingers crossed, hoping that she wasn't too, too stoned, hoping that she'd say the obvious.

She wasn't, and she did. "Okay," she whispered. "But . . . look. What's the sense getting our faces and our hands all dark, when the rest of us is . . . well, as light as *this?*" She touched the elbow of his green fatigues, and it was true. Her hands, unpainted, were no lighter than their clothes.

"Hmm," said Bobo, sounding as reluctant as he could. "You really think we should? I mean, you are the female—and a damned attractive one, at that, I must say. But . . . well, I guess you're right. I *know* you are. We're talking raw survival here, not country clubs or dancing school or kiddie games. We're both adults. The needs of all our teammates *must* come first. . . ." He started to take off his jacket.

Merribeth was pretty stoned, but not so much she didn't get the picture. Total camouflage? All over? She'd heard of body paint, but that was something different, something of a turn-on, wasn't it? This was for survival, like a sort of exercise; it could be sexy, but it didn't hafta be, like saunas, or a hot tub, couldn't you say? How the hell did she know—she had never done survival in her life before. Who had? She guessed that when you got right down to the nitty-gritty, life-and-death-type scene, a little thing like being seen bare-ass by a teacher didn't mean an awful lot.

"We'd better hurry up," said Bobo urgently, his shirt now off and starting on his belt.

Oh, what the fuck, she thought, and joined him, stripping down.

At first, it was a blast, it seemed to Merribeth. The paint was nice and greasy, and he slid it on her bod in gentle swirly strokes that felt real fine, she had to say. A little bit intense, in fact. She kind of liked the look it gave her, too, real snaky, you might say. Oh, if Tobe could see her now, she thought.

When he got done with her, she started in on him. He lay down on his front, and she began to paint his back; it was a lot like finger-painting time, in nursery school, but what she'd painted on back then was cold and white and came in pads, and didn't have no hair on it. To do his legs, she straddled him, and worked down to his boot tops.

At that point, she slid off him, leaned down, and whispered in his ear, "Okay, roll over, sir."

But when he did—uh-oh. She saw that there were . . . was a . . . complication.

Just be cool, she told herself; it's nothing personal, exactly. What she had to do, she told herself, was more or less shrug it off.

That thought—no sooner had it hit, she started in to giggle. She didn't want to think it anymore, or giggle anymore, but yet it seemed as if she had to. Shrug it off, she thought. That's really good. And, Wait'll I tell *this* to Tobe.

"What's the matter?" Bobo asked. He was lying with an arm across his eyes, just digging the sensations.

Merribeth went back to work: smearing, smoothing, swirling. She finished off his chest and reached his belly.

"There's one part here I'd better let you handle . . ." she began, but saying that *completely* cracked her up. She started in to laugh out loud, for real, and now there was no stopping it, at all.

"Hush," said Bobo, quietly but sharply. He moved his arm and looked at her. Oh, Lord. Oh, yum. "Sshh, shut up. You'll blow our cover. The enemy'll hear you."

Merribeth collapsed onto the nylon sheet, trying—but not making it—to keep from laughing. Bobo grabbed her by the shoulders. How to shut her up? He took a chance and aimed his mouth at hers, which brought him over onto her. She wriggled madly, trying still to keep from laughing, keep her mouth away from his, so she could breathe.

But then, all of a sudden, the situation took a turn—and no way for the better, so it seemed to Merribeth. Maybe she was being selfish, but still she had her limits, filling-teammates'-needs-wise.

"Whoops," cried Merribeth. She lurched and bucked and pushed up with her arms. Half-remembered bits of Willis lore had surfaced to her mind: Kick—chop—twist (was that it?)—spear—gouge?

"Yowch," cried Bobo, grabbing parts of him, himself, forgetting her. And she exploded from the thicket, running.

It was probably one of the easiest victories that any team has ever had in the history of Capture the Flag.

When Merribeth went—streaking (as they say)—across the midfield line, she flashed (excuse me) by a girl, a One, who'd crouched behind a tree.

"There's Merribeth," yelled Doris Mullady. "She's heading for our flag." And then, a little cattily, perhaps, "She hasn't got no clothes on." She started running in the same direction.

Of course, this news attracted other members of her team, like all of them, five guys. This they had to see. I mean, that is, they must protect their flag and capture the invader.

Merribeth, in something of a panic, ran on instinct, like a painted, shapely fox: stopping, hiding, circling a mudhole, cutting back. All around her, she could hear the slosh-and-go pursuit, and though she recognized their voices, and knew they weren't Bo, a girl still had her modesty.

"There she goes. I see her. This way."

"No, that's *me*, you idiot!"

Meanwhile, the other four kids on her team, hearing all this racket, assumed there'd been a change of plans. Instead of hiding out, their front line was attacking, so it seemed. Was that Bobo some kind of a Patton, or what?

Quickly, they conferred. One of them stayed back to guard the flag, the other three went forward, like a panzer tank battalion. In point of fact, the round-faced Swezey— zits, bad wind, and all—trotted straight to the opponents' flag (he had an excellent sense of direction), picked it up, and trotted back with it, completely unobserved, unchased, unthreatened. And victorious. Once across the line, and safely in the campsite, he put Bo's whistle to his lips and blew a set of double blasts.

Bobo, thinking hard enough to make his head ache, had dressed as soon as he was able to, and then picked up the tarp and Merribeth's discarded clothes. Following the sounds of her pursuit, he heard the double blasts, and so he stopped and thought a moment more.

And then he hollered, from between cupped palms:

"Okay, you people, that's the game. Everybody freeze, okay? You've all just seen—or heard, or been a part of, or been defeated by—an unexpected and unselfish piece of pure survivalism: invented, planned, and carried out by Merribeth, completely on her own." He paused to catch his breath and clear his throat. "Now Merri, you can hear me, can't you, buddy? I'll turn my flashlight on and stand it up between these rocks. Your clothes will be beside it. If you can hear me, just yell 'Number Two,' okay?" He stopped and waited.

Merribeth, with nothing much to lose, yelled, "Number Two," but not real friendly-like.

"Excellent," cried Bo. "Now, I'll keep talking—better yet, I'll sing—and you can home in on my voice. When you get to where you can see my light, yell 'Number Two' again, and I'll pull back and head for camp, and you can get your stuff on then, and follow me."

Bobo paused again, and hearing no objections, he began:

"For she's a jolly good fellow, for she's a jolly good fellow..." Bobo had a pleasant, mellow baritone.

In less than a minute, he heard another "Number Two," now quite nearby. He cut the music off.

"Now listen up, you little bitch," he hissed. "Remember this. It'd just be your word against mine. And everybody knows you're not Saint Agnes, sweetheart. The way it's set up now, you're one big hero—try to give me any trouble, you're a lying little whore."

And Bobo turned and strode toward camp. "That nobody can deny, that nobody can deny..." he sang. The one thing he had to remember to do was get that greasepaint off his body-works, before Brer Willis saw it.

68. The Ultimate Experience

"Now, boys," said J.B. Fairchild, at the dinner table, on the evening of the day that followed Merribeth's first overnight, "there's something I been meaning to bring up with you." He paused, a little too majestically, thought Bobo. "And that's this thing of putting kids in cages."

At Willis Rensselaer's suggestion, the dinner hour at FMI was changed the second week, from six o'clock to seven. He'd argued that they'd get another hour's training in, and Rita Fairchild (seldom on his side) had said she must admit the kitchen might be slightly cooler later. Bobo voted quickly for the change, which made it three to zero, with one abstention (of course the kids were not consulted, silly). He knew that Willis would have flown the coop—deserted— if he'd had to eat another meal to the accompaniment of the Sam N. Dreyfus Hour of Decency. Willis didn't disagree with most of what the Reverend Dreyfus had to say, it was just that he thought he hated southerners, a thing he'd learned to do in the military service. Almost every white person he met in the military, including all of his superiors, seemed to be southern, and they thought Willis was a stuck-up, overeducated Yankee faggot. Or so he thought, anyway.

For some reason, people often seem to hate people who

have the same faults they do, though they almost always claim it's something else.

"Jewell B. Fairchild is no gem, when it comes to depth of thought," Willis said to Bobo, "but compared to Sorghum Sam, the 'hell-fahr' man, he is the Kohinoor, the Hope, the Star of India—you name it. Rita's franks-and-beans with— God help us—pineapple chunks is certainly sufficient challenge to digestion without a side order of cornmeal mush about De Lawd warning some prehistoric Jew or other concerning the dangers of 'a-thay-istic com-yew-nizum.' I swear I'm going to booby-trap that son of a Panasonic bitch and join the Légion Étrangère, if I don't get the feeding hour changed."

J.B. thought that seven was a little late for chow, but he had gone along with the idea. What he did was start to listen to the Hour while he showered; then, after that, he'd open up a Coke and listen to the rest of it. When the Coke was about halfway finished, he'd fill the bottle with some Four Roses blended whiskey, put his thumb on top of the neck of it, and shake it up good. He'd have to stick his thumb *and* the neck into his mouth, to get the first fizzy shot of the stuff, but after that it went down nice and smooth. Before he went to chow, he'd put a couple of Sen-Sens in his mouth, so nobody'd get any wrong ideas. Eating at seven seemed to make J.B. real loose, and talkative, and aromatic.

"You don't see kids in cages in this country, and you shouldn't. I think we gotta cut it out." He pointed with his fork at Bo and Willis. "It ain't American. Here, what we do is give a kid a good smack, or a bunch of swats on the bee-hind, like it says to do in the Bahble. 'Spare the rod and spoil the child,' you bet. Why, the Reverend Dreyfus himself says that's the route you gotta travel with a kid, from time to time. And when you can't do that on accounta some bunch of mollycoddles down in Washington, D.C. or Hartford says you can't, why then you take away some privilege, or you make 'em do some extra drills or exercise, like we used to do in the Marine Corps. But you don't put them in no cages. That's more like something the Veetnams

190

would do—isn't that a fact, now, Willis? Over there, them monkeys do a lot of stuff like that to one another. But when you see a white kid in a cage, and know that he's American..."

"A cage is *certainly* no place for a young lady, under any circumstances," said Rita Fairchild, pleased to get her two cents in. She'd looked around the dining room while J.B. talked, and she had liked what she had seen. Her tuna casserole, with elbow macaroni, Velveeta cheese, a little curry powder, and the cream of mushroom soup, was going over great. She'd read the basic recipe in *Woman's Day;* she had thought to add the seedless grapes.

"The thing is, Jewell," said Bobo in his teacher's voice, and using, as he sometimes did, a name the student hated, "you often have to use a method you don't like to make a point that can't be made in any other way. Let's take, for example, the Second War"—Bobo held up two fingers— "and the atomic bomb. Given the way the Japanese were *then*, the sort of wild fanaticism that they had, it took the atom bomb to show them that we weren't kidding. You know what I mean? The one we dropped on Hiroshima let them know we had it; the one on Nagasaki proved that we'd absolutely wipe them off the planet, if they made us. They got the point, and they surrendered; now, they're fine. I've never had a better car than my Accord, I kid you not. I love it."

"I know," said old J.B. "That is, I know you're right about the bomb. And I'll go one step further and I'll tell you this." He winked. "I hate to say it, but—we haven't dropped our last one, yet. You mark my words." The jabbing fork again, a grape impaled on it this time. "No *way* the Russkis aren't going to try us. You think that buildup that they done is just for show? And I'll tell you something else: what with one thing and another, the chances are that one or two of theirs is gonna slide through some crack in our defenses—or window, like they say—and hit home here, and we are gonna have to suck it up and take it and hit back." J.B. made a small, regretful sound and shook his head. "Nossir, boys, it won't be pretty, notatall. But it'll be the *only* way in the world we'll ever get some peace, so that is what we're gonna hafta do."

Bobo nodded. "I'm afraid you're right," he said. "I wish I didn't think so, but I do. There's a gloomy, self-destructive side to Mother Russia; unfortunate, but true. The country's in a shambles—or the next thing to it—now. Bad harvests, a shortage of consumer goods, troubles in the satellites. The Kremlin knows it'll take a nuclear war to get the people's minds off their problems."

"I'm glad it isn't me," said Missus Fairchild, "that'll have to push the button, though."

"You know the reason you say that?" asked Willis Rensselaer. Rita started in to answer: "Well . . ." But he kept going, drowned her out. "A matter of conditioning and training. You aren't trained to take responsibility, to welcome it, to do . . . distasteful jobs like that. And you know something else?" He smiled at her. "You should be. Even women should be. *Everybody* should be." He turned to J.B. Fairchild. "We're going to get the cats on Tuesday, speaking of that sort of training. So that'll mean we can't put kids in cages anymore. We'll need them for the cats."

J.B. pulled an earlobe, and he looked down at his plate. "Well, that's another thing I been thinking about. This cats business. I'm just not too sure that all the parents of some of these kids are going to understand it. I mean, the chances are that some of them got cats themselves, an' . . ."

Bo and Willis both began to speak, but this time Bobo talked the louder, touching Willis on the arm to quiet him.

"Now, Jewell," he said. "We talked this through before, and you agreed we had to have a climax for the course, an Ultimate Experience. That can't be tea and crumpets, can it, now? You *know* these cats have had it, anyway; they aren't anybody's *pets*. Look. You've heard of the Harvard University Medical School, right? Do you know what they do with *dogs* up there, as a part of *their* students' training?" J.B. shook his head. "Well, let me tell you," Bo Bodine began.

192

Rita Fairchild hastily stood up and went to see her girls get out the ice-cream sandwiches, for dessert. She was allergic to cats herself, but she still hadn't liked the idea of this so-called Ultimate Experience, when she first got it out of J.B. In fact, they'd had an argument, and J.B. got real ornery, and so she'd decided to just put the whole thing out of her mind.

The training program was none of her business; it was entirely up to the men. Preparing tasty and appetizing meals was her business, that and looking out for Barracks G. The Institute was organized the way it should be, which suited her to a T. It was nice to be a woman, Rita Fairchild told herself. She enjoyed being a girl.

69. The Trouble

"Capture the flag, my ass!" said Toby with a snort. She'd had to laugh—was laughing still—at Merribeth's description of herself, in greasepaint, scooting through the woods. With everybody hot on her trail, you might say. But also she was outraged, very. "Capture your *ass,* that's what it was. Sexual harassment!" ("Her-ass-meant," she pronounced it, slowly; Merri smiled.) "Actually, it's worse than that. Attempted rape is what it really was." She stopped. They were walking on the running track, for after-dinner privacy. She made her voice real deep, a parody of Bobo's. "I shit you not, good buddy." Then back to normal, and in stride again. "That's what you've had pulled on you, d'you realize that? Attempted *rape!* He planned the whole thing. I'd bet anything he did. So it's even premeditated. You've gotta tell J.B." Her tone was light enough, but once again, the feeling in her gut was not.

"Oh, well," said Merribeth. "The thing is—see—there weren't any witnesses, and so it's like he said: his word against mine. You know how it is in school, Tobe. They always believe the teacher."

"Yes, but this is different," Toby said. "A lot more serious. I actually think these guys are dangerous. I mean it.

194

They are *creepy*. And us, for the time being, we're awful close to being prisoners up here. Zack and I were talking about it, and it's true. But we think J.B.'s a little different— you know that yourself. He's an asshole and a letch, but what he mostly is is dumb. He doesn't quite get the real picture, when it comes to Willis and Bobo. But we've got to make him start to understand. If we're going to raise any sort of hell about them when we get out—and don't think I don't plan to—we've got to start getting some stuff on record *now*—like, official whadyoucallit . . . *documentation*. And that means telling J.B., real close to when it happens, not sometime next fall, when—"

"But you didn't tell him about Willis doing that to you, did you?" Merribeth was shaking her head with about half a smile on her face, and for just a flash there, Toby thought she could see the way she'd look—oh, twenty years from then: pretty, still, but heavier, and not so full of fun and . . . trusting. "How come you didn't tell him, Tobe?"

Toby felt a flash of irritation; her thing was so much different. And was she really so sure of J.B.? Suppose it was her father, instead of J.B.—could she trust him? What a world. She'd trust Zack's father. Maybe. Probably. She watched her boot toe kicking at a stone embedded in the path that they were walking on. It could have been an arrowhead, but when it popped out, it wasn't.

"I guess I was embarrassed," she admitted. "What he'd say or ask me. How I'd end up looking; how I'd feel. *You* know."

"Yeah," said Merribeth, and put an arm around her friend. "And that's the trouble, always, isn't it?"

70. Undertakers' Kids

If you've ever known an undertaker's kid, you also know that undertakers' kids—most of them—don't feel the same way about death as the rest of us do. For them, death is a lot more of an everyday, easygoing, facts-of-life affair—one to a customer, and that's it.

This is especially true when the undertaker's place of business is attached to his home, as almost always used to be the case, and the kids grow up playing around his tools (yes, tools) and other . . . uh, stuff.

In big cities, like New York, though, things are apt to be a little different. The big funeral parlors in Manhattan are often staffed by people who live, and raise their kids, in Queens.

Those kids are no more familiar with corpses, chances are, than most of us are with the scene over at Frank Perdue's, a week or so before the big Fourth of July chicken sales.

Here's one of the most interesting facts I know about human nature: people can get used to almost anything, including ideas.

Another is that we can choose not to think about un-pleasant realities, if we don't want to.

Put those two together and you get a pretty good—if incomplete—explanation of why nuclear war might wipe us all out, someday.

71. Shooting Range

J.B. Fairchild had been brought up around guns. When he was a baby, there'd been a gun cabinet on the wall of the room his crib was in for a while. It had a glass door on it, so he'd actually seen guns before he could know or say what they were called, or what they did. His father went deer hunting with a buddy from work, for a week every year, in Vermont. He also went pheasant hunting some weekends in Connecticut, and every so often he brought home dead game, and J.B. saw it, and learned that it was good. When he was old enough to handle a .22, he got one for his birthday, and trips to a gravel pit, for practice and instruction from his dad. He always knew that he would graduate from tin cans to targets, to woodchucks, to deer and pheasants, and when the war came, he didn't have much of a problem adjusting to gooks. After all, he thought deer were beautiful (as well as tasty), and of course he never thought that about the North Koreans. Or the South Koreans either, if you want to know the absolute truth.

At the Francis Marion Institute, J.B. taught the kids to shoot much as he'd been taught, using bolt-action, single-shot .22 caliber target rifles. Those who showed an aptitude and interest could later move on to other weapons, specifically one of the four .30-06 service rifles, or one of the two 9mm Browning semiautomatic pistols that the Institute owned. Those Brownings retailed for over five hundred dollars apiece and were made in Belgium. They were pretty nifty pistols, J.B. thought. For one thing, they carried twice as many bullets as the old standard military .45; *and* you could use 9mm ammo in a lot of other weapons, like sub-machine guns, which was—or could be—handy in survival situations. However, being completely fair, he had to admit that if that Turkish guy over in Italy had been using a .45, they would've had to get themselves another Pope, no question. Nothing's perfect, J.B. thought: not people and not guns either. As he sometimes said to Rita, "If it ain't one thing, it's another."

He'd once said that to Bill Bartowiak, too, but *about* Rita, that time.

When it came to the kids who were shooting for the first time at the Francis Marion Institute, however, something pretty definite—and surprising—could be said: the girls were more successful than the boys. They learned faster, and they learned better. Not just safety rules and stuff like that. J.B. might have guessed that girls would be more careful when it came to handling a rifle so there wouldn't be an accident—being "muzzle-conscious," as he liked to say. But the actual shooting—hitting what they aimed at? And even under pressure, like in a little competition?

At first, J.B. just blamed the boys. He told himself this bunch they had were losers, too much into drugs and rock 'n' roll and sitting on their asses. And so he chewed them out and mocked them, challenged them and made them stay for extra practices. But pretty soon he realized they weren't all that bad; the girls were, simply, good. They didn't seem to like it all that much, the most of them, but they performed.

"Like little Annie Oakleys," J.B. told the guys at lunch, and Rita. "Of course, they won't make out as well with standard rifles as they do with them there varmint guns, but still . . ."

One fact that had definitely been true since the very first

199

day was that there were certain things he liked about having girls out on the firing line, lying on their stomachs in their tight little shorts, with their legs nice and wide apart. Oh, my, yes. Certain things, for sure.

J.B. would stand behind the eight stations on the range and check his pupils out. And then he'd give the range commands:

"Ready on the right?"

"Ready on the left?" And so forth.

The first week, he noticed that after he said "Load," and all the bolts clicked shut, that this one kid, Ernie Fazio— the one they started calling Luke a little later on—always crossed himself before he shot.

J.B.'s lips had tightened when he'd seen that. It seemed like such a typical dumb-guinea thing for a kid to do. He'd always thought Catholics were a bunch of show-offs, going around crossing themselves all the time. And they sure as hell didn't make all their foul shots in basketball, so you couldn't say it worked. There'd been guys who crossed themselves in Korea, when a howitzer shell came down nearby; it didn't work for all of that bunch, either.

Of course, it was true that he'd done a pretty fair amount of praying himself, over in Korea. Just about everybody had, if you wanted J.B.'s opinion, whether they admitted it or not. And *he'd* come through that war without a scratch.

It was also a fact that J.B. was one hundred percent in favor of having school prayers, too. The Reverend Dreyfus and him *and* the President of the United States were all together on that one. Hell, they'd sure had them in school when he was a kid, and it didn't kill anybody *then*. And even if he and the other boys in his class made fun of it and said a lot of the words wrong on purpose, they probably got something out of it. Look how easy he'd picked it up again in Korea, when he really needed it.

Praying and pledging allegiance to the flag were two things that *belonged* in school, as much as the ABC's and long division, in J.B.'s opinion. Crossing yourself like the Catholics did was something else again. If people were going to do that, they ought to do it in private, by themselves, or just with other micks or spics or polacks in their own schools. It didn't belong in regular public school, J.B. thought. The U.S. Constitution talked about the separation of the church and the state. That meant you kept the Catholic religion out of the public schools. And the Virgin Mary off the free-throw line, as he'd heard a fella say once.

Zack and Toby both enjoyed shooting the .22s, much as they hated to admit it.

"Of course it's a power trip," Zack said, walking back from the range one day. "I have a magic wand. I wave it: bang, you're dead. And a pretty clean job of it. I can keep my distance, nothing personal. Firing a missile or dropping a bomb would be even cleaner, of course, 'cause then you can kill thousands and thousands of people without even seeing one of them. It's almost like it isn't you that did it. *It* did it; I was only following orders, *Kommandant*." He raised one arm and goose-stepped up the path.

"With me, there's a certain zen to it," said Toby mystically. "You look into the scope and make a path of air— a tunnel—to the target. You send the bullet flying down that special path of yours and only yours—your bullet on your path—on to the bull's-eye, and beyond it..."

"...into truth, enlightenment, and carrot cake," said Zack. "Except that I happen to have read, and therefore *know*, that a rifle is a phallic symbol and you, being a girl, are trying to make up for your lack of...sexual artillery, let's say, by...hey, look out!"

She'd done a gentle "Willis" on the lad, the "Grab" part.

Louis Ledbetter didn't try to get into the reasons why he enjoyed shooting the rifle; he just enjoyed it. It was something he'd always wanted to do. There didn't have to be any big explanation for things. When he got really good on targets, he'd go out hunting something, somewhere. Something big.

That'd be a kick.

72. Droll Call

"He's *where?*" Belinda Plummer asked. She put a palm over the phone's mouthpiece and spoke, across the den, to Rodman. "It's Mr. Bo-Bo-Bowie Knife—Bodine."

She took the hand away. "Oh," she said. "On *bivouac*. This isn't a very good connection. I thought you said 'in Merrimack,' and I wondered for a minute what on earth going to Merrimack had to do with survival. Learning to fight the traffic, maybe. No, no—of course I'm joking. But how long's the *bivouac* apt to last, I wonder."

She listened for a while.

"Yes, I can understand that," she said. "But are we talking a day or two? A week? I mean, there must be some sort of master schedule, isn't there? How many days' food did they take, for instance—do you know?"

"Mm-hmm, mm-hmm, mm-hmm," she said. The palm came down again. "Flexibibble, flexibabble," she informed her husband, and made a face of comic fury and frustration.

"I see," she said. "Well, maybe I could speak to Toby, then. Toby Ayer?"

Listening. Listening.

"I understand," she said. "It's been cloudy down here, too, up until today. And I suppose Merribeth Scarpa's gone

202

stargazing, too. . . . No, I realize you said 'celestial navigation,' I was just being"—she gave a laugh her husband didn't recognize—"you know, a little frivolous."

She went quiet again, for an even longer time.

"I see," she finally said. "Well, could you do this, Mr. Bodine? Could you leave a message somewhere, under a cairn of stones, say . . . What? . . . No, another little jest, is all. With Mr. or Mrs. Fairchild, maybe, or *someone*, asking Zack or Toby or Merribeth to give me a collect call—a staff member could maybe stand beside them and make sure it *is* collect. That's if and when they're back on the base and have a minute or two between now and the end of the session that isn't taken up by some really vital element in the training program? Believe me, I understand how busy they are, and how busy *you* are, but . . ."

"Okay. Thanks very much," she said. "Goodbye."

Belinda Plummer hung up the phone and turned to her husband with her lips tightened and her head being rapidly shaken.

"He is *so* irritating," she said. "I know I shouldn't kid around like that, but he is *such* a pompous ass, so busy-busy-busy." She sighed. "To hear him tell it, no one has time to go to the bathroom up there, except for purposes of survival. Really. If you believe him, I'd be more apt to run into Margaret Thatcher at the Norwalk Bowl-a-rama than to catch my own son at the main lodge of the Institute."

"Um," said Rodman Plummer. "So vahtcha gonna do?" He'd been halfway watching a movie on cable, and drinking a Lite beer. The movie was *Zorba the Greek*.

"Nothing, I suppose," she said. "What can I do? There's only ten days more of it. I suppose they'll survive. Ha-ha." She tossed a whole-wheat pretzel at her husband. "It's just kind of annoying not to be able to reach him."

"That's the way it was in the service," Rodman Plummer answered placidly. "Used to drive my mother bananas when she couldn't get me on the phone. I kind of liked it, of course."

"That's because I wasn't your mother," Belinda Plummer

said. She stood up, switched her hips at him, and headed for the stairs.

Rodman Plummer nodded. He agreed with her. Zack had all the breaks: Belinda for a mother, and now Toby for a girl friend—what a pair. Not that he didn't deserve them. It was odd, though, that he hadn't kept in better touch. One letter in three weeks? Tomorrow or the next day, he would call up Harold Ayer, from the office; Harold Ayer would like that, and he would have the facts. Harold Ayer was probably in constant touch with Toby and that Fairchild. Rodman Plummer drank some beer and stared at the TV. Zorba the Greek would never have a kid at FMI, he realized.

73. Cats

It would certainly be fair to say that surprise was the first reaction of the members of the Teen Survival Session to the arrival of twenty or so heretofore homeless cats at the Francis Marion Institute.

They were not a prepossessing bunch—I'm speaking of the cats—even with the addition of the plastic Day-Glo orange collars that Bo and Willis sprang for at the Woolworth's in the nearby mini-mall, but still it seemed to Zack that "scruffy buncha pussies," Duke's reaction, was at least a tad more vulgar than it had to be. What no one knew at first, of course, was what these felines had to do with *them*.

A few kids tried to strike up friendships with the beasts; these were mostly girls who'd had a cat at home, or hamsters anyway. The cats, however, weren't interested in much of anything at all, except the food that Bo and Willis shoved inside their cages once a day and, from time to time, a little interanimal activity. They hadn't had a lot to do with people in their lives, and the contacts that they'd had were hardly what they'd call uplifting. People seeing cats like these would shout out loud and toss them sticks and rocks, and hard green apples, if they had them. Cats like these were not at all amused by people's games. They'd hustle under cars and hide behind the tires, mostly. Cats like these would never cross a person's path, if they could help it.

The facts about the place and purpose of the cats at FMI were first wormed out of Willis Rensselaer. By Louis Ledbetter, no less. It wasn't all that hard.

"What's all the cats for, Mister Rensselaer?" Louis had been sitting on the lawn beside the driveway—it was one P.M.—tossing lighted matches into the cages. Willis had passed by, munching on the Oreos he'd got with his red Jell-O (topped with blobs of Cool-Whip, bet your Rita Fairchild).

"Sunday brunch," said Willis promptly, with his half a grin. Louis was an animal—he knew that fact for sure, by now—but still, he had his points. He was an animal, for instance.

"No, no kidding," Louis said, and laughed. "Gimme three guesses, okay?"

"God, no," said Willis. "I wouldn't want to hear your ugly little fantasies. Suppose I simply tell you. *If* you promise not to breathe a word to anyone." The kids would have to know soon enough anyway, and having Louis Ledbetter tell them, by telling him not to tell them, would not only guarantee that everyone would know, but also save Bobo and himself from having to listen to the immediate negative reactions a few of them would have.

"Hey, listen—cross my heart on that one, Mister Rensselaer." Louis did some jabbing at his shirtfront.

"Well. What those cats are, little Lou-cifer, is a section of your final SAT." He laughed dryly. "Your Survival Aptitude Test. Six days from now, we're going to set them loose, and you and all your fellow fauns will start to . . ."

"Hey, Louis. What's this bullshit that I got from Luke? About you saying we were gonna have to kill them cats they put inside the cages, 'steada Arthur, here?"

Will and Bobo heard Rod Renko ask that question clearly. It was as clear as if they'd been in Barracks B. They'd put the little speaker on the table near their beds in Cottage 1, and turned the volume up to good-and-high. Rod must have even faced the microphone, they figured; they heard his little chuckle, and a sound that could have been the product of a palm slapped down on Arthur Barrett's shoulder. Willis had been surprised to observe that there were a few of the boys who didn't treat Arthur Barrett like the total oddball dork he was—who almost seemed to like him, even. This moron Renko, for instance. Professional-nice-guy Plummer. Not Louis, of course; Louis called a spade a nigger.

"Hey—I didn't say it just like *that,*" said Louis. "What I said was, first, they let them go, the buncha them. Then sometime—I don't know—a little later *we* take off. Everybody's on a team—you see?—girls as well as guys. Six teams, five on a side, right? And every team's got a color, like, black, white, yella, red, blue, and . . ."

"Green?" said Ernie.

"*Green,*" he said. "That's right. An' we all got knives and special pistols that they have. They got a spring inside, and what they shoot is little balls that break real easy— see?—and they got *paint* inside of them. . . ."

"Five points if you *kill* one?" Toby said to Zack. "Did Merri get that right? With a knife?"

Zack shook his head. "I'm not exactly sure," he said. "I think it's just you're meant to be—*you* know—at real close range. Close enough to touch them, say."

Toby stared into the almost-blackness where his voice was coming from. They were sitting on the floor of the tree house, and it was almost four A.M. Before the first week ended, Missus Fairchild didn't stay up reading anymore; she went to bed at nine and often snored by 9:05. Certain of her little ladies waited for about five minutes after that before they tiptoed out the door, and some did not return till almost reveille. The bug told Bo and Willis who was meeting whom and (sometimes) getting what, but they were not about to blab to Rita. They both were much too cool for that. They were *proud* of their young cocksmen. Jealous? Bo and Willis? Who said that?

207

"I see," said Toby. "Wonderful. If you forget your knife, it's quite all right to strangle one, or break its neck with one quick chopperoo. Terrific. That's just great. Everything I hoped for when I came up here: the chance to meet a cat in unarmed combat, hand-to-paw."

"Well, I guess the first thing we're meant to prove is we can stalk it," Zack explained. "The idea being that if we can surprise a wild cat—sneak up on it and touch it, see?—well, then we're pretty good. Or ditto if we run one down. I guess they think that if we can do that to a cat like one of these, we could probably do it to a person, too."

"And *killing* the cat? Where does that fit into the overall survival picture? Are we meant to eat it raw, or something? Like—wasn't it the Huns?—were meant to do with field mice? Oh, this is really beautiful," said Toby.

"I don't know about *that,*" said Zack. He touched her on the arm. "Look, Tobe. This isn't me. I'm just repeating what Louis told Rod that Willis told him. And what he said was that everyone in the session should be tough enough not to get squeamish at the thought of killing . . . *something.* That killing is an essential part of surviving. The *most* essential part, I think he said."

"That," said Toby, "does it. To hell with them. I'm getting out of here." She stood up. "I can just see me squaring off with some poor tabby: 'It's either you or me, Letitia.' This is just too crazy, Zack."

"Agreed," he said. "I'm coming with you." He hadn't wanted to suggest their splitting, first. He'd felt that they should leave for really quite a while—since Willis pulled that crap on her—but still he hadn't said so. Part of it—he knew that this was stupid, but he couldn't help it—was a little macho thing: he didn't quit, *he* didn't run away from things. He could take it just as well as or better than the next guy.

Another part was gallantry, or so he thought of it. This was Toby's deal lots more than his, and he had come only because she had to, more or less. That left it up to her to

208

say when they would head on out of it, or *if* they would; he shouldn't ever make her think that *he* was miserable.

And, finally, there was . . . Arthur, and some others. Maybe he was being superegotistical, but it seemed to him that he was helping *them* survive, in one small way or other. He'd hate to feel that he'd abandoned them, poor turkeys.

But now that Toby had suggested it, he couldn't wait. Sir Galahad—ahem, that's him—would help to get his lady fair away from this foul dragon's den. That was his knightly duty; it transcended everything.

He thought of bringing up, again, that maybe they should talk to J.B. first, and just ask him, please, to send them home—or tell him she was sick and had to leave. Then she could tell his parents, and . . . But then he thought perhaps they'd better not do that. It might, as she had said, alert their jailers, make it harder, or impossible. The sooner they got out, the better.

For the first time since he got to FMI, Zachary Izak Plummer felt . . . acutely . . . homesick.

By 4:55 A.M., they knew that "getting out of here" could not be done that easily—and not at all by them, by reveille. The gate *was* locked—and most securely—and where they looked, there weren't any wire cutters. Not to mention gloves and ladders and whatever other stuff they'd need, but hadn't thought of, yet. Not to mention *time*.

And just before they split for Barracks B and G, respectively, Toby posed another little problem.

"Oh, Lord," she said. "The cats. We can't just let them slaughter the poor things. We'll have to find a way to get them all out first. Or too. Or *something*." She glanced down at her watch. "Talk to you at Cals," she said. And fled.

74. Stakeout, Fakeout

"Hey! Listen up, you guys. I got a 'nouncement." Rod Renko raised his voice, so as to be heard over the general chatter. It was five minutes before lights out, in Barracks B.

"Good afternoon, boys and girls, this is your principal, Mr. Wimpleston, speaking," mimicked his old buddy, Duke.

"Shut up, ya shithead. I'm not kidding," Rod continued, talking louder yet, with now a little menace in his tone. "Here's the thing. Merribeth asked me to ask you guys—and this means me, too—to kindly stay the hell in the barracks tonight. All right? You got that? Everyone stays home. For just this one night only."

"Why?" "What for?" "How come?" some voices asked. Not that many people had been leaving the barracks that often lately, but tell people that they can't do something and right away they act a little pissed. Every Mr. Wimpleston knows that.

"I'm not going to try to shit you," Rod maintained. Having told them what they had to do, he now turned on the friendliness. "It's some of the girls," he confided. "Merri said they wanted to have this little party of their own tonight.

Private, women only, at the pond. I told her I was sure the guys'd go along."

"You bet I'd go along," said Duke. "At the pond? You think they won't be skinny-dipping?"

Rod took a swipe at him. "Well, so what if they are?" he said. "That don't have nothing to do with you, asshole. They got it all set up and organized, with special stuff to eat and everything. It's like a sorority party, or a showa, the way girls like to have. So what they're asking is they get some privacy, that's all. Which means *we* all stay in."

Of course a lot of boos and criticism followed, but anyone could tell it wasn't really serious. Rod Renko, *he* was serious, and they could go along with that. The thing made sense to them. Sometimes a guy'd like a night with just the guys, without a lot of girls around.

"Oh, one last thing," Rod said. He smiled. "To make completely sure we're all together on this thing, I'm gonna put my mattress right across the doorway, here. An' it's only fair to tell you, I sleep light. And once I *am* asleep, I fuckin' really *hate* to get waked up."

"Gee," said Willis, reaching for his running shoes. They were right below the table with the little speaker on it. "Do you suppose that we should tell J.B.? Or Rita?"

"Nah," said Bobo, searching for the flashlight in his locker. "They're a pair of party poops. And this is just a little swim-and-snacker. Good clean fun."

"Exactly," Willis said. "Dibbies on that maple near the dock. I bet they'll make a fire, but there's moonlight, too. A perfect night for . . . lifeguards, like ourselves."

"I think I'll hunker down," said Bobo, "behind that half-dead, leaning spruce, a little ways along the shoreline. You know the one I mean? And did I ever show you these binoculars? A miracle of modern science, if I've ever seen one. On a moonlit night like this, a guy could see a dimple on a maiden's little you-know-what. . . . " They started out the door. "Or even, yes, a *pimple*," Bobo said.

* * *

"Rod was perfect," Zack told Toby in a whisper. They were crouched in the rhododendrons by the main lodge, near the cages. "How did Merribeth get him to do it?"

"Piece of cake," said Toby, and she had to laugh. "Did you ever read *Lysistrata?* Just the threat was plenty. And he was okay about letting you out?"

"Sure," he said. "He woke up and tapped me on the arm, and said, 'Happy Anniversary, guy,' and that was it. Merri had a good idea there."

"Yeah," said Toby. "She told him it was our six-monther. She said Rod's a sucker for sentimental occasions. She is, too. She said it's because they're both from big Italian families. So he thinks we're up in the tree house right now, celebrating our little whoosies off. . . ."

That got to Zack, amazingly, her saying that. Later on, he figured that the danger and excitement had a lot to do with it—that, and the fact that he would so much rather have been doing what she said than what he was about to do. But anyway, he felt this sudden flash of pure, raw *wanting* Toby's body—wanting to be wildly, wetly, buckingly inside her, doing that one thing they hadn't ever done before. The symptoms, sure, were quite familiar to them both, by then, but not the almost-desperation that he felt.

Ye Gods, groaned Zack to Zack, without a sound. Is this the thing survival's all about?

"You got the tags?" he said to her, instead of all the things he wanted to.

She nodded, held them up so he could see. She'd found them in a cupboard in the kitchen; they might have been there from the old-time gun-club days. What they really were were key tags: cardboard disks with metal edges, and little clasps, quite like a safety pin, where you could put the key on. On every tag, all twenty-four of them, she'd printed clearly:

> URGENT—Call 448-3964 and say
> the Callipygians need *immediate assistance*.
> Guaranteed $100 Reward!

The number was the Plummers' phone at home; instead of keys, the little clasps could nicely hold the orange collar of a so far homeless cat.

When Zack had said a hundred dollars, she'd said, "Isn't that a lot? Suppose all twenty make it to a house and twenty different people call your folks? That'd be two *thousand* dollars."

"Well, first of all," he'd said, "it has to be a lot to make them call at all. It *is* long-distance, don't forget. And anyway, those cats are pretty wild; the chances are they won't get found—or caught, the way they'd have to be—by *anyone*. The third thing is, my folks'll leave the house, I hope, as soon as anybody calls, so there won't be anyone at home to answer. Unless the cleaning lady does, and that's just once a week, and she's not up on Callipygians, I don't think, and..."

"Right. Shut up," said Toby.

It took them quite a while to liberate those twenty cats. Zack used two hands to toss them, one by one, arcing high to clear the chain-link gate; he aimed them to the side—not down the drive—so bushes growing there might break the fall. It was like an out-of-bounds throw-in, in soccer, where you hold the ball high overhead and fling it long or short, depending; these "balls" had claws and wriggled, though, and tried to bite the thrower. None of it was easy, but they did it.

Twenty times, they trapped a cat inside a cage and held it in a jacket while they got its tag in place. Twenty times, the captive cat made yowling sounds, sounds that sharp-eared people could have heard, in nearby Cottage 1, had there been any sharp-eared people in it. Twenty times, Zack tossed, and cats soared and landed, struggled to their feet, and disappeared, while Bo and Willis cooled their heels and hopes, behind and up a tree, respectively.

75. Bad Sports

"Oh, Mister-sir-Bodine, sir?"

Willis knew that Bobo hated it when he—by using more or less the manner of address he'd had to use in boarding school, when he'd been just a kid, a student, and Bo had been his teacher—reminded Bobo that he was, that Bobo was, in fact a great deal older than he liked to think he seemed.

But at that point in the morning, Willis didn't give a shit. As a matter of fact, he was glad that Bobo hated it. He even hoped that Bobo knew that *he* knew Bobo hated it. Willis Rensselaer had been sitting up in the big maple tree overlooking the pond on the property of the Francis Marion Institute for more than five hours. It was almost three A.M.

"What is it?" Bobo barked.

Bobo had been better off, in one respect. He'd been on solid ground, which meant his feet had never had to dangle, while a branch cut off the circulation to them, and they went to sleep—to wake to pins and needles, later on. But on the other hand, behind the leaning spruce tree by the water's edge there were some biting insects, lots and lots of them. And R. Bodine, wilderness survival expert, had forgotten his repellent. Of course, I mean the artificial kind, that comes in cans and bottles.

"Well, sir," Willis drawled, in this bright-baby voice he'd chosen. "I've been thinking, *sir*. What I've been thinking is we might have been stood up, sir. Except that I'm not standing up. No part of me has stood up all night long. It's not what I expected, sir, Mister Bodine."

"Look, just shut up," said Bobo, getting to his feet. He circled around the fallen tree and walked toward the dock, and the big maple.

"Something must have happened—change of plans," he grumped. He reached the tree and stopped. He had to piss, and started to.

A brilliant flash went off. He jumped, and wet himself. He heard the whir of instant-print-emerging-from-a-Polaroid. That fucking idiot had brought a camera!

"Oh, well, sir," Willis said. "At least I'll have a keepsake from the evening, a memento. Lucky me. 'Mister Bo-peep has lost his sleep, but he still found...'" he started, in a singsong.

"Look, Willis, will you just shut up?" said Bobo. "This wasn't my idea any more than it was yours, so you can't blame me that they didn't show up. And what the hell do you think you're doing with a camera up there, anyway? Were you actually thinking of taking pictures of those girls, for God's sake?" He made an exasperated mouth sound. "And speaking of pictures, give me that one you just took. I didn't want to have my picture taken." There was no sound from the tree.

"Do you hear me?" Bobo asked. "Give me that picture!"

He knew he wasn't being a very good sport, but neither was Willis. And Willis had started it.

Willis Rensselaer dropped lightly out of the tree. He flicked his flashlight on and shone it on the picture in his other hand. He chuckled.

"Up yours, Mister Bodine," he said. His voice was soft, and not a child's voice anymore. "Of course, if you would like to try and take it from me, Dad..."

215

Bobo turned and walked away. Let the baby keep the picture, little shit. He'd settle that his own way, in his own good time. Willis had been disappointed, but for God's sake, so had he. There wasn't any reason to act crazy.

Always assuming Willis was acting. He *had* been in Vietnam.

Bobo had never been a big fan of the Vietnam War As wars go, it had been almost totally lacking in class.

76. Put Out

"You know what'd be fun to do, I'll bet?"

Harold Ayer said that, to Bill Bartowiak. They were sitting at the bar of Jeanie's Casa Linguine, splitting a small pepperoni pizza and knocking back a number of cold glasses of Miller High Life Beer, on draft.

Earlier that evening, quite a bit earlier, they'd played softball, and their team, the Off-Road Ramblers, had taken a terrific pasting from the Oakwood VFW, seventeen to two. It always used to be an even game with Oakwood, but now they'd taken in a bunch of ringers, and it wasn't anymore. The ringers all were Vietnam vets, which made them just a little bit colored and quite a little bit younger, and a hell of a lot better, in this easy-gliding, hot-dog style that black guys seemed to have. They laughed and talked it up and threw the ball around behind their backs, and ran like plain greased lightning, not to mention hit a lot of frozen ropes and caught it if they touched it. The old Oakwood vets, like Emil Desiderio, a few of whom still played, they laughed a lot more than they used to do, and gave them huge high fives and tens and called them Phil and Eddie, just like ordinary guys. Harold Ayer went oh-for-five and felt a little sick; Bill Bartowiak had split his pants, as well.

"No, what?" he answered Harold Ayer.

"Well, maybe take a ride up to the Institute. This weekend, even. Surprise old Fairchild and the kids. Look the program over. Let's face it, you're the President, and I'm a member of the board. Don't that mean that we're responsible—like, in a legal sense, and all that—for whatever's going on up there? I was thinking maybe some of the other guys on the board'd want to go, too. Hey!" Harold Ayer laughed out loud. "If we got a bunch of them to go, we could even have a little fun with the kids. Maybe make— what'd they call it?—a simulated attack, like we used to have to do in basic, remember? See what they been learning up there. Supposedly."

Harold Ayer swished the last couple of mouthfuls of beer around, inside his glass. He wouldn't want to say this to Bill, but he wasn't all that sure about the Teen Survival Session, now. *Or* Mister J.B. Fairchild and this "staff" of his up there.

The trigger for these feelings was the call he'd had the day before, from Mr. Rodman Plummer, Rodman as he called him now. He'd said to Harold Ayer to call him that, right after his secretary had put him on the line. ("Mr. Ayer? Mr. Plummer calling, Mr. Rodman Plummer, just one moment please for Mr. Plummer.") *Rodman* had been a little bit—hell, what was that he'd said?—"put out" by how he hadn't heard that much from Zack and how Mrs. Plummer couldn't even get in touch with him. Rodman sounded like a hell of a nice guy, Harold Ayer thought.

Now it so happened that his own wife, Florence, had been bending his ear on the same general subject with regard to Toby, and to shut her up he'd told her that he'd talked with Fairchild just that week, and everything was hunkydory. And he'd said the same to Rodman.

The first time that he told that lie, it didn't bother him at all, but when he told it once again, to Rodman, he got nervous. So what he'd done was try to reach this Fairchild that same night.

It hadn't worked. He'd gotten Willis Rensselaer—what

kinda name was *that?*—who'd said that Fairchild was away (an "exercise," he'd said), and so were Zack and Toby. But, he said, he'd seen them just the day before and they were fine-and-dandy and terrific students, picking up survival tricks like they were going out of style . . . and eager? Why, they were as eager as caged lions, always right among the first to volunteer for any tough assignment. And blah-blah-bullshit, had-to-run, but great-to-hear-from-him. And hung it up, ker-blam. Right in his ear. And him a member of the board.

Harold Ayer had been suspicious, not to mention pissed. Toby, volunteer? At FMI? Unlikely. And so he'd gotten this idea of getting Bill to go on up with him that weekend, arriving unannounced, and see for themselves just what the hell was happening up there, and were they learning lots of good survival stuff, or what. He knew there weren't any "visitors" allowed, but this was something different—like a general inspection, or what-have-you. It was just since he'd been drinking those Miller High Lifes that he'd thought of taking a whole bunch of guys along and *doing* something—like a "simulated attack"—that'd possibly make a fool out of certain people, this Willis Rensselaer, for instance.

"You know, that might be pretty good," said Bill. He pushed his empty glass across the bar, toward Jeanie's daughter, Toni. He pursed his lips together, and he pulled the lower one. Bill Bartowiak was thinking.

"Or maybe what we ought to do," he said, "is all of us pretend we're people from the city. Like, evacuated, see? We could make like we were in some sort of panic, running all around, and hollering, and stealing stuff. . . ." Put a few beers in Bill and he'd come up with some weird ones, sometimes.

"Yeah, but"—Harold Ayer put down a hand on Bill's right arm, the one he raised a glass with—"we don't *look* like city people, you know what I mean? And anyway, the kids all know you from the meeting, and lotsa them know me, from being friends of Toby's. We *could* get masks, but..."

"I guess you're right," said Bill. He sighed. The thought of acting like a city person in a panic still appealed to him, but he also knew he'd had a few beers, which meant he could get "carried away," as his wife liked to put it.

"Well, anyway," he said, "the place you're *really* right is where you said we ought to go and check this program out. I *am* the President"—he shifted on his stool and sat up straighter—"and the President's responsible. What *I* think is, we ought to have a meeting of the whole board up there, maybe this weekend, like you say. We could stay in the cottages, take our time, and look the program over, talk to different kids, like that. And have ourselves a good time in the bargain—play a little cards, *you* know. As for surprising them somehow—well, we can work that out." Bill pulled his lip again. He was pleased with how that sounded. "Our wives'll probably be glad to get rid of us," he added, thinking of Mary Bartowiak, Ms. Woman's Intuition. She hadn't let up on him ever since the meeting, where she hadn't liked J.B. that much, you might say.

"Yeah," said Harold Ayer, and started picking up his change. He wished that they were leaving then, that very night. Toby wouldn't volunteer for stuff up there; that Willis Rensselaer was full of shit.

As Harold Ayer had always used the term, only girls "put out"; but he and Rodman *were* put out, by golly.

220

77. Sub Species

After twenty-two straight (by that I mean *consecutive*) days
of it, most of the members of the Teen Survival Session
had gotten used to getting up for calisthenics at five o'clock
in the morning. They didn't like it, still—of course—but
they'd gotten used to it.

"Kinda like you would an ampyatation," Rod's friend
Duke summed up their feelings, in his sensitive and phil-
osophic way.

So, given people's increased state of wakefulness, lots
of them remarked (though not out loud) on Bobo's insect
bites that morning, and the fact he wasn't smiling near as
much as usual. Merribeth and Toby even slipped each other
winks. Willis Rensselaer, also on the platform, always looked
the same, as if he would gladly bite your head off, or if
yours was not available, a toad's, a chicken's, or a painted
turtle's. J.B. clapped his hands between each exercise, the
way he had on every other day, and tried to roll his stomach
underneath his rib cage.

It fell to Doris Mullady, halfway through a body twist,
to notice that a cage door hung partway open.

"Hey!" she cried, to no one in particular. "Looks as if
the cats got out!"

221

All the students stopped, and stared in that direction. Bobo dropped his arms; Willis trotted over to the cages.

Everyone could see that they were empty, but Willis opened all four doors and stuck his head in each of them, in turn. When he had finished doing that, he took the last cage door and slammed it shut with all his might.

Because there wasn't any latch on it—just a hasp—the door rebounded open, at great speed, striking Willis smartly on the elbow. That made him leap (and Bobo hide a smile) and grab the door—the top of it—and give it one enormous yank, enough of a yank, in fact, to pull its screws right out, the ones that held its hinges to the doorframe. The door came off, and Willis hurled it toward the flagpole with a shout of effort. Although he'd recommended short words to the kids, when hitting, the one he chose himself was four full syllables, beginning with a synonym for Mom.

By this time, student voices were a-buzzin':

"Gee, howja suppose they ever did it?"

"Maybe, when whoever fed them, or whatever . . ."

"Someone musta *let* them out, I bet."

"Where d'ya think they got to, anyway?"

"So whatta we do now?"

Willis had rejoined his colleagues on the platform, and the three men huddled for a minute while the kids kept talking back and forth and calling, *"Here* puss-puss-puss-*pussy!"*

Finally, J.B. called for their attention.

"I've been informed by Mr. Rensselaer," he said, "that he himself closed up them cages after suppertime, last night, and put a heavy staple, like, in every whatchacallit. What I'm saying is, there doesn't seem like any way them cats could open up them doors theirselves."

To which the young survivalists said things like:

"Oooo!"

"Accomplices!"

"An outside job!" Etc.

"So what we'd like to know is this: did any of you-all see any strangers on the grounds, like yesterday, last night?"

old J.B. asked. "Anyone atall?" Will and Bobo had the students skewered with their eyes, but old J.B., he just seemed puzzled by the deal.

"Well, what I'd like is for everybody to keep their ahs peeled this morning, wherever you are on the grounds, and see if we get a glimpse of a cat anywhere, or not. Seems like the first thing we need to know is where the dang things *are,* all right? So, maybe like at lunchtime anybody who's seen a cat, or more'n one, can tell me that, and where they seen 'em—and we can take it from there. Don't forget, they got them yeller collars on, so they shouldn't be too daggone hard to spot.

"And now, let's get on back to Cals"—he stuck his chest way out—"if you please, Mister Bodine."

After Cals, they ran—the boys at an exhausting pace, in silence, and the girls a lot more comfortably, with shouts of "Hey, I t'ink I taw a puddy cat!" and "Kittee-kittee-kittee-kittee-*kittee!*"

When they had breakfasted, the kids were split up into different groups, to practice different sorts of specialties. Willis Rensselaer took ten of them for bayonet instruction, which hardly anyone enjoyed and almost everyone believed was out-of-date, like Waterloo, or World War *One,* for God's sake.

But Willis liked the weapon, really liked it. He'd explained to Bobo and to old J.B. that he felt the bayonet developed something that he called "the spirit of killing," in a really admirable way.

"You just can't kid yourself," he said, impassioned by the subject, almost lyrical. "Fighting with a bayonet is honest conflict, face-to-face, an intimate relationship. *I* live; *you* die. Both of us are people, not abstractions; all nations are the same, all colors—our gooks and their gooks. The bayonet can make life very real and valuable. Not to mention slippery," he said, and slid a semi-smile across his face.

Willis had devised a bayonet assault course that the kids were forced to run, tilting at these dummies that he'd made, each of which had outlined "target zones": the head, the chest, the groin—the usual.

"The bayonet attacks the human centers of command, the places that we get our orders from," he'd tell the kids. "The brain, the heart, the balls—or ballsesses," he'd say smirking. "When anyone is threatened in those spots by one of these"—he held up his double-edged and brightly sharpened, pointed blade—"he tends to panic. *She* does, too," he added delicately, "unless she's looking for a cut-rate hysterectomy." Some days he'd lead them through the course, stabbing, slashing, screaming like a wild man.

A lot of people found that pretty scary, that performance, though Merribeth, with feigned indifference, shrugged and rolled her eyes. "Whatever turns you on," she said.

On the morning of the Catescape, Willis reached his wildest. "Today, we're going to *wipe those dummies out,*" he told his squad. "Destroy them, shred them, get at their insides."

And so he led them up and down the course till that was done, and everyone was hoarse and limp and soaked with sweat, and panting in a state of near exhaustion. Sawdust, straw, and bits of tattered uniforms were strewn along the course.

Yet when he said "Dismissed!" they all had energy to head on off, away from him, at once. All, that is, but Louis.

"Say, Mister Rensselaer," he said and sidled up. "I don't know if I should say this, but . . ." He stopped and waited, head half lowered, looking from the top part of his eyes.

"Well," said Willis calmly, "put it this way. If you don't, I'm going to take this shiny little tool of mine and stick it maybe halfway up—"

Louis cut him off abruptly, looking at him squarely now and nervous-laughing all around the words.

"Last night," he said. "It may not mean a thing—you know?—but last night Plummer left the barracks after lights. Probably around eleven. Renko said that nobody could leave, on accounta some party the girls were going to have, but Plummer, he went out. I saw him go. And you know what

224

else? There wasn't any party. I asked around—oh, three, four girls. Real casual, you know? I'd just walk up to them and go 'Have a good time at the party last night?' And I swear, none of them even knew what I was talking about. So what I was thinking was, maybe Plummer—him and his girl friend, even—might've . . ."

"Louis," Willis Rensselaer advised, "you just pay attention to your glands and your digestion; let me do the thinking. You haven't got the forehead for it." He took his bayonet, detached it from the wooden rifle mock-up that they used, and with a sudden wristy motion, not unlike a Ping-Pong backhand slam, he brought the flat of it across the boy's rear end.

Louis leaped and yelped and covered up the yelp by laughing. "Yessir, Mister Rensselaer," he said. "I just thought that maybe you . . ."

"Uh-uh-uh-uh-*uh*," Willis scolded. "There you go again." He made a rapid motion with his empty hand. "Thank you, Louis. I enjoyed your song. But now, buzz off, you little scorpion. Isn't that your mama calling? Or whatever it is you lovely creatures have."

The exercise had made him feel much better.

Missus Rita Fairchild liked a lunch of soup and sandwiches, along with salad bar, and fruit or Jell-O for dessert, with cookies. But kids would not eat soup in summertime, she found, and so she just stopped serving it. It was no skin off her ear. That day, the sandwiches were heroes, which meant club rolls instead of bread, with slices of American process cheese and luncheon loaf and carton tomatoes, with shredded iceberg lettuce and either Miracle Whip or bottled Italian dressing, for a change. For dessert, it was the canned Bing cherries in heavy syrup, with pecan sandies.

J.B. wasn't all that upset about the cats' getting away, it seemed to Rita Fairchild, but the other two sure were. They hardly said a civil word the whole lunch long, just argued back and forth about such things as circumstantial evidence and unsupported allegations and the kind of threat

225

it'd take to get the truth from kids like these. Bobo asked the other two to let him try a favorite strategy of his; it wouldn't cost them anything and—who knew?—it possibly might work.

Willis, still, was into twitting Bobo. "I know *exactly* what you're going to say to them," he said, "and let me tell you this: that kind of thing went out with narrow ties and tea dances, for Christ's sake. This is 1982 now, Dad."

But J.B. told him, sure, go ahead, and Bo stood up and chimed his glass and said:

"I thought you'd like to know"—a frank, but fleeting, smile—"that we know certain things about the cats. They didn't just escape; they were released. They're gone. There were no strangers on the grounds last night; it was an inside job. And in this room are those who are responsible. Of course you know exactly who you are." His gaze went slowly around the room, with one wise eyebrow cocked.

"Now, it'd be a cinch for old J.B. to stand up here and make a bunch of threats and start a big investigation. And before you know it, we'd have changes in the atmosphere we've worked so hard for: suspicions, accusations, all that inquisition jazz." Bobo liked to toss off slang like that. Like one of them, he thought. "But he is not about to take that route. All of us up here agreed that if we were another kind of group—the Pittsburgh Steelers football team, let's say, or employees of U.S. Steel or Exxon—well, that might be the thing to do. But not for us it isn't.

"We're a different breed of . . . *person,* we survivalists, at FMI; we have a different sort of contract with each other, a different sort of Rappaport." Bobo smiled; nobody got it, nobody laughed. "Mutual interdependence is the name of our game—united we stand, divided we . . . die." He drew the corners of his mouth way down and gave them one quick nod. Bag the humor; sock it to 'em.

"What that means"—good teachers always clarified—"is that when one of us makes a mistake, we all have to suffer for it. That's a hard fact of survival, good people, and we might as well get used to it, right now. For example:

226

seeing that we haven't got those cats, we'll have to have another sort of Ultimate Experience. It may not be as good—by that I mean as *interesting*—but that shouldn't really matter. We ought to pay *some* price for what was done to us, by one or more of us—in other words, ourselves. And it won't kill us, that's what matters; we'll survive. What we're going to do is simulate a very different set of circumstances. Still survival stuff, of course, but different."

There was some nervous changing of positions, and a throat or two got cleared.

"The thing we're going to try to do," said Bo, "is act as if we've had a four-day notice of a nuclear attack. On Hartford. Because the bomb will fall that close, we can't stay here; the fallout would be deadly. We don't have vehicles for all of us, and anyway the roads would be a mess, with every car in Hartford trying to get away on them, and cars from all the other towns, and so forth. So what *we* have to do is put on packs and arm ourselves and walk the hell on out. If we can cover fifty miles a day, we'll be in fairly decent shape. We'd be well up in Vermont," said Bobo.

"Which means"—Bobo looked around the room again and smiled a joyful-looking one—"tomorrow morning that's exactly what we're going to start to do, walk to Vermont: fifty miles a day, full packs and weapons. Of course, because there isn't any *real* emergency, we can't go marching off outside the fence with guns and everything. So what we'll do instead is walk our fifty miles a day in here. Ten full circuits of the track and set up camp each night. It should be quite a test—experience—for us; difficult, but possible. A few of us may lose a pound or two—okay, you gals?—and get a blister here and there, but when we're finished we'll be real survivors, don't you think?"

As Bobo talked, the clients at the Teen Survival Session looked increasingly . . . distraught. This was Connecticut, July—thus hazy, hot, and humid. Vermont, well, that had sounded nice, but fifty miles a day to *nowhere*? So when he finished, groans, objections, pleadings all came out of them. It wasn't *fair*, a lot of voices said, to make *them* suffer on accounta someone else ("some idiots," in fact) uncaged a bunch of mangy cats. It wasn't *their* fault, was it? Why should they . . . ? And *fifty* miles a day . . . ?

Some said they'd rather be irradiated.

Bobo raised a soothing, peaceful palm.

"Hey," he said. "Believe me, I don't blame you. But look at the alternatives we're faced with. I, for one, refuse to be a cop up here, to start suspecting my companions, setting traps for people"—Merribeth could not resist a loud, fake sneeze—"trying to catch them in a lie. Hell, that'd ruin everything we've worked for."

He paused, appeared to think. "Of course," he said, "there is one other possibility. Let's say whoever let those cats go free just did it as a joke—or because they had a special thing for cats"—he did a number with his eyes— "or some other dumb fool reason. And now they maybe *see* that it was dumb, and maybe that it's not exactly fair to put their good survival buddies through this . . . other exercise, just because they chose to take the law into their own hands, so to speak. Well, if that person or persons was man or woman enough to stand up and admit it, well, then I don't think that there'd be any need"—he seemed to check this out with his Director—"for all the rest of us to strap those great humungous packs on, in the morning. . . ."

Zack later compared the moment to the way you dove into a swimming pool in May, when it had just been filled, before the sun had had a chance to mellow it a little. You gave yourself a one-two-three, and made your mind a blank and . . . did it. ("A blank is right," said Toby, at that later time.)

He even raised his hand, as he got up.

"I'm the one who did it, sir," he said.

Bobo couldn't help but sweep his searchlight of a smile past little-snotty-smarty Rensselaer.

"How about that, sonny?" he said, *sotto voce*.

Before a lot of people in the room had got through gaping over Revelation 1 ("Plummer? Jeez, he's the *last* guy that you'd think'd do . . ."), Toby'd gotten to her feet, as well. In retrospect, she called her action "Scudsyesque," but at that moment she was only spitting mad.

"Letting those cats go was my idea," she snarled at the head table. "*I* did it; he just helped. Maybe someday—God forbid—I'll have to kill a cat in order to survive, but doing it for practice is . . . just *gross*."

And she sat down again—so Zack did, too. She'd desperately wanted to say "perverted," but at the last second, she'd chickened out, not being one hundred percent sure that it wasn't "*pre*verted." No point in making a fool of yourself when you're proclaiming a principle, she thought.

Again, there was a buzz of conversation. Reactions swept across the room, leaving little whitecaps of emotion. Relief and gratitude were first; everyone was spared from torments indescribable. But—come to think of it—the threat of that huge horror of a march had been invoked *because* of what they'd done, those two. And no one in authority had ever said—announced to all of them—they'd have to *kill* the cats. Louis's story was a rumor, nothing more. And it might've been . . . well, kinda fun, to see if they could stalk the cats and splatter them with just a little harmless water-color paint. You really *could* say, if you looked at it a certain way, that Zack and Toby *had* more or less put their own wishes ahead of the group's—so a lot of people thought. Which wasn't good survival, was it, after all?

Human nature being what it is, the question "Who do they think they are?" did occur to more than one survivor (of the first three weeks, two days of Teen Survival Session).

The other questions of the moment were (1) what, if anything, Zack and Toby would "get" for their misdeed, and (2) whether the staff could round up another bunch of cats.

The answers to those questions, and still other ones, would be decided in the way that everything had been, all Teen Survival Session long. Democratically, by vote of those of legal voting age, which is to say the staff, except for Rita Fairchild. Let *her* vote and the next thing you know you'd find her in your bathroom.

They met in Cottage 2, before the evening meal, that very night.

"I'll tell you God's own honest truth," said old J.B. (That was the same "God" that had given the atomic bomb, as a special gift, to the American people, according to him and Phyllis Schlafly. Even Sam N. Dreyfus didn't believe *that*.) "I'll tell you God's honest truth: I'm just as glad there ain't no cats to kill, no more. Like I was saying, boys, I'm just not sure atall that killing cats might not-a-been more trouble than it's worth. If, say, the people down below—the board and them—decided it was wrong or bad for us to have the kids do that, you know whose ass'd be collecting unemployment in the fall. For you guys, this is just a summer job, but me, I got my future and my family to think of."

As a general rule, J.B. thought about his "family" only when the word rolled off Rita's tongue, with ugly emphasis, but now (his whiskey-Coke in hand) he nodded solemnly and stolidly, a crewcut pillar of society, you bet.

Allied once again, Bo and Willis both had joined him in a drink, though neither of them found a whiskey-Coke to be his cup of tea.

"Of all the juvenile libations," Bobo later said, with feeling. And then, in baby talk, "I t'ink I'd wike a wum and woot-beer, pwease." He'd not forgiven Willis for that moment by the pond, but a united front was vital to the program—to making Fairchild swallow their new plan for it, that is.

Willis had forgotten their small tiff, by then; the morning and the afternoon had seen to that. His head was full of so much nastiness—new stuff forever seeking to replace the old—that little incidents like that were quickly moved along, like so much shoddy merchandise in discount stores. As he sipped his drink (it wasn't sweet enough for his peculiar tastes), his eyes, from time to time, would flick across the room at J.B.'s Panasonic, from which the voice of Sam N. Dreyfus could be clearly heard, as if he were a part of their discussion. Willis wished that he could reach right through those speakers and then, in stereo, press both his thumbs against the preacher's windpipe—very slowly cutting off this source of warm and Karo-flavored chatter. Either that, or hold him down and stuff his mouth and nose compactly full of fine old pecan pie, so that he couldn't make a sound, or take a breath, in fact. The Rensselaer Amendment to the Clean Air Act, thought Willis.

"You know," said Bobo, lighting up a lantern of a smile, "the more I thought about the cats, the more I saw your point. You may not believe this, but . . . I'm glad they're gone, myself." What the fuck, he thought, no point crying over split cats; it was time for old J.B. to have another brainstorm.

"Of course," he rambled smoothly on, "we can't admit our feelings to the kids, or have it look as if the three of us *condone* what those two did. As you were saying just a week or so ago, kids have got to get some punishment sometimes, when they go wrong. So what we have to do, it seems to me, is work *that* out—their punishment—and then to figure out some climax for our session."

"Well," said J.B., "perhaps some sort of field day would be good—different kinds of competition, see?—in stuff that they been doing here, like riflery, and startin' fires . . ."

There was a vintage J.B. Fairchild "idea," Willis thought: a field day. Gee-whiz, double-golly-oh. Bobo was right: taking the difference in their ages into account, J.B., not Rod Renko, was by far the dumbest asshole in the place.

But here was Bobo, nodding his fool head off and grinning ear to silly ear.

"Uh-*huh*," he said. "That'd be *great!* And taking your idea one step further, we might be able to set up one huge climactic event in which the kids'd have to incorporate a whole bunch of different survival skills at the same time. . . ."

"Like a relay, sort of?" asked J.B. excitedly. "Or a kind of marathon-lak, where you have to run and stalk and cook a meal, and shoot and set up camp. . . ."

"You've got it!" Bobo said. "That's perfect!" He seized old J.B.'s hand and pumped it up and down.

J.B. looked both pleased and slightly puzzled. The voice of Sam N. Dreyfus—as sweet as marzipan, as ominous as okra—filled the momentary silence.

"An ah fo' an ah, and a tooth fo' a tooth. Hand fo' hand, and foot fo' foot," he said. It was a favorite text of his: vengeance is y'all's.

But Bobo, standing up, flicked off the radio and patted it approvingly. "And there," he said, "you have the rest of it: how to punish Ayer and Plummer, and also make the punishment constructive, useful—like you said, *American*. They released the cats, so they can take their place—eye for an eye and a foot for a foot, just like the Reverend Dreyfus put it. Talk about your perfect quarry—beats a bunch of cats all hollow! Ayer and Plummer—both of them are pretty doggone good survivalists. What a challenge for the kids they'll be! What a perfect exercise." Bobo shook his head. "J.B., you are too much—you're just a genius, pure and simple." Willis bobbed a half a nod to *that*. "Let's see. Suppose we let it last two days, give them—what?— two hours head start, say? The others try to stalk them, shoot 'em with the CO_2 guns. Zack and Toby can't get hurt—we'll even give them goggles for their eyes—and at the end we'll see what color paint they've got the most of on their clothes. Fabulous! It'll be like two full days of survival hide-and-seek. Each time one of them gets shot, we make the hunters come on back to base for fifteen minutes; then off they go again. Hey," said Bobo, eyes alight, "how about some trophies for the winning team, okay?"

Like other teachers, almost everywhere, Bo was very big on prizes.

J.B. ran a palm over the top of his head. What Bobo had said hadn't been *exactly* the kind of field day he'd been thinking of, but it incorporated a lot of the same ideas, for sure. And the two kids being punished would get a whole lot out of it, too. There could be times, up the road there, where being good at hiding—from a bunch of city people, say—might be essential to survival. As a matter of fact, about the only thing wrong with his idea that he could see was that it didn't hardly punish Zack and Toby much at all.

"Well..." he said, expecting to go on and make that point.

But Bobo hadn't finished, quite. "I know we all agreed," he said, "that putting kids in cages is a no-no. But maybe just this once it is appropriate. Symbolic, you could say. I really think those two would almost *like* it—showing they could take their medicine, like that. It'd be just for a day or two before the field day. And other kids would see there's such a thing as justice—law and order—in this world of ours, that no one 'gets away with it'—not here, not now, not anymore. Ayer and Plummer pay their debt and have their slates wiped clean. They take their medicine where everyone can see it going down." Bobo held out a plausible hand. "And furthermore," he said, "it fits the crime. Where once we kept our twenty cats gone wild, we now have two young lions, right?"

That very night, Willis was pleased to say to Harold Ayer that Zack and Toby were "eager as caged lions"; it was just about the high point of his day. And it *was* true that Z & T were caged, by then; they'd gone there after supper, amidst a lot of laughs and kidding, sure. During their confinement—J.B. so announced, to titters, during supper—they wouldn't have to use a cat box, though. Four times a day, they'd be let out, for exercise and visits to "conveniences": once after every meal and just before lights out.

And something else: unlike the cats (again) they wouldn't "bunk together."

"It wouldn't do if folks was kept awake by...yowlin'," J.B. said, and chuckled in his hand.

Even Missus Fairchild smiled at that one. She'd heard much cruder stuff on Johnny Carson.

78. Matty Crews's Hav-a-Hart

In 1639, old Matilda Crews's umpteen-times-great-grandfather had up and moved himself and family and household goods from the New Haven colony to North County, Connecticut, because he'd thought that one of the Reverend Davenport's sermons was boring. That's the sort of root she sprang from. Of course, it wasn't called North County back then, or anything else, other than "way the hell and gone up north, someplace." Jeremiah Crews had settled on the best-looking piece of land he could find and, being the sort of nonconformist that he was, he (over)paid the local Indians: a deck of playing cards, a mirror, and a bugle. In the years since then, the Crews family had sold off chunk by hundred-acre chunk of it, for real cash money, which meant that old Matilda Crews was left with just the semi-swampy worst remainder, a wooded piece a short ways up the road from what she called "The Friendly Moron's Institute."

Matty Crews, as everybody called her ("Rhymes with 'batty,' get it?") was a genuine eccentric. Just check her bona fides: she (first) was rich; she lived alone; she never mowed her lawn; she had an outhouse; she didn't own a car, but hitchhiked back and forth to town. She also kept raccoons as pets and was—as she proclaimed herself—a "pacifistic anarchist." This meant that she found government in general ridiculous, absurd, incompetent, a pain, but that she'd never raise a finger to overthrow it. It was widely believed that she subscribed to *Mother Jones*—and also *House and Garden*.

Like almost everyone else, she thought that the Francis Marion Institute was a CIA training area, but that never stopped her from taking rides from people like Harold Ayer and Ricky Renko and Bill Bartowiak, when they were first putting the Institute together.

"Don't think I don't know what you're up to," she'd always say to them, and shake a finger, scoldingly. And they would slap their thighs and laugh and talk about the weather. Hence: "The Friendly Moron's Institute."

Matty Crews always kept a large Hav-a-Hart trap set in her garden, during the summertime, to protect her sweet corn from the "*wild*" raccoons that sometimes came to call. Whenever she'd catch one—the trap just caught the animal alive, unharmed—she'd put it in one of her big, comfortable cages and feed it canned salmon and homemade granola until the corn had all gone by, at which point she'd release it.

Its raccoon relatives would listen to its story, smell its breath, and roll their bandits' eyes around. If Matty Crews forgot about the closed-up trap, in early fall, she'd sometimes be awakened in the middle of the night by the clanking sound made by one or two raccoons trying to figure out how to get into the darned thing.

79. Cagey

The worst thing about being in the cages, Zack and Toby later agreed, was that for the first time since they left their playpens, they were in a place that they literally *couldn't* get out of. It wasn't anything like being in class, or even in a car going sixty miles an hour on the Interstate; in both those cases you *could* leave, if you wanted to badly enough, and besides, you were there of your own free will, sort of. No, in this situation they were locked inside a cage—two cages—with padlocks on the doors, and if someone didn't unlock the padlocks, to feed them or to let them out, well...tough. It was possible to die from being caged.

Being locked in a cage calls for a whole new relationship with yourself.

"You know something?" Toby said, the second day. "About the only way we can prove we still exist is to do something—like scream and shout—that'd make them react to us. Except when they react, we're nothing. We have no effect on the environment at all. Do you realize that?"

Zack looked through the wire at her. She was sitting in the farthest corner of her cage, her legs drawn up, her head upon her knees. She had on a pair of yellow shorts and matching yellow T-shirt, just as he did. Bobo'd brought them to the cages the first evening.

"Here," he said. "The cats, poor things, had only collars, but you two get a uniform. You can give me the stuff you're wearing in the morning."

"I think I'll stick to what I've got," said Toby, pointing at her olive drabs. "Blue would be all right, or even purple, but yellow's not my color, really."

"Gosh," said Bobo, "what a shame. 'Cause if you're not in uniform—this uniform—by morning, why then you'll have to go the cat route. That means a Day-Glo collar. Only. Period. Willis said he'd help me slip one on you, gladly. And slip the stuff you're wearing off, of course." He smiled enthusiastically. "I shit you not, good buddy."

By midnight, they had changed. It made another way that they were different, special, strange.

Now, Zack was somewhat worried. Tobe was not adjusting well. She was much more of a free spirit than he was, he thought. To him, being put in a cage was, in a way, just another part of life that had to be put up with. His father had this expression: "That's just the way it works," which he used to explain—or not explain—a lot of the things (e.g., presidential appointments, the SATs, medical education) that one had to adjust to or "keep a stiff upper lip" about. There wasn't "any point in making waves," Rodman Plummer sometimes said. "Life isn't perfect," he would add, thinking he'd passed on a useful truth.

Zack had never gone to boarding school, but he knew he could have handled it.

"The thing *I* realize most," Zack said to Toby, "is tomorrow we get out of here. They're going to let us go, and they are *never* going to catch us."

Toby lifted up her head and turned to look at him. Her eyebrows were up, and she might have been holding her breath; she had that sort of desperate look about her.

What they'd been considering was just refusing to play the game at all. If they didn't run, the other kids couldn't stalk them or shoot them with paint guns; that'd be too

237

ridiculous. Merribeth had snuck by to say that a lot of them didn't want to, anyway. If they staged a sit-down strike, they figured, the worst thing that could happen was that they'd stay in the cages until the end of the session, just a few days down the line.

But was it? Was that—really—the worst thing that could happen? After a day in the cages, and this uniform business, they'd found it easier and easier to convince themselves that Bobo and Willis would never let it go at that. It wouldn't be like them at all to just let a couple of kids ruin their precious game plan. Toby and Zack were both imaginative. Bobo himself would have been proud of some of the possibilities they came up with, though of course they didn't tell the worst of them to each other. But Zack had become sufficiently alarmed by *his* imaginings—and Toby's, little squaw's, were worse—to cause him to decide to lobby for a change in plan.

"Look," he said—he whispered. No one was around, and they were pretty sure the cages weren't being bugged, but in a cage, you whispered. "They're going to give us a head start. Two hours, did they say? We're in just about as good shape as anyone. Or better. Plus, no one knows the layout here as well as you do—'cept for old J.B., perhaps. Places we can hide, and stuff like that. What I was thinking was, if we can find some tools, just a pick and shovel really, well, we can dig our way out, underneath the fence."

Toby let her knees go, straightened out her legs. She stared at him. She blinked and stared some more. "I can't believe I never thought of that. Of course." Zack could almost see the energy come rushing into her. Like Popeye, when he'd eat the spinach. "That'd be a hundred times easier than getting over it," she said. "The fence is set in poured cement, but not an awful lot of it. A foot, at most; I saw them pour the stuff." She turned her hands to fists and shook them both at him, and then she smiled and crawled across the cage. Zack could see her nipples, up against the yellow shirt.

"We'll need some food." She spoke in rapid bursts of

238

whisper. "And tools. And maybe a diversion of some sort. You know, a plan to get them all someplace, to give us time to . . ." She ran a finger down her face. "Let's see . . ."

Zack closed his eyes and took in one deep breath, and smiled. They weren't out—far from it—but at least he had the old familiar Toby back: the standard, working, energetic, optimistic model. He knelt and gripped the wire between their cages, puckered up his lips, and stuck them through the mesh, in her direction. She laughed, and knelt herself, and met them. As kisses go, it wasn't much, but what the hell: they were excited already.

80. Gun Collecting.

Speaking of the special guns he'd heard that they were going to use to shoot the cats, Louis told an audience in Barracks B: "They got a spring inside." Counting intentional lies as well as other oral factual errors, plus mistakes on written tests in school, that was the 2,683rd time he'd been wrong in his life, so far.

The guns were powered not by "a spring," but by carbon dioxide. They had brown plastic grips and steel-blue barrels, and they fired dye- (*not* "paint-") filled plastic balls that were about half an inch in diameter. Their manufacturer claimed that they were accurate and useful to a range of thirty yards.

The members of the Teen Survival Session signed out these reasonably long-barreled handguns by teams, from the Institute's "armory." With the session drawing to a close, almost everybody's mood was easygoing, loose, relaxed. This so-called Hunt would be no tougher than you made it; certain people planned to find a quiet spot and simply smoke a joint or two, hang out and take it easy. Shoot at Zack and Toby? Hey, forget it. They were "okay kids" to some, and even "real good friends of mine" to others. Turkeys were for shootin', man.

Of course there were a few—well, quite a few—who planned to play the game as Will and Bobo planned it . . . make that *ordered*. One of this variety was Louis.

Louis was a Green; as luck would have it, so were Rod Renko and Arthur Barrett. When the Greens signed out their pistols, Willis had some fun, at Rod's expense, pretending that he just could not believe that "that" was Rodney's signature.

"Look," he cried, and held the sign-up sheet on high, so everyone could see it. "He's actually *misspelled* his own last name! Can you believe it? Don't just take my word for it—you look at this yourselves. Now isn't that an *i* between the *e* and *n?* It looks like one to me, all right. Dear Lord, I thought I'd dealt with idiots before, but this thing here . . ."

Everybody gathered around the desk to look and point and make remarks and laugh, and Louis, given such an opportunity, didn't hesitate an instant. He quickly reached and took a Browning semiautomatic 9mm pistol from off the shelf—one of the two that lay there in plain sight—and slid it in the waistband of his pants, in back, where it was covered by his jacket. A box of ammunition fairly dove into his pocket.

And in a little while he signed up for a dye gun, too.

Arthur Barrett was the last of the Greens to get his CO_2 pistol. Almost predictably, he was a little late in getting to the armory, but not so late he didn't see some things he wasn't meant to.

81. Cat Nap

Matty Crews had had her supper. Then she'd baited up the Hav-a-Hart and set it by the sweet corn. For bait, she used two fresh bay scallops, fried in butter, and with mushrooms; she'd eaten eight, herself, for dinner, and she knew they were superb. Anything she trapped would feel, she felt quite sure, enriched by the experience.

Then she took a white enamel saucepan from her kitchen shelf and went to pick some raspberries. Her patch was just around the corner of her house, and not far from the garden.

Matty Crews's memory was not what it had been. She'd forgotten (just for instance) why she liked Eugene McCarthy, and whether Jackie Gleason had died or not. But still, her ears remained what she called "snooping sharp," so when the trap clanged shut, she heard it.

"Hmmm," she said out loud. "I wonder what I've cotched me this time."

She knew it could be a raccoon, of course, though coons preferred to dine in darkness. Rabbit was a possibility, but rabbits didn't eat fried foods, or fish, any more than chipmunks did. Might it be a skunk? Matty Crews had never trapped a skunk, nor even seen one, other than a goner by the roadside. And she hoped she never would. Years before, she'd bought a big tall can of Sacramento Tomato Juice, because a friend of hers had said she ought to have one, just in case of skunks. Matty Crews could not remember why, though. Maybe if you gave a skunk tomato juice to drink, it wouldn't spray your dog. Except she'd never had a dog. She'd have to ask the friend again, if she could think which friend it was that told her.

In any case, she had to go and check the trap. She tiptoed quietly around the corn.

"My land," said Matty Crews out loud, when she had looked. "A kitty-cat."

And so it sort of was: a tiger, crouched down in the Hav-a-Hart, and looking mean and lean and wary. But also taking dainty bites of scallop fried in butter.

"Just look at you," said Matty Crews, most warmly. "A *very* pretty kitty in a *lovely* sporty collar."

The cat did not seem calmed by Matty Crews's flattery. Matty saw that it was very, very wild. She also saw the tag clipped on its collar, and some writing on the tag. To read it, all she'd have to do was find a way to separate the cat and collar. Peacefully, of course.

"Pas de sweat," said Matty Crews, bilingually.

She lifted up the trap and put it in an empty cage. She also slid into the cage a saucer of warm milk, which she had first enriched with half a powdered Nembutal. Then, using two long kitchen forks, she opened up the trap and let the cat step out into the larger cage. It wasn't long before it started lapping up the warming, narcoleptic treat.

Matty Crews checked out the tag again. She'd read it half a hundred times and knew it quite by heart, but still . . .

". . . the Callipygians need *immediate assistance*," she read out loud. She was sitting in her favorite easy chair, a dark-gray velvet one, with tidies on the arms and back. Clearly (she believed) the message came from people at the Friendly Moron's Institute, people that the CIA were holding there, for interfering, governmental reasons. Her mind was ninety-nine percent made up: she'd dial the number on

243

that tag. The CIA was seldom in the right—though always *to* the right, of pacifistic anarchists.

But first, she felt, she ought to sleep on it, the way her father'd always said a person ought to do. The morning would be soon enough to call, provided she remembered.

Matty Crews bemoaned her failing memory. Back in school, say sixty years ago, she'd always been a whiz in world geography. But nowadays she wasn't even certain-sure where Callipygia *was*.

82. Game Plan

By the time the hour came for Zachary Izak Plummer and Cristabel Ayer to play the Fox for all the Teen Survival Hounds, they had their game plan perfectly in place. It was simplicity itself.

Details, step by step, as follows.

Merribeth, the ever-faithful friend, would stash their uniforms—fatigues—and money, if she had some, in the tree house; they would go there first, though not directly. No, what they'd do, when they were dis-encaged, was head off, slowly, toward the woods and into them, then quickly circle back along the fence and scoot on up the big old maple. Once they had fatigues on, covering their yellow shorts and shirts, plus caps, they wouldn't have to be so spooky; from a distance, both of them could pass for lots of other people.

Then, next, they'd slide around to where the tools they'd need were kept: a shed beside the garden, next to the garages. No one ever hung around the garden of his own free will, and the cars in the garages simply sat there all the time and had their batteries run down. At Teen Survival it was walk-trot-sprint-crawl-gallop; it might have been 2001 B.C., the way a person never ever drove, up there.

With tools in hand—two shovels and a pick, let's say—

245

they'd duck back in the woods until they reached a certain distant spot along the fence that Toby'd chosen. Say half an hour's digging and they're out. Of course the Hounds would find the hole, but not until some further time had passed, enough and more (they both believed) for them to reach the nearest town, where they could call a cab to zoom on down the Interstate. If, as well might happen, they were short on fare, Zack was sure he could convince the driver that his mom would pay the rest. But even if he couldn't, they would have enough to get them well away—to someplace where they could call someone to come and pick them up.

A person learned a few survival skills by being young, American, and living in the suburbs.

83. Game

"The best laid schemes o' mice and men / Gang aft a-gley," wrote Robert Burns, the Scottish poet, proving he knew Life, and also Gaelic. Zack and Toby (neither of them greatly like a mouse, and to the state, mere children) had better luck with theirs, at first. They exited their cages, in the presence of a small—and part-supportive, part-derisive—crowd, at six A.M., and disappeared at once into the woods. Then, safely out of sight, they swung on back around the lodge and up into the tree house. Clothes and money, both, were there, and "personal effects" like keys and wallets. The money was a tidy sum, beyond their expectations. Merribeth had held a going-out-of-session pot sale; talk about "a friend in need," *n'est-ce-pas?*

So Zack and Toby slipped into their olive drabs and headed for the place that tools were kept, with less than half an hour down the drain.

At which point things ganged totally a-gley.

Outside the garages—thus beside the little toolshed— was a red Accord sedan, its hood as open as the upper jaw of any hungry crocodile. And bending into it was Rutherford Bodine.

Zack and Toby stopped, reversed, and crouched behind

an aromatic dark-green dumpster. What on earth was Bobo doing there? And—more important—how long would he keep on doing it? Five minutes' watching and they had their answers.

Clearly—tragically, for them—the guy was tuning up his car.

In common with a lot of males who grow up in America, Bobo was an automotive know-it-all. Mister Goodwrench *hated* him. Bobo never sought his help; he'd tell him what to do, in tones that made it clear he'd fix the thing himself, except that he had more important, taxing work on hand. If Mister Goodwrench didn't have a sign that said he couldn't, Bobo'd often stroll through the garage, peering in the nearest motor job, making mournful clucking sounds, even as he shook-shook-shook his head. Every guy who worked in every service station Bobo ever patronized thought he was a Grand Prix prick.

When working on his own machine, Bobo made a small, satiric playlet of the job, complete with props and costume that he kept inside the trunk. By the time Zack and Toby got to be his audience, everything was perfectly in place.

First of all, he had this little plastic AM radio, a table model, old and cheap, with one cracked knob he'd wrapped in friction tape, the whole thing covered with a layer of oily grime. The radio was always on, and set to any nearby station that played music. On top of it he put an almost-empty Hires root-beer bottle, with three unfiltered Camel butts suspended in the dregs.

Over his survival shirt and shorts, Bobo wore his costume, a mechanic's coverall, in charcoal gray. On one shoulder, he had sewn a patch, his college coat of arms; *Lux et Veritas*, it said. And on his breast, in script and bright-red thread, there was his *nom de* greasepit: *Rutherford*, of course. In the pocket of his coveralls, in back, there was the rag he'd use to wipe the oil and grease off on: a hand towel from the Plaza. He also wore a one-size-fits-all

Boston Red Sox baseball cap, but backward, so the bill sloped down his neck.

While Zack and Toby knelt and watched, Bobo worked methodically, completely in the role: whistling a tune quite different from the radio's, talking loud and dirty to a spark plug, honkin' in a clotted red bandanna. Time went by; he farted twice; he sure was in no hurry.

Toby said to Zack, "It looks as if we've had it, in the tool department. Present company excepted," she tacked on.

He whispered back, "And this is it, the only place, you said?"

"Far as I can think," she said.

"How about if maybe I distract the guy, somehow? Then you could run on in and grab a pick and shovel?" Zack's tone was not convincing, even to himself.

Toby made a mouth. "Or how about you just look over his shoulder and say, 'Don't shoot, Marshal. I want to take this one alive.' Maybe that'd work," she said, and shook her head, but also smiled. She didn't look defeated by a long shot, Zack was glad to see.

"Yeah, well, I don't see a lot of sense in staying here," he whispered. "If we can't dig out, we're going to have to try to hide, right? And that means getting some food somewhere, as well as going to wherever it is, which you know a lot better than me, and..."

Toby took him by the arm. "Wait," she said. "You just made me think of something. Food. There are survival supplies in the tunnels. And not just food, but packs and hand tools, all sorts of stuff. Little spades, like for digging foxholes, you know? Maybe even picks, I don't remember. Come on."

So while Rutherford Bodine, oblivious, deep inside his car, kept rocking to the music of Chicago, Toby led Belinda Plummer's boy around behind the big main lodge, and down, and in its sloping cellar door. That was where the tunnel system started.

As Toby'd said to Rodman Plummer, the tunnels that her father and his friends had made were mostly used for storage. They could be used (she'd said) as shelters, too, in case of nuclear attack. Perhaps.

"I'd hardly call them *livable*," said Florence Ayer, one time. "*Survivable*, perhaps—I wouldn't know, of course," she said.

To Zack, they seemed like horizontal mine shafts, in the movies: walls and ceiling braced with timbers, sheets of plywood nailed to them, in places. The floors were more or less like wooden catwalks, so the stuff they'd stored on them would stay up high and dry.

And what a lot of stuff there was: crates and cardboard boxes, jerricans and barrels, some of them well labeled, others not. Later in the summer, it was planned, Florence Ayer equivalents would come and organize this hodgepodge of supplies. Women had a flair for work like that, work that called for tidiness and following directions. "Like filing, in an office," Harold Ayer explained to Ricky Renko. Men, he said, were better when it came to making policies, and that—the life-and-death decisions. "You never see a woman at a SALT or summit conference," he said. "And most of them are smart enough to know it's not their kinda thing. They're just too soft—God bless 'em," Harold Ayer concluded, with a wink.

Zack and Toby had only a Ray-o-Vac to help them in their search, but even with a ceiling full of fluorescent lights, it would have been slow going. The first thing they established was: there wasn't any crate or box that bore a nice big label "TOOLS—for digging" on it. That meant they had to open everything that wasn't marked, and so they found the following, in quantity:

- portable chemical toilets (in long-lasting, easy-to-wash polyethylene), with chemicals

- kerosene space heaters (polished chrome reflectors, full front safety guards)

250

- radiation emergency anticontamination kits (mask/respirator, filters, goggles, coverall, etc.)

- germicidal drinking-water tablets

- convenience foods, in heavy-duty No. 10 cans, with special storage atmospheres

- jumbo packs of assorted latex condoms: lubricated, colored, ribbed and not (Zack covertly broke the seal on one and grabbed a handful, thinking what the hell, you never know)

- uniforms, all olive drab

- bandages, adhesive tape, tampons, Excedrin Plus, Right Guard *and* Secret, lipstick and eyeliner and shampoo and conditioner, Oil of Olay, Preparation H, Crest, Dr. Scholl's—the basics

And finally, finally, finally the entrenching tools, those little olive-colored spades that you can dig a foxhole with, provided you've a lot of time, or terror, on your hands. Zack and Toby helped themselves to four of them, believing—as so many people do—that lots of something bad can somehow total up to something good. They also found and freed two backup flashlights, and some extra-long-life batteries.

Toby checked her watch, when this had all been done.

"There isn't any point in starting digging now," she said. "We've only got half an hour left. So what we'd better hurry up and do is hide, just like you said, and that means taking food. . . ." She looked back down the tunnel. "Those cans are kind of gross, and anyway, we haven't got an opener," she muttered, talking to herself.

Suddenly, she snapped her fingers, turned to Zack, and winked. "Hey, I've got it," she exclaimed. She pointed to her head, above the ear. "Smart kid," she said. "Over in the skeet shack—you remember?—there's jars and jars of nuts, for protein. Plus all those sour balls, for energy. Not

251

to mention tons of beer and soda. For replacing essential bodily fluids, of course."

Zack grinned. "I read about a woman in an airplane crash who lived on toothpaste for a month," he said. "She probably lost weight but didn't get a single cavity. We, on the other hand..."

"Come on, Cassandra," Toby said, and started down the tunnel, spades in hand.

Forty minutes later, they were sitting in the old abandoned cellar hole, underneath a tarp well strewn with leaves and brush. Unless a searcher came within, oh, fifteen-or-twenty yards of them, their hideout was invisible. Their larder—four jars each of Mixed Deluxe Dry-Roasted Nut Assortment, and Natural All-Pure-Fruit-Honey Sour Balls, along with six-packs (two) of Sunkist Orange Soda, and two of Löwenbrau—was large enough, they felt, to see them through a lot more time than they would ever have to be there.

Their plan, in fact, was to emerge at four, the next A.M., and be outside the fence by 5:15. Knowing fellow Teen Survival Sessionists, they were fairly sure that few would be abroad (read "up," "awake") at such an early hour, if they didn't have to be. Not only did they like their sleep, but also—face it—they discouraged kind of easily. If, as it *would* happen, no one even got a *glimpse* of T and Z for one entire day, the game would quickly lose excitement and be—ultimate disaster—*boring*.

Being bored was what they'd had enough of, all of them, already.

"Rather than be bored, I'd take my chances at the dentist," Duke once claimed. "Maybe I'd get nitrous—right?— and even if I didn't, hey. Pain is *never* boring," Duke maintained.

84. "...two in the (am)bush"

For more than three weeks, it had driven Louis Ledbetter a little bit insane, trying to figure out what Toby and Zack were planning to do. Not about survival or their sex lives, not about their choice of college or career. About *him*.

How would this matched set of suck-butt little jerk-offs plan to stick it to him?

As weeks went by and they did nothing, nothing, nothing, Louis realized that was it—their plan. They'd make him sweat, the four weeks that the session lasted, saying nothing, being oh-so-cool, just keeping him, like, under their surveillance. Then, when it had ended—and he had had to bust his ass for four full fucking weeks—they would turn around and blow the whistle. Cops would come, with cuffs and warrant, maybe Murder One.

So, up until the time that "Zack and Toby got encaged" (a line of Duke's), as cat replacements in the Ultimate Experience, Louis had his mind made up on what he'd better do. And that was get a running start, the day the Institute let out. What he had in mind was California—hey, why not?—he always said he had to go there sometime, anyway. He'd leave while they were eating breakfast, calmly walk on out the gate and keep on going. All he'd take would be a change of clothes and cash, whatever he could find. Kids were really careless with their money.

But all the stuff involving cats and cages—and *confessions* (Louis almost shit a brick when he heard Zack and Toby say right out that they had done it)—all that stuff had made him see that maybe there was still (or *now*) a better way, a permanent solution. Running, disappearing was all right, but that way he would always be a fugitive. The other way—if he could find the means to bring it off—would mean he'd never *ever* have to worry. Take out Zack and Toby and there wouldn't be no witnesses to anything, other than his buddies; he knew *they'd* never bring it up, 'cause that would mean their asses, too. Minus Zack and Toby, it was business—life—as usual. All he needed was the means, and then he *had* the means, almost like a present he'd been fated—*meant*—to have.

His team, which got the green dye in the little balls that went inside the CO_2 guns, they didn't make a difference, either way. They'd had one meeting, just like Bobo said they should, to get together on the strategy they'd use, when they could start to hunt, at eight A.M. What happened was that no one but himself was into it at all, as far as he could see. This Renko kid, the muscle one, who could have been a problem—the size of him, and with his girl friend such a bosom-bud of Toby's—he frankly said that having such a hunt was nothing but a crock, in his opinion, and he wasn't going to do it for a minute—("fucking") period. And furthermore, he said—he looked at Louis when he said it, too—he didn't want to see no green on Zack or Toby, neither, at the end.

He, himself, Rod Renko said, was going to go someplace he didn't care to specify, with certain of his friends, and have a party. Both the girls assigned to Green said that seemed supercool to them.

The other members of his team were turkeys. Jerry Something was a feeb who liked to talk about some game he played with friends at home that had to do with ancient history, or something. Arthur Barrett was that useless load

254

of chicken, a big fat spaz who wasn't good at anything. A couple of times, after the meeting, he tried to start a conversation with Louis about the Hunt, what'd be the best way for a person to go about it and all, but Louis knew that he was only sucking up to him by acting like he cared. Arthur Barrett couldn't hit a parked Impala with a cannon from across the street, much less a moving human target with a dye gun. Louis told him that he didn't know, and that probably the best thing he could do was hunt up his own wang and shoot that off a time or two.

Actually, Louis had given the matter of the Hunt a great deal of thought, and he was pretty sure he'd found the way to do it right. It helped to be an animal. It helped because he could pretend that he was being hunted, he was quarry. What he thought was that they'd go to ground, lie low awhile, and let whatever hounds there were get tired and discouraged. Then they'd make one lightning move, under-over-through the fence, at some place distant from the lodge, and not far from an outside road.

(It was a lucky thing, in a way, that Zack and Toby didn't know that Louis had thought this whole thing through so much the same as they had. It would have been depressing. Like having to agree with H. Cosell, *verdad?*)

And so, at eight A.M., when other people started off briskly to hunt, or seem to hunt, Louis angled off alone, not going fast at all, a day-pack on his back, with extra clothes and food, and most of all the Browning from the armory: the *means*. He had his dye gun, kiddy's toy, in hand.

Louis spent an easygoing day, checking out the two or three most likely spots along the fence. He sat in each of them awhile, looking up and down, trying to put himself in Zack and Toby's shoes some more. He saw, or sometimes only heard, some other hunters in the woods, but he was careful not to call attention to himself. No one shouted out a sighting or a hit. By nightfall he was settled in the single spot that seemed the best to him.

* * *

Louis didn't much enjoy the night. The woods were much too noisy, full of other creatures, animals and birds. *"Shit."* He said that almost prayerfully, a time or two, when there were sudden nearby sounds. He may have dozed off once or twice.

But when, come dawn, in misty silence, shadowlight, he saw both Zack and Toby creep up to the fence, in olive drab, with tiny spades, he didn't say a word.

He just reached out his hand and picked the Browning up, his semiautomatic pistol, made in Belgium. He'd loaded it the night before. It held exactly fourteen rounds, lucky-seven each, if need be.

85. A Page from Toby's Journal, dated May 18

I think it's just a fact that adults are a lot more paranoid than kids about the Russians, and black people and oriental people and even Indians. Kids can give them competition when it comes to radiation or other environmental stuff, maybe, but seldom are you going to meet a kid who's freaked out by the thought of having Cubans in Angola.

Older people seem to think the worst of other people. Maybe that's because they're so much more experienced. I can't believe it's that they know themselves much better, and are afraid that other people may be lots like them. What they seem to be saying is all other people are *different* from them.

Kids certainly get depressed, though. A lot of people I know are worried sick about the way they're doing things now and what on earth they *will* do, later on. *Hopeless* is an easy way to feel—like, "nothing works." Sometimes, kids go out and kill themselves or get messed up by chemicals because the world (and that's the adults' world) seems so enormously fucked-up.

But what kids *don't* do, at times when they're afraid, or

generally bummed-out, is go out getting guns or making fortresses someplace. That's a thing for adults, certain kinds of adults. Adults are the natural survivalists. Maybe that's because they love themselves so much, or think they're powerful, that they can *do* stuff, win—that they're invincible, you might say. It's more or less as if they feel that they can outlast or outsmart or outtough the other people— those ones they don't like. I guess they don't think as much about the superhuman dangers. Like, how do you outlast (outsmart, et cetera) a bunch of rays?

Most kids in the same situation would rather listen to some tunes and smoke a little grass, or drink some beer, or go to a show—take their minds off whatever it is, somehow. Maybe this is being lazy or short-sighted of them, but maybe it's simply being realistic. Sometimes I think that every person in the world today is just as helpless as a baby and that whatever's going to happen to the world or his country isn't going to be decided by himself, or any other person. It isn't like I believe in predestination, or anything really— I don't know—*"superstitious,"* like that. It's more that once things start going a certain way, there doesn't seem to be any stopping them. I *hate* thinking like that, but I can't help it.

86. 4:03 A.M.

Belinda Plummer was awakened by her husband's snoring, so she thought. He didn't snore that often. She decided to go to the bathroom. She had to anyway, sort of, and it would wake him up, and he'd roll over, off his back.

Sure enough, when she returned to bed, the guy was lying on his side.

"Hi," he said, in his sleepy-mumble voice, and, "You all right?"

And she said, "Yes, I'm fine."

Neither of them went right back to sleep, though both of them assumed the other had, and didn't say another word.

Florence Ayer was sitting in the nurse's station drinking coffee. So far, she'd had a quiet shift on Woodbridge 3, the floor where patients were who'd just had major surgery. A lot of the sickest people in the hospital were in beds on Woodbridge 3.

Nurse Ayer looked at the clock. Legend had it that most babies were born in the inconvenient early-morning hours, but she knew that that was nonsense. Sure, sometimes life begins at two or three or four A.M., but not as often as it ends then; that was her experience. A lot of people's bodies seemed to just give up, break down, toward daybreak. As if they didn't have the strength, or will, to run for one more day.

Florence Ayer stood up. She put her coffee down and stretched. Through the window, down the hall, she saw the gray of very early daylight. It looked to her as if Woodbridge 3 had made it, and she smiled.

Harold Ayer was glad his wife was out on duty. He'd had a dream—about Korea, maybe—and he might have just been shouting, at the end of it.

87. Help-less

When Arthur Barrett saw Louis Ledbetter take the Browning 9mm semiautomatic pistol off the armory shelf and stick it down his pants, he didn't make anything of it other than the obvious: the kid had swiped a gun, a real one. He bet the kid—he knew his name was Louis and he hated him—would take the gun on home with him and show it to his friends. Maybe use it in a stickup. Not a bank or a bar or a gas station even, probably more like a Burger Chef, that kind of place. Maybe a 7-Eleven. Possibly he'd shoot someone; Arthur wouldn't put it past the guy.

The last thought must have stuck in Arthur Barrett's mind that day. His mind was not a bad environment for thoughts, ideas, imaginings. That very night, it sprouted.

Ohmigosh, thought Arthur Barrett, lying in his bunk. This Louis plans to shoot down Zack and Toby, just for fun—for practice, you might say. Zack, the nicest guy he'd ever known, by far. Louis didn't like Zack, not at all—not him or Toby, either. The Hunt would be a perfect opportunity.

Arthur hardly slept at all that night. He tried to think what he could do. Historically, the answer'd always been: not much.

261

Well, first of all (he thought) he couldn't tell the staff; he wouldn't dare to. They never would believe him, number one, even if they knew the gun was missing, even when they saw that it was gone. The people on the staff had labeled him a loser; they looked at him a certain way, spoke to him a certain way. They expected him to fail at anything he tried; he heard that in their voices when they said his name. They hated him—they'd put him in a cage and hadn't minded when some other kids did . . . *that* to him—and they seemed to like Louis, at least Mister Rensselaer did.

If he told them about Louis's taking the gun, they'd probably think *he* did it and was just trying to put the blame on Louis, to get even with him. They'd call him a stool pigeon and a squealer, and it was perfectly possible that Mister Rensselaer would decide to make him *really* squeal, somehow. He could imagine Mister Rensselaer saying that: "I'm going to make this squealer squeal until he can't even *whisper,*" and then doing something awful, painful, horrible to him, over and over and over.

No, thought Arthur Barrett, sometime after midnight, talking to the staff was not the answer. Suppose the staff reacted as he feared they might, tortured him and stuck him in the cages, too, again—how would that help Zack? Maybe he could warn him, cage-to-cage, but warning him would do no good that he could see. Zack and Toby were already hoping, planning, to avoid being seen by any of the hunters, he felt sure. Knowing that one of the hunters had a real gun wouldn't do anything but freak them out *completely.*

Arthur decided that he'd have to tell Rod Renko. Rod wasn't nice, not in the way that Zack was, anyway, but more and more he hadn't seemed too hostile. He'd tell him first thing in the morning, Arthur B. decided.

It didn't work. He simply couldn't get the guy to listen—pay attention—for the longest time, and when he did . . .

"Rod," he'd started, shortly after reveille. Rod had passed him twice, going to and coming from the "head," and hadn't even seemed to hear. Then, partly dressed, he'd leaned against his upper bunk, his head down on his folded arms. Rod just hated getting up in the morning; Arthur wondered if he'd gone right back to sleep, like that.

"Rod . . ." he said again, and touched a bulging biceps.

"Whoever it is, just get the fuck away." Rod's voice was muffled by his blanket. "I don't care if it's fuckin' Brooke Shields; it's just too goddamn early in the morning."

"Rod, please," said Arthur, bending closer to his ear. "It's important. It's about Louis, and——"

If Arthur Barrett hadn't had an overbite, he probably wouldn't have had a perpetually wet lower lip, the sort of lower lip that, in grade school, causes other kids to ask you "Do you serve towels with your showers?" when you speak to them excitedly, at times.

Now, Rod Renko took his head out of his arms and bellowed, "Goddamnit, Arthur, quit slobbering on me, will you, for Christ's sake?" Other people laughed, of course.

An hour later, after he had had his coffee, Rod recalled the look on Arthur's face, and felt a little bad about it.

"Hey, Art," he called, across the barracks. Cleanup was completed; the beds were made, the floors all swept, the clothes were all hung up. Rod was about to leave, with his friends, on the Hunt—or, sticking to the facts, an all-day party. "What was it you wanted to ask me? Earlier, you know?"

A lot of people turned and looked at Arthur. They didn't really care about his answer; it was more or less a reflex. A question had been asked, and now they waited for the answer. Louis was among the ones who waited.

Arthur shook his head. "Nothing—no. Forget it," he replied.

Everybody left, in all directions. It was almost eight o'clock, by then.

263

88. Only the Good Dye Young

Louis Ledbetter, lying on his stomach, had his arms stretched out in front of him, as he'd been taught (by old J.B.) to do, at pistol practice on the range. His left hand grasped his other wrist; his right hand held the pistol, pointed like a giant metal finger, straight at Zack and Toby.

It wasn't going to be anything like it was in the arcade; everything was different. There wasn't any point in trying to kid himself. Out here in the open, in the country, it was harder to concentrate. The sounds were not the good, familiar sounds; it didn't even smell the same.

Louis took a few deep breaths to calm himself. He was excited and he didn't want to miss. Missing even one of them could mean a lot of trouble, more—if that was possible—than what he had already. Hitting them did *not* mean trouble; hitting them meant getting out of trouble. Anyone with any sense at all knew you had to take care of Number One, especially when Number One was innocent. Protecting someone innocent was always justified—like self-defense or if you kill a guy who's trying to rape your sister. Unless he did this thing, right here, he'd be unfairly crucified. He

264

wasn't going to let that happen. The facts were just that simple, and so was the solution.

Once you put your quarter in, the game started, and it was up to you to play. Fish or cut bait, his father said. Well, he was at that point right now. The quarter had gone in, and what he had to do—yes, had to do—was start, right now.

Looking down the barrel of the Browning, Louis noticed Zack had started digging. Toby, she was nearer, also in a semi-crouch. Her head turned back and forth, sometimes looking at the hole that Zack was making, sometimes peering down along the fence. He'd thought to take out Plummer first, figuring that he—a guy—was lots more dangerous and, like, *tougher*. Plus, as a guy, he'd have the sense to run, the moment that he heard a pistol shot, where she—dumb broad—might freeze, or wait to see if she could help, the way a nurse or something would. But now he thought that maybe he'd hit Toby first. She looked real antsy, readier to split, while he was all caught up with digging.

He had a good grip on the stock, his finger tight around the trigger. This meant he could control the game, just as if he were standing at the console. He had the power—a different shape, was all—right there in his hand.

Yeah, that'd be the best. Toby was a sitting duck. Chances were he'd finish her with just a single round: heart shot, easy, left of center just a hair, her tit would be the perfect target, what there was of it. Then he'd throw a stopper into Plummer—aimed, for sure, but quick. If he had to put a couple more in him, to finish it, no problem. He moved the pistol barrel back toward Toby, got the sights up on her shirt. Let's see; he wanted *her* left side, not his; that wasn't tit at all, just target.

265

The real truth was, he didn't want to do it. He didn't think he could; he didn't feel that easy surge of power. But if he didn't, he was—well—as good as dead, or worse than dead, you could say. Before he thought again, he started.

Louis didn't even hear the sound at first. He was in another world, sucking in that big last breath, the one he'd hold before he fired. All night he'd had to deal with noises in the bushes, fuckin' birds and animals.

This time the noise persisted, though; it wasn't sudden-over, like when a bird decided to take off. And also it was getting louder, louder.

It broke through Louis's concentration, that noise did, and he turned his head to face it, see what it could be.

Before his eyes could focus, he had caught the dyeball squarely on the nose, up high. It hurt, it hurt like hell; his first thought, riding on a bright-red flash of pain, was Oh, my God, I'm shot, I'm killed. But the ball had also burst; his eyes were filled with thick green dye. His arms jerked up spasmodically; the gun went off, a bullet headed upward through the leaves.

"Jesus," Louis screamed. He dropped the Browning, started pawing at his face.

He didn't even hear the awkward stumble-steps, as they careened away.

As always, when he could, he turned and ran. As always, running added to his terror. Even after four weeks' practicing, he didn't do it well.

He stumbled, sprawled—and lying on the ground, immobilized, heard only birds, and wind, a tractor in the distance. Before he'd turned to run, he'd looked to see that Zack and Toby had disappeared. They were all right, unharmed, at least for now; Louis had been stopped from killing them. Amazingly, he'd won—and it was much more than a game.

Slowly, he got up. He put the dye gun in his holster, brushed some leaf mold off a knee. He blinked his eyes and

266

wiped his mouth and started for a pleasant, shady place he knew of, near the pond. He went quite slowly, and he didn't make a lot of noise.

Bobo would have been surprised how quietly he walked, for Arthur Barrett.

89. Regrouping

Toby and Zack were born in 1965 and 1966, into families that weren't particularly hip or with-it, when it came to life-style. Rodman Plummer, for example, would never wear anything other than white, light-blue, or tan boxer undershorts, or a jockstrap, while Harold Ayer went to his grave believing only Jews liked bagels.

What this meant was that most of the dynamite words and expressions that marked the interpersonal pathways of the sixties and early seventies—like *nonjudgmental, confrontation, body language, here-and-now, consensus,* and *self-actualization,* that bunch—didn't mean anything major to Zack and Toby, anything capitalized—like, Wow.

It also meant that when what was, recognizably, a pistol shot went off not far from where they were (both of them crouched down beside a chain-link fence) neither of them asked herself (or him-), "How does that pistol shot make me feel?" or "What are my various alternatives, in response to that pistol shot, given this particular and open-ended set of circumstances?" No, instead of asking those, they both took off; pretty soon they stopped and checked for blood and nuzzled one another. Honest? Natural? Aware? A pair of foxes couldn't have done better, so it seems to me.

Later, they discovered both of them assumed that Willis, Bo, or possibly J.B. had shot at them, or *over* them, perhaps: that warning shot you read about in stories. Of course they didn't know (and never knew) for sure, any more than Louis ever knew who'd made his face turn green. *His* best guess— his only guess, let's face it—was Rod Renko, the only Green who might have dared *and* cared enough to do it. Goddamn big buttinski could have blinded me, thought Louis.

In any case, what Zack and Toby did was head back to the cellar hole, posthaste. They had. to let their pants dry (Toby later said, in jest, to brother Devon), regroup, and figure out a better plan, a bold new stroke of some sort.

It didn't work out that way. The plan that they came up with was a salvage job, an old idea Toby'd had to start with. It floated, more or less, into their minds, sometime toward the close of day. Floated? you may ask. Indeed, indeed. Swept along and bobbing on a sea of Löwenbrau, five bottles worth, apiece.

90. 448-3964

Matty Crews spent the next day making raspberry preserves, so it wasn't until late afternoon that she had a chance to get the weight off her feet. She headed for her favorite easy chair and sank down in it with a sigh.

And onto a Day-Glo cat collar, with one open silver buckle.

"Oh-my-dear-oh-my," said Matty Crews, rising, feeling, and remembering.

The number, 448-3964, was on the tag, which she had placed beside the phone, as a reminder. The phone was in a closet in the entrance hall. She went to it at once.

"Shit Miss Mitchell," muttered Matty Crews, in transit, scolding her bad memory with this mysterious and magical expression. It always cheered her up, somehow.

She dialed, and reached, the Plummers.

91. Bill Bartowiak's Plan

The Board of Directors of the Francis Marion Institute consisted of eight guys—eight *great* guys, as a matter of fact, all of whom had known each other since the week before forever, most of them from even before they were married. All of them liked a good time, but also knew when to get serious, where you had to draw the line. They were all real men, which was something of an endangered species in this day and age.

Although some of the above statements might sound like opinions—or even nonsense—to another observer, they were plain and simple facts to Harold Ayer. And if you didn't believe him, you could ask anyone else on the Board of Directors of the Francis Marion Institute. They'd tell you, sure as Bob's your uncle.

If it was a certain Friday evening in July, you could have asked them all at one time, if you happened to be in the North County Diner, because they were all there, sitting around three pushed-together tables, in the back. They'd driven up in pairs, in four different four-wheel-drive vehicles that were parked outside, and if you hadn't seen those vehicles with their heavy show-bars, extruded-aluminum running boards, custom steel (chrome-plated) bumpers, and

3,500-pound-single-line-pull winches mounted on their fronts or backs, you might have guessed—from looking at the men—that maybe they were going to a National Guard weekend, or maybe a reunion, better. Because all of them were dressed, at least in part, in military gear: khaki, olive green, or camouflage. Of course they didn't wear insignia of any sort, like stripes or bars or badges, name tags, even. So maybe it was fair to say they looked like hunters more than soldiers. Also, most of them were drinking beer, which Guardsmen might or might not do, before a weekend. It certainly appeared to be a fact that whoever the eight men were, or whatever they were planning to do, they were enjoying themselves.

"...so when Bill called up, I said to Mavis, 'Look. I know I said we'd get together with the condo guy this weekend.'" George Zagaris looked around the tables, grinning broadly. "This is this—whachamacallit—*time-sharing* crap, where you put down, I don't know, something like seven thousand bucks and that means you can stay not just at yours but at any one of these condos for a week, every year, for your entire life. It's probably a great idea but, *you* know, seven big ones, for Christ's sake. 'The thing is,' I say to her, 'I've gotta take a raincheck on it. Something important's come up, and we're having a special board meeting, up to the Institute.'" George Zagaris shook his head and laughed. "Mavis hit the roof," he said. "'Raincheck?' she hollers. 'Whatya think this is, the chicken special down to Finast?' And then she says, 'You and that damn board. You know who's really Chairman of the Board? Well, it ain't Bill Bartowiak, it's me! B-O-R-E-D,' she goes, 'bored with you and bored with all your damn excuses.' Oh, brother, was she pissed, or what?" George Zagaris winked and smiled some more. Everybody liked hearing him tell stories about his fighting with his wife. That Mavis had some kind of a mouth on her. Not to mention knockers out to here.

"Anyway," said Ricky Renko, dad of Rod, "what's the final word on what we're going to do tonight?" He spoke to Bill Bartowiak. "Harold, when he called me, said we'd probably do, like, a sneak attack—just more or less to see what kind of smarts the kids have got, in terms of their reactions. Like what they call contingency planning, down at the office."

Seven pairs of eyes were switched to Bill, and Harold Ayer, his closest buddy, recognized that little smile of his the first. Not very often, but from time to time, Bill would get a thought—an inspiration, you might say—that he really did believe was pretty doggone good, and sometimes, also, funny. And when he got a thought like that, why it'd take an atom bomb, at least, to make him leave it go. That little secret smile was like a road sign: here it comes.

And so it came about that when the men departed from the diner, half an hour later, they all assembled by the back of one red truck that had a chrome-and-vinyl cap on it, and outsized wheels. There, each of them received a different shirt, big enough to cover up the one that he had on—some striped, some polka-dotted, others in a garish solid color— and also a new hat (wide-brim, cap, or pork-pie, great variety, again). And also, finally, just before they got into their vehicles, every man was handed, and put on, a painted rubber mask, that realistic kind of mask that covers your whole head.

Although their shirts and hats and caps were all completely different, their faces, now, were all the same. Every member of the board was now the entertainer Sammy Davis, Jr.

Yes, as Bill Bartowiak had planned it all along, the Francis Marion Institute was about to be invaded by some city folks.

273

92. Toby the Torch

Toby turned to Zack and put her finger to her lips and raised her eyebrows high; it was barely light enough for him to see her eyebrows. She'd done this lots of times between the cellar hole and where they were, which was almost at the little house beside what used to be the skeet field.

It wasn't that her friend was making lots of noise; he wasn't. In fact, for the entire trip, he'd taken real slow, quiet steps, trying to walk the way he'd read the Mohawks used to do, putting down the outside of each foot before the rest of it. In order to do that, he had to concentrate like mad, which made him frown and press his lips together. He looked peculiar, that's what Toby thought, as if he might throw up, and so she put her fingers to her lips partly to remind him to throw up quietly, if he had to.

Then, too, she was a little bombed, and that made everything seem sort of . . . well, ridiculous. Herself, him, being shot at, being bombed, and creeping through the woods—just everything. Making this finger-to-mouth gesture, over and over, seemed to her like a pretty hilarious thing to do, right in keeping with the rest of it. She wasn't the least bit afraid. As a matter of fact, the main thing she felt other than bombed was incredibly sexy. She'd seen Zack dip into

274

that box of condoms in the tunnel, and though she wasn't sure she wanted to fuck him or anyone else at this exact point in her life, she wondered what he'd do if she asked him to quit walking on the outside of his feet and stop and model one for her right now. She took another gander at his face. Legend had it guys his age were always ready, eager, and available. Her mother'd said it wasn't quite that simple. Chalk another up for Mom Knows Best. Probably better to take one thing at a time, anyway, Toby thought, and they were almost there. One "thing," she thought. Merribeth would like that thought. She almost giggled.

For the last hundred yards or whatever it was, Toby pretended she was a hooker, switching her ass back and forth in as seductive a way as possible. That was hilarious. Of course he didn't even notice.

Once they were in the skeet house, they started in directly on the work they'd planned. It was very close to dark inside, but still they stayed down near the floor as much as possible, in case of passersby. They didn't need to see much, anyway.

First, they ripped to cardboard shreds the cartons that the soda and the beer had come in. They ripped up all the cases that the jars of nuts and sour balls had occupied. They took the stacks of round clay pigeons out of their big boxes, too, and tore those boxes up, as well.

When they had finished doing that, the only things left in the closet were the boxes of shotgun shells. They moved these from the closet, too, but didn't bother to unpack them. Then, on the closet floor, they made eight stacks of clay pigeons, each about eight inches high. The stacks were several inches apart, and described about three-quarters of a circle, like rocks around a campfire, with the open part facing the closet door. On top of them they put a round chrome grill, and then on *it* (where old-days gunners once placed porterhouses) they stacked up all the shotgun shells, box after box after box.

Under the grill, instead of charcoal, they put shredded cardboard, mixed with paper, lots of it. The paper came from piles of magazines they'd found: ancient *Field and*

Streams, old *Rod and Gun*s, two or three *New Yorker*s, and (quite near the bottom) just a single dog-eared *Photographic Annual*.

Then, using more of that same stuff, they made a mound about a foot wide and a foot high that stretched across the room from the closet to the front door. To keep it more or less in shape—piled up and straight—they tipped over a bunch of straight-backed wooden chairs, frontways, so that their ladder backs were just above the mound.

By the time everything was ready, it was really pretty dark outside. Toby struck the match, the only one she'd need (good scout!), and lit this foot-high paper fuse they'd made, from right beside the outside door.

They closed and locked this door behind them, then they scooted for the cellar hole, where they had left their spades.

93. Bad Actors

When the four four-wheel-drive vehicles driven by Bill Bar-towiak, Ricky Renko, Harold Ayer, and George Zagaris pulled up to the gate of the Francis Marion Institute, it was twilight-going-on-to-dusk. Or, in other words, there was just about enough light to see that the gate was chained tight-shut, said chain secured with a Master padlock, No. 5, in fact.

"Shit," said Sammy Davis, Jr., sounding very much like George Zagaris. It was, in fact, that long "shee-yit" of mockery—contempt—rather than the shorter "shit!" of anger or frustration. He bent and took hold of the hook at the end of his winch cable and held it up interrogatively to his companions.

Sammy Davis nodded, seven times.

He put the hook around the chain, came back, and did the necessary things inside his truck, backing up and letting out some cable. Then he started up the winch.

The cable tightened. There was a pause and then a snap. The hook jumped back and landed on the ground, halfway to the truck, about. The gate swung open. Sammy Davis made a circle of his thumb and forefinger.

Driving without headlights, Bill Bartowiak led them in.

277

In all four vehicles, someone said to someone else, "Funny they don't have no sentry," or something very close to that. And got the laughless answer "Yeah" ("Sure is," "Uh-huh," and "Yup"). Instead of driving right up to the lodge, they stopped by the garages, right where Bobo'd worked on his Accord, the morning of the day before. On foot, they came around the toolshed toward the lodge, each of them sauntering along in what he felt was city-style. Later on, perhaps, they'd start to run around in panic, but not until they had a proper sort of audience.

Which it didn't look as if they'd have, real soon. The lodge was dark, completely so, and so were nearby Cottage 1 and nearby Cottage 2.

"Where the goddamn hell do you suppose that everybody is?" asked Sammy Davis, Jr., of his clones.

Well, the answer to that question, for almost everybody, was meant to be the same: "out in the woods, someplace." For good reason.

At the end of the first day of the Hunt, with no sightings reported and the teenage session members looking surly, smashed, or stoned, the staff had said that things had better shape up, "fast and fancy." Their Ultimate Experience was falling apart on Willis and on Bobo, and J.B. was fixing them with that kind of marvelously contemptuous and almost pitying look that manages to contrast the benefits of wealth, culture, and a college education with those of good old homespun horse sense, all in the flick of an eye—you can guess in the favor of which. And they were simply hating it, of course.

And so, specifically—the staff had laid this on the teens, the second day of the Experience—everyone was made to go and draw some "trail food," three days' worth, and plan to spend that time ("of course it could be less") going through the forest, bush by bush if necessary, until they "put some colors on those kids." No one was to use the beds, the bathrooms, or the kitchen stove before there'd been some "countin' coup," said Bobo, master of the lingo of the old frontier (he thought). He, J.B., and Willis also would be roaming through the woods, making sure that there was active hunting going on.

That was one reason for the staff's being out there, anyway. The other was that pistol shot of Louis's. Willis, who rose early as a bird—a raptor of some sort, of course—heard the shot and recognized the sound. He'd gone and checked the armory and found the Browning population cut in half, and when he gave that news to Bobo and J.B., there'd been an argument of sorts. Who would take the gun, and why? Whom had it been shot at? Bobo thought that Zack and Toby might have gotten it, somehow; Willis, closer to the type himself, had other candidates in mind, including Louis. J.B., a classicist at heart, preferred the "mysterious stranger" theory, say a tramp or derelict, for instance. He knew that if he mentioned KGB they'd laugh, but, hey, don't rule it out, he thought. The Reverend Dreyfus had reminded him the week before that there'd been Russian agents on the school boards of two towns somewhere— New York, he thought it was, or Massachusetts. Trying to get the kids to read a lot of filthy books, he'd bet.

Anyway, what all that added up to was: Willis said they had to all be firearmed out there, the three of them. They owed it to the kids, he said. With that, he grabbed the other Browning, and old J.B. was not averse to strapping on his service .45. Bobo felt a little foolish carrying a single-shot bolt-action .22 rifle, but he didn't intend for a minute to fire the damn thing, and it was either that or a .30-06. For some reason, the third option, "or nothing," never did occur to him.

What all this added up to was that the only person left behind, in the more or less central compound of the Francis Marion Institute, was Missus Fairchild. And she was not just "left behind" the way a kid might leave behind a summer reading list before taking off on an extended cruise on the family ketch (or his older sister her diaphragm, let's say). No, Rita Fairchild had a job to do, a duty. She was sitting

279

in the window of a darkened Cottage 2, on lookout, holding in her hand a walkie-talkie. If, by any chance, some teen survivalists came back, and tried to use their beds, or bathrooms, or the kitchen stove, she was meant to get in touch with old J.B. at once. The staff would "take it from there."

When Missus Fairchild saw the members of the board come sauntering up the driveway . . . well, even in the dusky dark she knew they weren't teens, or *her* teens, anyway. The way they walked had lots to do with that, and also their . . . apparel. Missus Rita Fairchild had often told her friends that she didn't have "a prejudice-bone" in her body.

Her first thought was: perhaps these men are waiters, thinking that the gun club still was here, and hoping there were jobs.

Her second was: she'd better call J.B.

"Shady Lady calling Alpha Uno Corn-yo. Shady Lady calling Alpha Uno Corn-yo. Come in Alpha Uno Corn-yo. Over," she whispered urgently into the little black box in her hand, slightly mispronouncing the third word in the staff's "handle." She'd chosen her name first, so that Willis jumped right in and said what theirs would be, and smiled at her, the way he did. Well, she just happened to know that "Alpha" and "Uno" both was Latin, and meant "A-1," together. So it wasn't hard to figure out that "Corn-yo" was also Latin and meant something like "command post" or "leader." Aside from Willis, only Bobo knew the word was *coño*, which was Spanish, and meant "cunt."

"Alpha Uno Corn-yo to Shady Lady. Alpha Uno Corn-yo to Shady Lady." J.B.'s voice, distant and staticky, came out of the box. "Speak up, goddamnit, Rita. You sound like your head's stuck up your sassafras. Over."

Missus Fairchild's eyebrows shot straight up her forehead. This time, she talked in a very normal tone of voice. "I only thought that maybe you'd just like to know that there's eight fellas walking big as life right by the lodge this very minute, as pretty as you please. Perfect strangers, each and every one of them."

Rita Fairchild smiled a small one to herself. Be rude to

her, was that what he was going to be? And not just, like they say, in privacy, but broadcast on the airwaves. Who could say how many folks might listen in and hear her being talked to in a way no lady ought to be? That's what comes, she thought, from hanging out with ones like smart-mouth little Willis. Well, she could rain on his wise-ass parade.

"Oh, just one other little thing, Jewell dear." She stretched the moment out, enjoying it immensely. "Those fellas I just mentioned? You probably don't care, I know, but all of them is big buck colored people. 'Bye," said Missus Fairchild, pushing the antenna down and switching off her little walkie-talkie.

By the time she had finished with her message, Bill Bartowiak and the rest of the board had stuck their noses into the big main lodge and turned on a couple of lamps and confirmed their suspicion that it was, in fact, empty. It was also neat and tidy, which the board read as a definite plus for the program. The kids had been taking care of the place; it didn't look anything like most of their rooms at home. A really definite plus: after Doomsday, there'd be a lot of tidying-up to do. Harold Ayer wasn't too surprised. His wife had told him more than once about her getting compliments from other kids' mothers concerning Toby's manners, helpfulness, and training. Being "well-brought-up" and that. It was just at home she acted like a slob, sometimes. Well, not a slob, exactly. A little careless, maybe you could say.

Leaving the lodge, the board next walked the path to good old Barracks B (for boys); it was just as dark as the main lodge. Outside, on the little porch of it, George Zagaris made like he was Wyatt Earp or Marshal Dillon, one of them. He creased his hat, and opened up the door and swaggered through it, walking with his legs all bowed and hands out to the sides, above imaginary six-guns. Everybody laughed at that a little. Someone hit a light. The place was neat, but empty.

Barracks G was next, a little ways away. This time it

was Ricky Renko, front and center; he made it law-and-order time: *Untouchables*, or *Kojak*, or that *Hill Street Blues*.

"Okay, babies—this here is a raid," he snarled, jumping in the door real quick, his finger jutting from his hip, and followed closely by the boys from the squad room.

How could he have known that five of Merribeth's best customers, aka the Red team, had recently said "Fuck it" to the Hunt and entered through the other door, around the other side, like, just a toke or two—or three, or four, or maybe more—before?

Stoned to the eyeballs, sitting in the dark, Duke Merillo, one of Rod's best buddies, sort-of-thought, What the hell is Mister Renko doing here?

Then someone on his team flashed on a flashlight. Duke and all the rest could see it wasn't Mr. Renko, after all. *They* weren't Mr. Renko. They weren't anyone that anyone had seen before . . . exactly. But on the other hand . . .

And then, as Duke began to giggle, three fellow potheads hollered, "Queers!" and picked their dye guns up, and aimed, and fired. Right away, the teammate with the flashlight dropped the thing, and all five kids leaped up and scrambled for the door—the same back door they had come in by. The joint, abandoned and forgotten, simply lay there on the floor and smoked.

In the main front doorway, there was cursing and confusion in the darkness.

"Hey, shit, I may be bleeding . . ." "Something hit me, too." "What the hell is that I smell?" "Jesus, whaddya suppose . . ." Et cetera.

The board backed out the door and off the little porch outside it. Someone got his lighter out, and pretty soon two others did the same, and so, by Bic-light and the stars, everyone could see the bright-red splashes on the shirts (one shiny blue, one yellow polka dot on white) that Harold Ayer and Ricky Renko wore. It looked so much like blood it struck them almost dumb—can you believe it?

"What the . . ." started Harold Ayer. He touched the stuff and brought his finger to his nose and sniffed.

"Right there, niggers," said the voice behind him. "Fuckin' hands real slow behind those woolly little heads."

It's probably crazy to think that Harold Ayer recognized Willis Rensselaer's voice from the phone call that he'd made some nights before—and reacted to the memory of having disliked the guy, and what he'd had to say, and having had the phone hung up on him. Harold Ayer couldn't tell you himself whether hearing Willis Rensselaer's voice had anything to do with his reaction or not. He really couldn't swear to it one way or the other; he later told guys that, a lot, when he retold the incident.

And neither did he, or Ricky Renko, or any of the other members of the board, know for sure how much being called "nigger" like that contributed to what *they* did next. Possibly a lot. It'd be nice, for instance, to think that being called "nigger" that way gave Bill Bartowiak, George Zagaris, and others, in a clear and sudden flash of empathy, new insights into how it felt to be a black, and scorned for no good reason whatsoever. And filled them with a fine, fresh fury, at what they now perceived to be so many persons' inhumanity to personkind.

Wouldn't it be nice to think that?

And to also believe that from that moment on these eight men were able to deal with all their fellow citizens in a spirit of decency and charity and kindness, untainted by the slightest whiff of prejudice?

Go ahead and think that if you want to. Please, I wish you would. Sure, I suppose there's another possible explanation, but who needs any more of that crap? Not this world and not this story, either.

But, in any case, what happened was that in the dim illumination provided by those three Bic lighter flames (and also by the stars), Sammy Davis, Jr., full of grace and rhythm, both, made a left-foot pivot, dancer-smooth, and drove his polished Country Squire walking shoe squarely—make that *pointedly*—precisely to the balls of Mister Willis Rensselaer (whose trigger finger *might*, perhaps, have frozen at the sight of so much blood).

This kicking action, on the part of Harold Ayer, seemed to galvanize the group. Almost as one, Sammy Davis, Jr., turned and flung themselves into the fray. When they'd been stationed in Korea, they'd learned some local hand-to-hand techniques, and though they hadn't thought of all that stuff in years, a lot of it came surging back, directly to their hands and feet. As George Zagaris later said, "Once you've learned to do it on a bicycle . . ."

And so they pummeled not just Willis Rensselaer, but also Rutherford Bodine and also old J.B., up one bearded side and down the shaven other. It's true that Bill Bartowiak, just as he had started one big fist streaking toward the gut of old J.B., did have the thought, My gosh, that's old J.B., the guy I hired for the job. But then it was too late, and old J.B. was going "Oof," and Bill was thinking, What the hell, he'll never know, and anyway he shouldn't play with guns, while chopping with the other hand across his (former) buddy's nose.

In almost less than it takes to tell the tale, the staff was in retreat, or better make that *flight* ("Lucky thing for me I'd did that runnin' every day," J.B. later told his oh-so-sympathetic bride), leaving the Board of Directors of the Francis Marion Institute behind to get their breathing back in order. The first thing that they did, of course, was pull off those hot rubber masks and get to be themselves again.

Which let them hear, as plain as plain could be, the sound of gunshots in the distance, followed by a big explosion.

94. Dachshunds with a Badger on Their Minds

Luckily for everyone named in this narrative, as well as, oh, maybe fifteen million others who've had small roles or none in our story, the explosion heard by the Board of Directors of the Francis Marion Institute, the staff of same, Missus Rita Fairchild, Rodman and Belinda Plummer, Matty Crews, and all the kids enrolled in the Teen Survival Session including Toby and Zack was not the sound of a nuclear device going off in or around Hartford, Connecticut. Instead, it was the infinitely less deadly result of all those boxes of shotgun shells in the skeet house being reached and ignited by the absolutely first-class little fire that had sprouted in the place. Pretty soon all of those mentioned above, except for Matty Crews and Zack and Toby (and the fifteen million, natch), were headed for the flames (the board now altogether maskless, hatless, city-shirtless), joined by elements of the sheriff's office and the North County Volunteer Fire Co. Later on, of course, there came the State Police.

Matty Crews stayed squarely where she was, thinking unkind thoughts about the government, while Zack and Toby

285

dug like dachshunds with a badger on their minds. If only they had known about the gate, they could have wandered out of it and met the Plummers driving in the driveway, but, alas, they didn't, so they dug. Or not "alas," depending how you look at it. The digging was good heart-lung exercise, and spending all that money on a cab was more or less in line with the administration's efforts to stimulate the economy, I suppose. Everything depends on your point of view; we've had that out before.

In any case, they arrived at the Plummers' house on Catamount Hill a little after midnight. It was dark.

95. Home Sweet Egg

Zack rang the doorbell in his father's favorite shave-and-a-haircut tempo before he used his key; he wouldn't want to alarm his parents. And when they were inside and at the bottom of the stairs, he hollered, "Mom! Hey, Dad! It's Tobe and me. Don't we even rate a cold calf sandwich?"

He got no answer, naturally enough. They turned on lights and found his parents' room was empty, with the bed still made. Back downstairs, they roamed into the kitchen, used the fridge at length (and also, yes, in depth), and finally sharp-eyed Toby checked the pad beside the telephone. There, in Rodman Plummer's writing, was the line "the Callipygians need immediate assistance."

"Wow," she said. And, "Great. A cat got through to someone." And she pointed.

Zack looked and nodded, smiling. "Yay," he said. "They must be up there now. You think I'd better try to call? Just so they'll know that we're all right?"

"Yeah," said Toby. "Better had. Poor them." She shook her braids and laughed, but not as if she found the situation funny. "I bet your father's raising fifteen different kinds of hell. They must be going crazy."

Zack found the number, dialed, and got a Trooper Novack

of the State Police. His name, and Toby's name, were not unknown to Trooper Novack; his parents, Trooper Novack said, were somewhere on the property, joining in the search for them, as also was (surprise!) his girl friend's father. Zack told him he and Tobe were safe and sound, at home, and please to tell their parents. Trooper Novack said he surely would and they should stay right where they were—they got it? Zack thanked him very much and said that they'd be happy to; they were pretty pooped, he said, so probably they'd just sack out and see their parents later, or maybe in the morning. Trooper Novack said they should do just that, and meanwhile he'd hang up and call the searchers off. He knew it couldn't hurt a guy's career to tell a man like Mr. Rodman Plummer what, in all the world, he wanted most to hear.

Toby looked at Zack, and vice versa.

"Bed?" she said. She was feeling tired, and hungover, and relieved, and (unaccountably) a little pissed, and some other things that were harder to identify, right off.

And he said, "Well, I guess we *could*."

"You think that we could use The Egg?" she asked. Saying that, she realized that she didn't feel completely safe, yet. So that meant she wasn't all that relieved, after all. And she wasn't really tired, or really hungover, or actually pissed, either. She didn't know how she was feeling. "Upset" might cover it.

And he said, "Huh? The Egg?"

"Yes," she said. "D'you think your father'd mind? I don't know. I'd just like to hang out there for a while. It'll be at least three hours before they all get back."

Zack shrugged. "Sure," he said. "I guess it'd be okay. It's pretty cozy down there. I'd just have to turn on a couple of things, like the power and the fans. It might be a little stuffy for a while." Being in The Egg might be better than being in the big house; he could see that. He decided to take along a beer.

"You want one?" He'd opened up the fridge, held out a Heineken's.

Toby made a face and shook her head. Then she sucked a breath and made a little gesture with her hand.

"Yeah," she said. "I'll take one."

96. Well Bred

The Egg *was* stuffy for a while, too hot for all the clothes that they were wearing. They took off their fatigues, which left them in their yellow shorts and shirts. It seemed a week ago that they had put those on, backs to one another, in the cages. Zack knew he felt a little shy, again; he didn't know quite why. He'd seen Tobe in her bathing suit a lot of times; the yellow shorts and shirt were much more clothes than her bikini. It was probably The Egg, he thought. It was so separate from everything. They might as well have been on another planet, or the only people left on this one.

Toby went and sat on one of the built-in bunks, leaning up against the bulkhead, with her brown bare legs tucked underneath her fanny. She took a sip of her beer and realized at once that it was the last thing in the world she wanted to drink.

"I guess it's all starting to hit me," she began. Zack was still standing, moving up and down the center aisle, doing this and that, checking out the fans, the different lights, the water. He was also trying to figure where he ought to sit. Toby's way of sitting on the bunk, leaning in a corner more or less, with both knees sticking out—it didn't look exactly welcoming.

"Aren't you going to sit down?" she asked him.

Her tone made up his mind. He went to the bunk across the aisle from her and stretched out on it, holding the bottle of Heineken's on his chest.

"I mean, do you realize," she said, "that our parents sent us up to that Teen Survival Session because—I don't know—they thought that maybe it'd help us to live some kind of longer, better life in case there ever was a terrible disaster, and what happens? We came a whole lot closer to dying than we ever did in all our lives. I guess getting born was the second most dangerous thing I ever did, and I didn't choose that, either."

Zack nodded, chewing that one over.

"Of course, to be completely fair," she said, "it wasn't our parents that made us act the way we did, up there. Exactly. It was more as if we said we'd rather *not* survive, if it meant doing—or not doing—certain kinds of things. *Being* certain ways—you know?"

Zack agreed with that. "Boy, that's what it came down to, wasn't it?" he said. "It almost makes you wonder how a person ever *can* feel safe." He had the feeling, pretty much all of a sudden, that the things they were talking about were really major, having to do with a lot more than their getting away from a bunch of crazy people at a summer camp. He felt a little short of breath, the way he'd get before a soccer game.

"Nowadays, you probably can't," said Toby. She pushed her hair back from her face, and sighed.

"What do you suppose we'd do," she said, "if we knew the Bomb was on its way right now? Here we are in The Egg and everything, but in five or ten minutes, say, the Bomb is going to come down somewhere in Hartford. What would you say we ought to do?" She stretched her legs out and rolled over on her side, facing him.

Zack stared at her and blinked. He had an answer ready for that one. It was something that most guys had talked about, with one another.

"I'd want to make love with you," he said.

291

I don't know. But I'd want to make love." He looked at her some more and had to smile. Not at what he'd said—because she was so beautiful.

Toby nodded. She could feel his words and smile in different ways, in different places. She felt like crying and—she was surprised by this—very, very sexy, once again.

"But that'd be so sad," she said. "Our first and last time. 'Did you feel the earth move, darling?'" Suddenly, it was almost hysterically funny; she talked louder and faster. "But you know how you hear the first time's a big disaster for a lot of people? Wouldn't that be just our luck—can you imagine it?—double-dip disaster?"

She *did* laugh then, closing her eyes and shaking her head, but Zack, now sitting up and facing her, didn't feel it was so funny, either.

"Well," he said, trying to make it sound offhand. He *did* believe what he was going to say, didn't he? Of course he did; he *must*. "Maybe what that means is that we ought to do it now, instead. Before there's any pressure, or whatever. That way, we'd be practiced up—ready for anything." He made a macho funny face and laid a palm over his heart. "*Semper paratus* is our guide . . ." he sang. The Coast Guard hymn; he didn't really know the words.

Toby opened up her eyes and looked at him. "Come here," she said. She put her legs down so that he could sit beside her on the bunk.

He went, and put his arms around her as he sat. They lolled back on the bunk. His mind felt pretty much messed-up, as if he'd lied to her somehow, a thing he'd told himself he'd never do.

"You know," she said, when they had kissed, but lightly, neither one prolonging it, "as soon as you start thinking of *surviving*, which means, like, after something awful happens—sure, I mean the Bomb—then everything's fucked up. There's no such thing as a normal life, or growing up, or anything like that." She made a sort of gulping, laughing

"Making love—this is what *I* think, anyway—
￼ything to do with stuff like that, all the

horrible stuff. Practicing up so we can both be sure of having the big O right at the moment of meltdown, or something. It's absolutely *crazy*." Toby struggled to sit up. She stood.

"I think it's time to get this stuff off." She smiled. "Besides, you've never even seen me naked, yet."

She took her shirt off, threw it on the floor. She pushed her shorts down, all the way. They lay there by the shirt: two wrinkled, dirty, yellow things.

"There," she said.

He shook his head in wonder, admiration, understanding. Then he rose and did the same.

"There," she said again, "that's good. Zack." She pointed at his chest and slowly looked him up and down. He'd never felt so valuable in his entire life.

"And Toby," he replied, and looked at her again.

She put her hand out and he took it, and they shook, nodding as they did so. And then they turned and joined their hands a different way—his right, her left—before they smiled again and took two breaths and walked directly down the aisle and out The Egg's big thick lead door.

Belinda Plummer, had she been there, would have understood, and maybe cried some happy tears.

The night outside was clear, and full of stars.

JULIAN THOMPSON helped a group of teenaged people start their own high school in New Jersey, in the early seventies, and he worked there for a few years doing teaching, counseling, college admissions, and the bathrooms. Now, though still devoted to the academic calendar, he writes novels and lives with his wife in Vermont.

NOVELS FROM AVON/FLARE

THE GROUNDING OF GROUP 6
by Julian Thompson

Coming in May 1983!
83386-7/$2.50

What do parents do when they realize that their six-teen-year old son or daughter is a loser and an embarassment to the family? If they are wealthy and have contacts, they can enroll their kids in Group 6 of the exclusive Coldbrook Country School, and the eccentric, diabolical Dr. Simms will make sure that they become permanently "grounded"—that is, murdered. When the five victims discover they are destined to "disappear"— and that their parents are behind the evil plot—they enlist the help of Nat, their group leader, to escape.

AFTER THE FIRST DEATH
by Robert Cormier
62885-6/$2.50

This shattering thriller is about a group of terrorists who hijack a school bus in New England and hold a group of children hostage—forcing each one to make decisions that will affect not only their own lives, but also the nation. "Marvelously told...The pressure mounts steadily." *The New York Times* "Haunting...Chilling ...Tremendous." *Boston Globe*

TAKING TERRI MUELLER
by award-winning Norma Fox Mazer
79004-1/$2.25

Was it possible to be kidnapped by your own father? For as long as Terri could remember, she and her father had been a family—alone together. Her mother had died nine years ago in a car crash—so she'd been told. But now Terri has reason to suspect differently, and as she struggles to find the truth on her own, she is torn between the two people she loves most.

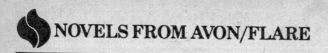

NOVELS FROM AVON/FLARE

I LOVE YOU, STUPID!
Harry Mazer   61432-4/$2.50
Marcus Rosenbloom is a high school senior whose main problem in life is being a virgin. His dynamic relationship with the engaging Wendy Barrett, and his continuing efforts to "become a man," show him that neither sex, nor friendship—nor love—is ever very simple.

CLASS PICTURES
Marilyn Sachs   61408-1/$1.95
When shy, plump Lolly Scheiner arrives in kindergarten, she is the "new girl everyone hates," and only popular Pat Maddox jumps to her defense. From then on they're best friends through thick and thin, supporting each other during crises until everything changes in eighth grade, when Lolly suddenly turns into a thin, pretty blonde and Pat, an introspective science whiz, finds herself playing second fiddle for the first time.

JACOB HAVE I LOVED
Katherine Paterson   625210/$2.25
Do you ever feel that no one understands you? Louise's pretty and talented twin sister, Caroline, has always been the favored one, while Louise is ignored and misunderstood. Now Louise feels that Caroline has stolen from her all that she has ever wanted...until she learns how to fight for the love, and the life she wants for herself. "Bloodstirring." *Booklist* A Newbery Award-winner.

Available wherever paperbacks are sold or directly from the publisher. Include $1.00 per copy for postage and handling: allow 6-8 weeks for delivery. Avon Books. Dept BP. Box 767. Rte 2. Dresden, TN 38225.

NOVELS FROM AVON ◆ FLARE

FACING IT

Julian F. Thompson   84491-5/$2.25

Jonathan comes to Camp Raycroft as the Head of Baseball, hiding the fact that he used to be the best left-handed prospect in the country—before The Accident. Then he meets Kelly, the beautiful dancer, and suddenly his life changes. He realizes he must tell his secrets in order to earn love and trust. By the author of THE GROUNDING OF GROUP SIX.

JUST ANOTHER LOVE STORY

R. R. Knudson   65532-2/$2.25

When girlfriend Mariana tells Dusty they are through, he decides it is easier to die of a broken heart than it is to live with one and tries to drive his car off a pier into the Atlantic Ocean. However, Rush, a champion bodybuilder, just happens to be there to save him and convinces him to try pumping iron in hopes of winning back Mariana's love.

I NEVER SAID I LOVED YOU

Jay Bennett   86900-4/$2.25

Peter has always intended to follow the family tradition and become a lawyer, until he meets beautiful, golden-haired Alice, who convinces him that he's listening to everyone else but himself. Now he has the problem of deciding for sure what he really wants without losing Alice's love.